Trembling With Fear

Horror Tree 2017

Edited by STUART CONOVER

and STEPHANIE ELLIS

Artwork by ANDREW BUTCHER

Copyright © 2017

These are works of fiction. Names, characters, businesses, places, events and incidents are either the products of the author's imagination or used in a fictitious manner. Any resemblance to actual persons, living or dead, or actual events is purely coincidental.

Cover art: Andrew Butcher

ISBN-13: 9781720228998

Horror Tree ... 9
Trembling With Fear ... 9
Foreword ... 10

JANUARY ... 13

Count Your Blessings - Ken MacGregor ... 15
Masks - Jess Landry ... 19
Second Skin - Liz Butcher ... 19
Nuisance Neighbours - Angeline Trevena ... 20
Dr Carey's Hygienic Alternative Meats - Carl R. Jennings ... 21
The Cinema Experience - Nicole J. Simms ... 24
Benny - B.B. Blazkowicz ... 24
Program Delete - Robert Allen Lupton ... 25
Separated - Patrick Winters ... 25
Champ - Kevin M. Folliard ... 26
Deep Woods - Chad Vincent ... 28
Just Like HVN - Daniel Pietersen ... 28
The Shambling Dead - Franklin Murdock ... 29
Interred - Ryan Neil Falcone ... 30
It Sleeps - Stuart Conover ... 34
Tryst - Amanda Bergloff ... 34
Turning Tides - KC Grifant ... 35
Young Love - Rose Blackthorn ... 35

FEBRUARY ... 37

Hello Mr. Magpie - Ross Baxter ... 39
Ghost of a Smile - Ken MacGregor ... 43
The Greatest Love - Paul Starkey ... 43
Bath Time - Stephanie Ellis ... 44
Mrs Margolis - Greg Moss ... 44
Kameraden - Richard J. Meldrum ... 45
The Real Bogey Man - Liz Butcher ... 48
Hunger Moon - Jennifer Canaveral ... 48
Granny Gwen - Hillary Lyon ... 49
The Tender Spot - Andy Brown ... 49
Life and Limb - Kevin Holton ... 50
Confectious - Matthew R. Davis ... 54
Mental Check - Patrick Winters ... 54
Valentine Surprises - Brendan O'Dea ... 54
The Adelphi -Alyson Faye ... 55
The Paper Clip - Mathias Jansson ... 58
Swift Retribution - Robert Allen Lupton ... 58

The Monster from Moorsville - Erik Bergstrom   59

MARCH   61

Down to a Sunless Sea - DJ Tyrer   63
The Very Best - Catherine Berry   65
Awakening - KM Zafari   65
Kindness in the Aftermath - Rob Francis   66
Resurrection - Chanelle Pina   67
Separated Again - Patrick Winters   69
Starting Over … In Style - Rose Blackthorn   69
The Survivor's Museum - Andrea Allison   70
Bound - Emma Taylor   71
The Hag of the Mists - Frank Coffman   71
The Heart Song - Timothy Rock   72
Till You Do - P.J. Kryfko   74
Just A Dream - Andy Brown   74
The Black Spot - Brendan O'Dea   75

APRIL   77

The Gift - Paul Wooldridge   79
Bathtub - Maci Mills   82
Burn - Liz Butcher   82
Norman's Bunny - Alyson Faye   83
Paying the Bills - Kevin Holton   84
Oddworth's Silent Partner - Madison McSweeney   88
Raking - S.C. Cornett   88
What Follows in the Fog - Erik Bergstrom   89
The Watchers - Jess Dosser   90
The Unremarked Return - Ken MacGregor   95
Kill Shelter - Richard J. Meldrum   95
The Fart - Mathias Jansson   96
The Impossible Visitor - Carl R. Jennings   96

MAY   97

The Worm Turns - B.B. Blazkowicz   99
Burnt Soup - Stuart Conover   102
No Funny Business - S.C. Cornett   102
A Walk In Sunlight - Richard J. Meldrum   103
Sight - Liz Butcher   103
The Good Son - Mathias Jansson   104
Ageless - Mary Jo Fox   104
The Lights - Matthew Gorman   105

Mother Knows Worst - Ruschelle Dillon   109
Kaidan - Patrick Winters   109
Necrovore - Frank Coffman   110
Altarstone - Robert Allen Lupton   111
Time With Ethan - Ryan Benson   115
Worms - David Turton   115
Out Of Time - Kevin Holton   116

JUNE   117

What the Dog Tells Me - S.L. Edwards   119
Flight 666 - Liz Butcher   122
The Angry Tree - Jacob Mielke   122
The Power of Suggestion - Richard J. Meldrum   123
Footprints - Judson Michael Agla   123
Cargo - Alexander Lloyd King   125
The Glow in the Mirror - Amanda J Evans   127
Formative Experience - Kevin Holton   127
Posted: No Hunting - Robert Allen Lupton   128
Mr. Jackson - Justin Boote   129
The Itch - S.C. Cornett   132
Soul Mate - Alyson Faye   132
The Long Road to Immortality - Kev Harrison   133
Jagged Little Teeth - Stuart Conover   137
Roses Are Red: Volume 1 - Justin Boote   138
Monsters - Patrick Winters   138

JULY   139

Silver & White - Justin Shioshita   141
Time of Death - Richard J. Meldrum   143
Darkness and Light - Amanda J Evans   143
Date Night - Alyson Faye   144
The Elephant Curse - L.S. Engler   145
Roses Are Red: Volume 2 - Justin Boote   147
Just A Taste - S.C. Cornett   147
They Glistened Black In The Sun - Stuart Conover   148
To The Sea, The Sorrow - Daniel Pietersen   148
The Companion - Carl R. Jennings   149
To Die For - Stephanie Ellis   150
Diao Si Gui - Patrick Winters   151
Glass Slipper - Robert Allen Lupton   154
Dabblers - Sarah Doebereiner   154
The Summon - Mathias Jansson   155

Now I Lay Me Down - Ruschelle Dillon   156
Hunting Him Down - Michael A. Arnzen   158
The Day Was Hot The River Inviting - CR Smith   158
Exit - Bart Van Goethem   159

AUGUST   **161**

Portrait In Blood - Steven Carr   164
Just Right - Robert Allen Lupton   166
Lightning Need Only Strike Once - Richard J. Meldrum   167
Guilty - Sarah Doebereiner   168
Anything Storage - G.E. Smith   169
Nest Of Bones - Alyson Faye   172
The Twins - Matthieu Cartron   172
Roses Are Red: Volume 3 - Justin Boote   173
Arrogance - Bryan Nickelberry   174
Roadkill - Ruschelle Dillon   176
Picture Perfect - Catherine Berry   176
Notes From The God Chair - Steve Bevilacqua   177
In The Woods – On The Hunt - Pernell Rogers   181
Sympathy Dish - Sara Tantlinger   181
Bloodlust - Kevin Holton   181

SEPTEMBER   **183**

Commander of the Clew - Nick Manzolillo   185
Story's End - Sara Tantlinger   188
Bugs - Justin Boote   188
Love's Last Kiss - Robert Allen Lupton   189
You Must Not Remember - Jason D. Grunn   190
Rose Red - Alyson Faye   194
Mystery - Richard J. Meldrum   194
Eat It - Brianna M. Fenty   195
The Greenhouse - Kevin Holton   197
The Chase - Pernell Rogers   197
A Simple Accident - Richard J. Meldrum   198
Weeds - Christina Dalcher   199
Last Will And Testament - Stephanie Ellis   201
The Dead Of Night - CR Smith   201
Metronome - Paul Isaac   202
Choosing - Tim J. Finn   202

OCTOBER   **203**

Anubis - Diana Grove   205

Bugs #2 - Justin Boote   209
Reaction Time - Kevin Holton   209
Time And Time Again - Richard J. Meldrum   210
Washed Up - Matthieu Cartron   210
Acceptance - N.O.A. Rawle   211
The Monster - Guy Anthony De Marco   211
You're Just His Type - Kristin Garth   212
Savior - Richard J. Meldrum   215
One Person - Andrea Allison   215
The Basement - Patrick Winters   216
The Marionettes - Carolyn A. Drake   217
The Eye - B.B. Blazkowicz   219
Host - Sian Brighal   219
Charcutier - James Appleby   220

HALLOWEEN EDITION   **221**

The Pumpkin Club - Justin Boote   223
The Cold Uncertainty of Love or Real Love in a Cold Climate -
Martin P. Fuller   226
Hungry Pig - Jarrett Mazza   229
In The Pumpkin Patch - Ross Smeltzer   236
Our One Night a Year - Chris Campeau   238
Trick or Tarantula - Kevin Folliard   241
I Remember Samhain - Chad Vincent   241
Good Carving Depends On The Pumpkin - CR Smith   242

NOVEMBER   **243**

Just A Little Bloob - G.A. Miller   245
Bugs #3 - Justin Boote   248
Let Down Your Hair - Robert Allen Lupton   248
Break Her Back - Richard J. Meldrum   248
Charla Nash - Agnes Marton   249
Tea Party - Alyson Faye   250
Pink Poodle - Kevin M. Folliard   250
In the Woods - Steppen Sawicki   251
The Scutterings - Martin P. Fuller   252
No Ordinary Game - N.O.A. Rawle   254
Crimes of Passion - Michael Parker   254
His Cousin's Tale - Ethan Hedman   255
Two If By Sea - Jennifer Canaveral   259
The Parasite- H.B. Diaz   259
How To Prepare Roadkill - CR Smith   259

DECEMBER   261

The Last English Speaker - James Burr   263
Scarecrow - Alyson Faye   266
Jack in the box - Mathias Jansson   266
Fracture Clinic - Richard J. Meldrum   267
David and Goliath - Richard J. Meldrum   268
Through The Jungle - Stuart Conover   271
Sunday Roast - Stephanie Ellis   271
Little Louis - Erik Baker   272
Outlast - Kate Bitters   273
Kitty Cat - Alyson Faye   277
Date Night - Richard J. Meldrum   277
The Ebbing Tide Calls - Daniel Pietersen   278
Barfight- Fred Rock   279
Tristan - Stuart Conover   281
Redundant - Stephanie Ellis   281
Not Even a Mouse - Ruschelle Dillon   282
The Hanging Lights Sway - Andrea Allison   282
Dad - G.A. Miller   283

CHRISTMAS EDITION   285

A Letter For Santa - Jessica Shannon   287
X-mas Twist - Michael Baldwin   290
Dead Watch - R. M. Smith   293
The Day Before - Charles Reis   299
Five Letters To Santa - David Rae   302
Clack! - DJ Tyrer   306
The Grungle - Kevin Folliard   307
Wrong Night - Adam Millard   308

HORROR TREE

The **Horror Tree** is a resource for horror authors which was created in 2011. The main goal when starting the site was to include all of the latest horror anthologies and publishers that are taking paying submissions. A resource useful for both new and experienced publishers alike looking for an outlet for their written material! Each anthology that we list should have a set deadline as well as offer compensation in the form of direct payment, royalties, or at the very least a physical contributor's copy.

Since that time, we have expanded to include articles on every aspect of the writing process, fiction, guest posts, blog tours, and more!

Please be sure to visit us at http://www.horrortree.com

TREMBLING WITH FEAR

Trembling With Fear is a branch of **Horror Tree** which publishes original fiction every Sunday morning. In it, we have a minimum of one short story and three pieces of flash fiction on a weekly basis. We are not a static publication however, and have recently introduced serials as a new feature and no doubt there will be other developments. Please remember to check our *Trembling With Fear Submissions* page for details on how to submit.

We welcome all forms of speculative fiction though we do have a focus on darker works. The outing was added as a way to give authors a fresh set of horror to keep their minds working in new creative directions, readers a place to find new short work to check out on a weekly basis, and help grow our community.

This anthology marks the collection of all work published in our first year and hopefully this will be something we're able to continue every year going forward!

Both **Horror Tree** and *Trembling With Fear* are run by volunteers who freely give up their time to bring you the best of the dark side. Want to help? Please get in touch via the above address.

FOREWORD

Ladies, Gentlemen, Lovers of Speculative Fiction,

Thank you all from the bottom of my heart for continuing to read and share our *Trembling With Fear* posts. To be totally honest I started the fiction section of Horror Tree on a whim. It was an experiment that I thought would be good for authors and readers but had no idea if it would take off or not.

Thanks to all of you, these posts have been highly read and shared meaning we've been keeping it going and growing!

Most authors will tell you that one of our greatest tools is to also read. My initial goal for *Trembling With Fear* was to give authors some bite-sized fiction to get your minds going, another outlet to publish their work, and to increase networking with our little community.

I feel like we've been able to hit all these points at this time! Not only that, but we've made it to print!

I'm going to be honest with everyone for a moment here. About half way through the year, even while things were going great with *Trembling With Fear* I was about to call it quits. From having two kids, to being overworked at the day job, to my slew of side jobs, to dealing with debt, and attempting to get some fiction written I was at my breaking point.

At that point I made one of the best decisions for the site - I reached out to Twitter and asked for help. I spoke with a few people and ended up feeling that I really clicked with Stephanie Ellis who has become our wonderful editor and am glad I did.

I had always tried to provide feedback on rejections and network with our authors, but Steph hands down has me beat on handling everything. Without her amazing addition to the team I don't think we would have made it through the first year with plans to grow into the second.

So, thanks to the readers for continuing to come back and enjoy fresh fiction every Sunday. Thanks to the writers for tirelessly sending in your work and giving us all more entertainment. Finally, another huge thanks to Steph for helping me not lose my way with *Trembling With Fear.*

It has been a hell of a year seeing *Trembling With Fear* grow into its own on the Horror Tree and it we're looking to see it continue growing over the course of the upcoming year!

STUART CONOVER

Dear *Trembling With Fear* Readers and Contributors,

Wow! Our first anthology. When I first joined **Horror Tree**, I certainly never expected to be involved with this. Like so many of you, I have been aware of this site for a few years now. It became, once I discovered it, my go-to place for market news. It was where I found anthology and magazine submission calls—for free. Until that point I had subscribed to a UK publication, *Writers News* and occasionally purchased the *Writers' & Artists' Yearbook*, searching for outlets for my work. I spent the money and came up with zilch. The home for my writing was not to be found in those hallowed pages so I scrapped the subscription and the book and simply relied on **Horror Tree**. This gave me a level of success I had not expected, with my stories being printed in magazines and anthologies chosen from submission calls on this site; it also gave me leads to other sites and opened my eyes to the world of speculative fiction; it gave me a home.

Then I spotted *Trembling With Fear* and sent in a drabble, noting Stuart's comment of it being a way to show support for **Horror Tree**. Something I was more than happy to do in a world where chasing profit appears to be the be all and end all. **Horror Tree** is Stuart's labour of love and one which so many of us should be thankful for. It made it a bit of a no-brainer then when Stuart asked for more help, in particular with editing TWF, and here I am.

Today, TWF is still a way of supporting **Horror Tree** but ultimately it is there for the writer. It provides a platform for writers to show their skills, to hone their dark natures, to get feedback from readers and now with this anthology, extend their reach. This anthology contains *all* of the stories published in TWF on the **Horror Tree** website; it is a physical record of your output and something we are particularly proud of. We hope you will be too.

TWF is also about community. I've seen you build and weave our network on twitter and other websites, online friendships are forming and it's been lovely to see the support you give to each other (and to me and Stuart!).

So, thank you for making me welcome at TWF, for working with me and making it an enjoyable experience and thank you to Stuart for creating Horror Tree in the first place.

STEPHANIE ELLIS

JANUARY

COUNT YOUR BLESSINGS

KEN MACGREGOR

It's the thirst that gets you. Before today, if you'd asked me what the most terrifying thing was about the sea, I'd have said "sharks."

And they are. Terrifying. Especially when they breach. You'd think you would focus on the teeth, right? Hundreds of sharp yellow cutting tools, in rows, attached to the only actual bone in the animal's body: the jaws.

But, no. It's the eye. You can only see one at a time, because the head of that fish is too damn big. That endless, ebony orb that stares back into you. It is sizing you up, that look. It is wondering what you might taste like. How many bites does it take to get you all the way down? To slake the endless hunger.

I'm not sure what kind of sharks they are. They're big, gray and scary-looking. Great Whites? Tigers? Makos? How the hell do I know? I'm not a sharkologist.

Yeah. They're bad all right. But, sharks are a distant third to the really scary things about being lost at sea.

Second to worst is the sun. You try to cover up, but of course, when the ship went down, you were only wearing swim trunks and t-shirt. Your head, arms, legs and feet are slowly roasting out here. Mine. Sorry. I've been adrift for a couple days. I get confused. Maybe my brain is getting cooked inside the toaster oven of my skull.

The sun's bad, all right. First, I was deeply red and my skin was sore. Now, I have blisters: second-degree burns. Can the sun cook my flesh all the way? Will I be Cajun-Blackened Jeff Sturges?

Which brings us to our winning entry in the *'what's the most horrible thing about being lost at sea?'* contest. The thirst. It tastes like agony.

I'll tell you the worst part: all you can think about is water. And, all around you is … yep: water. Only, you can't drink it. The salt content will kill you. I know this, intellectually. But, just look at it, sloshing against the sides of the raft, sparkling in the sunlight. So pretty. Just one little taste can't hurt.

Nope. Not going there. Not yet anyway. Maybe later. Keeping my options open. I'm crafty like that.

My father used to say, "Count your blessings." When I broke my index finger, he said, "Hey. At least it wasn't your whole arm." It was a grim sort of optimism that pretty much defined who he was. So, I'm counting my blessings.

One: I'm still alive. That's pretty cool, considering the other three people who were on the boat are not. Alive, I mean.

Two: I have the raft. This is a big one. If I were just floating in a life-jacket or something, I'd have been shark-food by now for sure. If not, then I'd be dead of hypothermia.

That's all I got. Two blessings. My dad would say, "Hey. At least it's not zero."

Something bumps my raft. Could the sharks be getting bolder? If they bite my inflated craft, I'm screwed. That'd be the end of both my blessings, I bet.

Of course, if I die, I won't be so damn thirsty anymore.

I am reminded of that one guy in Dante's *Inferno*. You know, the one in the water up to his chin, but every time he goes to drink it, the water disappears. Or, as long as I'm on a classic literature kick, that poem that goes on forever—I forget the name. The line I'm thinking of goes, '*Water, water everywhere, and not a drop to drink.*'

I'm betting the two writers spent some time at sea. Maybe a long time, all alone, surrounded by miles of wet, shiny, oh-so-tempting poison.

I could just take a tiny sip. Not enough to do any real damage. Just, you know, wet my lips a little.

No. Bad idea. Stop it, brain.

Another bump. This time, I could feel it slide under me, all the way across the bottom of the raft. Whatever that is, under me, is getting more curious. Or more bold. Or just trying to scare the piss out of me. Well, joke's on you, shark. Too dehydrated to pee.

I miss my phone. Not that I would be able to get a signal out here, but at least I'd know what time it was. What day, too. I mean, the sun has gone down and then back up twice now. So, it's been at least forty-eight hours since the boat developed that fatal leak and went down to the bottom of the ocean with my $300 phone and my three friends.

Well, my friends didn't sink right away. They lasted a good while. Constance almost made it into the raft with me. It was damn close. She could still be alive.

If I hadn't shot her.

All the blood in the water is what probably drew the sharks in the first place. Now, they were hanging around, hoping for more food.

I didn't mention the gun earlier when I was counting my blessings. That's because I used all but one bullet already. Eight shots in the clip and one in the pipe. That's the expression, right? Picked that up from movies. So, yeah. I burned seven of them in rapid succession. Three in the bottom of the boat, one in Cliff's head, two in Carla's ample chest and one in

Constance's leg. It was a terrible shot, but she was attacking me at the time.

She fell to floor of the sinking boat, clutching her thigh with both hands. She looked more pissed off than hurt. But, it gave me enough time to pull the cord on the inflatable raft, jump in and shove away.

She dove in after me. You have to admire that kind of tenacity. She got an arm over the edge of the raft. She was spitting and swearing, if you'll pardon the pun, like a sailor. I calmly put the barrel to her forehead and she shut up.

"I'm sorry, Constance," I said to her. "No passengers."

I pulled the trigger. She looked surprised and indignant as she slipped beneath the surface. I guess I would be, too.

So, if you're keeping score at home, that's eight bullets. Out of nine, total. I have one left. Not really a blessing. More of an unpleasant alternative to dying of thirst. Or to drinking the salt water. Or being shark bait.

The raft is moving. I mean, it's always moving a little, but now, it's more like, um, *traveling*. I grab the solid rubber handles so I don't get tossed over the side. Looking into the water, I see something I don't understand. There's a thing under me. It's not a shark. Too big.

Maybe it's a whale? It could be. I mean, from here, it looks like an endless expanse of gray flesh. If I were forty feet up, I might be able to see what it was more clearly.

We pick up speed, my tiny raft, the monster we ride, and I. Wind whistles in my ears. My sunburnt skin recoils from the sudden cold breeze.

I hang on. What else can I do?

We're going up, rising out of the water. Now, I am forty feet up, but I still have no idea what I'm riding on. It's not a whale. Too big.

I didn't think there *was* anything bigger than a whale.

Something else is breaching the surface behind me. It's even bigger than the beast I'm on. We climb higher. The mind-boggling mammoth behind me keeping perfect pace as more of it emerges from the sea.

Eyes the size of city parks. Nostrils big enough to inhale skyscrapers. Below them, teeth. Hundreds of them. Big enough to eat the world.

I realize where I am. My raft is not riding a separate thing. I ride the monster's tongue.

Okay. So I was wrong. The thirst is not the worst.

I am about to be swallowed whole by an impossible monster. Maybe this is my Hell. My punishment for murdering my faithless friends. Well, Cliff, Carla and Constance, you three cunts, you have your vengeance.

Of course, I had *mine* first, you cheating assholes.

As the mouth closes over the withdrawing tongue, over me and my raft, I think, *Hey. At least I still have the one bullet.*

Laughing, I say it aloud.

"Count your blessings."

MASKS

JESS LANDRY

The face looking back at her through the mirror was perfect.

She ran her fingers over the smooth ridges of her cheeks. She traced the contours of her flawless jawline. She admired the ruby hue of her lips, accentuated by her porcelain skin. She watched them curl into a smile. She hadn't smiled in ages.

She brought her fingers over the nose, stopping on the bridge. The slightest of bumps protruded from under the skin, burrowed like the pea under the princess's mattress. The smile faded from her lips.

She ripped the perfect face off and went to fetch another.

SECOND SKIN

LIZ BUTCHER

Malach breathed a contented sigh as he listened to the hypnotic whirring of the sewing machine. He paused, lifting his work to admire the faultless seam. An untrained eye would never know the pieces came from two separate people. Malach stroked the skins, recalling their donors—long since disposed of. He wondered why he'd wasted years working with inferior materials. He was making up for lost time now. Years he'd spent, collecting the thirty victims he needed for the thirty-piece pattern. It was his masterpiece. Malach pressed down on the pedal, relieved as the whirring drowned out his victim's screams.

NUISANCE NEIGHBOURS

ANGELINE TREVENA

Ellen pressed her hands over her ears. Why did they have to bang so loudly?

She poured two glasses of wine and carried them back through to the living room where Tom was browsing her CD collection.

"Into heavy metal?"

"It drowns out the neighbours."

She winced. They were at it again. "They must be really noisy. It's quite rural here. How far are your nearest neighbours?"

Ellen looked out at the rutted garden, each lump of the lawn marked with a popsicle stick. She hummed thoughtfully. "Not as far as you'd think, and not as restful as I'd like."

DR CAREY'S HYGIENIC ALTERNATIVE MEATS

CARL R. JENNINGS

Hello friends! Do you find yourself unwilling or unable to pay the outrageous prices for the more traditional sources of meet such as beef, chicken, pork, lamb, fish, and venison? And don't even get me started on veal—that is if you can even find it! Nor do you want to risk using another source to feed your family, such as rats or insects? Do you have any idea how filthy the average rat is? Disgusting!

I was in the same boat as you not too long ago, that's why I started *Dr* Carey's Hygienic Alternative Meat! Before you press that skip button I'm not talking about those soy-based 'fake meat', like some dirty vegetarian. I'm talking about good, old-fashioned flesh-and-bone meat. But, I hear you thinking in puzzlement, I'm not using any of the usual meat sources, what is actually in *Dr* Carey's Hygienic Alternative Meat? I hope you're sitting down for this revelation because it's going to knock your socks off! *Dr* Carey's Hygienic Alternative Meat uses only the best, responsibly sourced human remains!

But, I hear you cry in astonishment, why would I ever eat human meat? Therein lies the brilliance of *Dr* Carey's Hygienic Alternative Meat! Have you had a look around lately? Getting a little crowded in all the habitable areas on this planet, isn't it? I mean, how do you think we came to this shortage to begin with? With sheep fields being converted to low-income housing, cattle ranges being used for prisons, and pond farms being filled in for retirement villages? How could we not find ourselves in danger of losing the venerable institution of the carnivore!

Dr Carey's Hygienic Alternative Meat, like a rising phoenix, pulls from all of those sources—the prisoners, the destitute, and the old—in order to fill the gap in the market and your stomachs. All of the dregs of society, the drains on all of our hard-earned money, can now serve a purpose once again! And, after all, isn't that what life is all about?

If social responsibility isn't enough to convince you to take out your credit cards just yet, let me give you and your growing hunger even more reasons to buy as many pounds of *Dr* Carey's Hygienic Alternative Meat products as you can afford.

Years ago, my great grandfather, Pappy Carey, owned one of the Midwest's premiere cattle ranges. As a young kid I would sit on my father's knee as he told me story after story of delicious cows in fields as far as the eye could see; of juicy, succulent steaks and hamburgers that they, and their wallets, all thrived on after a slaughter.

After much searching of the internet and libraries, I can proudly say that I have replicated the best practices of Pappy Carey's cattle farm! All of our meat is as safely and cleanly prepared as it was in the good old days.

But let's say you aren't convinced yet; that my excellent lineage and exhaustive research hasn't assured you of *Dr* Carey's Hygienic Alternative Meats' tastiness and fitness for consumption. "But *Dr* Carey," I hear you cry, "I don't want to eat the same thing as a filthy and worthless Wastelander—killing and eating each other to survive!" Well, do I have good news for you: All of our alternative meat products are tested for diseases such as AIDS, HIV, all forms of cancers, viral infections such as the flu, and much, much more. Such dedication to the safety of my customer has lead, I can now reveal, to having secured the world's first approval to serve our alternative meat products by the USDA! That's right, folks, your own government has placed its stamp of blessing upon all of *Dr* Carey's Hygienic Alternative Meat products.

But, I hear your stomachs wail, how would I even prepare human meat? Well fire up those burners and ovens, get out those pots and pans, because *Dr* Carey has taken care of that for you too, folks. With each order of *Dr* Carey's Hygienic Alternative Meat, I'm going to throw in a downloadable copy of our new e-cookbook, *Dr Carey's Hygienic Alternative Meat Preparation Guide*. In it, I have recorded over two-dozen ways to cook our products as developed by the world-renowned chef, the late Phillip de la Nourriture. Now you too will be able to cook a scrumptious, delectable, and hearty alternative meat meal for yourself and your family.

And if you still don't find yourself sold on the viability of my alternative meat then listen to this: if you order one pound of *Dr* Carey's Hygienic Alternative Meat today you will receive not one. Not two. Not three.

But four pounds of alternative meat for the price of one! There are many choice cuts to choose from: thigh, calf, buttock, breast, shoulder, and more! You may also choose from our line of budget processed alternative meats, including the triumphant and along awaited return of the traditional American hot dog!

And, for those of you that have already ordered *Dr* Carey's Hygienic Alternative Meat products from your local grocery warehouse and have found it to live up to the hype and more, why not try our brand new Customer Loyalty Program? For an insanely low monthly fee you can have your favorite cuts delivered directly to your home, straight from our facilities, by our high-tech fleet of drones. From the basic Standard Level to the exclusive Gastronomer Level, with which you'll receive pictures and videos of our choicest stock so that you may pick out your source personally!

I'd like to see a kale farmer do that!

All of our products are backed up by our satisfaction guarantee: if you are not completely satisfied by your alternative meat product for any reason then call our fast and friendly customer representative hotline to receive a credit on your next order.

Remember *Dr* Carey's Hygienic Alternative Meat the next time your stomach growls for something red-blooded. You owe it to society but, more importantly, you owe it to your own taste buds.

THE CINEMA EXPERIENCE

NICOLE J. SIMMS

Nicholas laughs, eyes fixed on the big screen. The cinema had always amazed him even when they were simple silent movies. He had adored the Charlie Chaplin movies, *City Lights* being his favorite. He sips his drink and frowns. Removing the lid, he studies the empty drink container. He pokes the slumped girl next to him; their eyes lock.

"I need more," he says. The girl sits up and raises her arm. "Thank you, darling."

Baring his fangs, Nicholas pierces her flesh. He then holds the girl's wrist over the drink container. The girl whimpers. Yes, Nicholas loves the cinema.

BENNY

B.B. BLAZKOWICZ

Benny liked him some coffin nails.
He would take two, four,
sometimes even more.
Friends implored he take no more.
Lest he would achieve, a one-way vacation to the morgue.
Benny loved those coffin nails,
even when his health it failed.
He woke up one morning feeling sore.
Benny saw his stomach by the door,
with skin and hair on the floor.
To no avail and to his dismay,
he saw a ribcage full of nails.
A skeleton, he was begotten!
So, Benny bought himself a coffin.
For he knew his ship has sailed,
built out of his favorite nails.

PROGRAM DELETE

ROBERT ALLEN LUPTON

Jim was a hacker, a former Catholic, and a drunk, not necessarily in that order. He hacked into the Vatican and fought his way through security and found a file called *Intelligent Creation Control Data*. While he was searching the file, alarms went off and the Vatican system started to access his computer and location.

"Screw this," said Jim and he hit the key to delete the Vatican's files. The percentage deletion popup raced across his screen and when it showed eighty-five per cent, his desk, computer, and room disappeared. Jim's last words were, "Damn, I wish I hadn't done that."

SEPARATED

PATRICK WINTERS

It's ten o'clock and my husband won't stop pounding on the front door.

He's been out there for the whole last hour, calling out to me, begging for me to let him in and take him back. That he still loves me. He promises that we can go back to being how we once were. I want to believe that, but I know better. I'd shouted at him to go away, to just leave me alone. He started to get angry after that, shouting louder and knocking harder. It's scaring me.

My husband's been dead for over a year now.

CHAMP

KEVIN M. FOLLIARD

"Somethin' slippery between my toes, Mama!" Gracie called from offshore. Her head bobbed in the shoulder-deep ripples of Lake Champlain. Gracie squealed and tossed her head. "Oh! I think it's a fish!"

Mama scowled from her folding chair and flipped a page of her paperback. "Probably leeches! You wouldn't catch me in there! No ma'am!"

"Fuddy duddy!" Gracie called. "The water's beautiful, Mama!" Gracie dunked and spun on her toes, drilling into the murky bottom. She bopped back above water and surveyed the hills, ripe with towering firs. A pine breeze cooled her wet head. "I could stay in this one spot forever!"

"Hmm." Mama didn't look up. "You always were a little fish, ever since you was a girl. Never leave the lake. Never leave the pool. Never wanted to go home and go to bed, where it's soft and warm."

"No, ma'am!" Gracie insisted. "When's the last time you been in water, Mama?"

"Never." Mama sipped her diet cola. "Never once."

Gracie giggled. "Liar!"

"Never told a lie, neither," Mama insisted.

"You told me about the Tooth Fairy, when I was young," Gracie said. "That was a lie."

"Tooth Fairy's real." Mama flipped a page.

"She is not!"

"Who else would give a dollar a tooth? Not me."

"Might be right there." Gracie floated onto her back. Wisps of cloud crept through the sky like molasses. "You'd like it in here, Mama."

"Leeches, 'n slime, 'n bacteria. You'd best wash up good back at the motel."

"I might roll around in your sheets first! Germs deserve a comfy bed too!"

"You'll be sleepin' on the roof of the car."

Gracie squeaked with laughter.

Suddenly, a wall of liquid gushed up and cascaded over Gracie. She floundered and took a gulp of lake water. Her toes fluttered in the mud. She coughed. Gagged. Struggled to stay upright. Water flecked from the back of her throat until she cleared her windpipe with a loud hack.

Gracie rubbed her eyes. A foamy ridge glided over the surface of the water, tapered towards shore, and washed over brown sand. Frothy, V-shaped ripples lingered.

"Mama! What in heaven was that?"

"Mmm?" Mama remained fixated on her book.

"Mama, did you see what caused that big wake?"

"Big who?"

"Mama!"

Mama finally looked up, eyes sagging with exhaustion. "What!"

"Somethin' moved in the water. Somethin' huge!"

Mama huffed. "Your big mouth. Been movin' all day." She returned to her book.

"I'm serious." The shimmering stillness of the blue water returned. Gracie tip-toed through the murk, toward shore. "I never felt somethin' movin' underwater like that before. Felt like a whale cruisin' past."

"You never felt no whale cruise past you before." Mama shook her head.

"Well if one did, it would have felt just like that! A big bus of a thing pushin' all the water around it."

"Always had an overactive imagination."

Gracie's big toe slipped over a flat broad surface. "What in Sam Heck?" She ran her toe along the smooth, wide object. "Feels like someone sunk a rubber doormat here!"

"Nobody sunk no doormat."

"You don't even know what I'm talkin' about, Mama. I'm standin' right on it." Gracie put her full weight down on the slick surface. Immediately, a green hump and slithering tail erupted like geysers. Gracie plummeted backward. An enormous flipper breeched and slapped the water.

Mama finally glanced up as a long neck craned from the churning water, ending in a toothy snout and shiny obsidian eyes. The beast snarled, jerked its thirty-foot neck at Mama, and plucked her from her chair.

Mama's paperback landed face down on the surface of the lake. The beast's neck twisted and plunged Mama under. Its trunk shifted from shore with a shove of its front paddles, and it dove back into the deep.

Gracie bobbed and trembled in the beast's wake. The paperback absorbed water and sank. And it wasn't until the book disappeared into Lake Champlain that Gracie found the power to scream.

DEEP WOODS

CHAD VINCENT

Snow falls sideways in damp flakes, wind howling. His feet slog through, pant legs getting wet, getting cold. Must keep moving. Something internal drives him forward, a fire that evades the raw wind at his face.

'*Can't remember if I'm running from or heading towards,*' the clouds in his mind collide in a thunderstorm of confusion.

His body gives pause as a wave of exhaustion throbs muscles into spasms, giving time to glimpse at his surroundings. Behind, deep ruts follow in the form of hurried prints. Crimson blotches dapple his backtrail.

Then comes the echoless howl of the wolf, again.

JUST LIKE HVN

DANIEL PIETERSEN

An alpine breeze rustled Simensen's hair. She looked up the valley to the mountains, snow-topped and hazy. Perfect. Behind her, the chalet processed its morning diagnostic routines. She sighed. The voices had been telling her that she needed to leave for days now. She'd procrastinated, but today was it. She'd be sad to leave. She lifted the gun-shaped device to her temple, sighed once again, then pulled the trigger.

She disappeared.

She dropped the v-manipulator into its charging cradle, started removing the haptics. A screen behind her scrolled text, then blinked: CH VALL HVN 777 – QA COMPLETE TECH SIMENSEN

THE SHAMBLING DEAD

FRANKLIN MURDOCK

I'm alone when they come for me, holed up in my house after the war ripped through our town, those strange chemicals rolling along the ruined landscape. They've all turned, friends and family, into the shambling dead.

But the dead have memories … they know I'm here.

I hear their hissing, smell the death. But before they can reach me, I detonate the pipe bomb I'd been holding since the beginning. Although I'll die and they won't, I relish knowing they'll be reduced to pieces, unable to kill or feast, just a gibbering graveyard beneath a town we all once loved.

INTERRED

RYAN NEIL FALCONE

My god—they're going to bury me alive!

Phil Kersey's mind churned with turmoil moments after awakening to find that he was lying in a coffin, unable to move. That he had no recollection of how he came to be in this predicament was as disconcerting as the paralysis itself. Even his eyes were unresponsive; in an attempt to get his bearings, he slowly took stock of his surroundings using his peripheral vision. The room he was in had the unmistakable décor of a funeral parlor.

This was a funeral. *His* funeral.

The shocking epiphany was interrupted when the open space above his coffin was suddenly occupied by a looming figure. It took a moment for his unfocused eyes to coalesce on the somber face of his brother-in-law. Curtis was his daughter's godparent, a frequent golfing partner, and an even more frequent drinking buddy. More importantly, he was also a doctor.

I have to signal him … let him know that I'm not dead …

He first tried to speak, then to lift his hand to get Curtis's attention, but nothing happened either time. Instead, he remained silent and motionless as the gurney the coffin laid upon was pushed down a lengthy corridor. From the way his head was positioned, he could see that the man pushing him was his wife's oldest brother, Perry, a mortician. His heart began to race when Perry began to discuss perfunctory burial arrangements with his wife.

How had he gotten here? What the hell had happened? It took the full measure of his concentration to block out the blinding intensity of the migraine he was experiencing, which shrouded his memory.

I'm a pharmaceutical sales rep. I have a wife and a daughter and drive a red Porsche. My wife calls it the 'mid-life crisis-mobile' and complains that the vanity license plate is tacky … I was driving home from a sales conference when …

He shuddered involuntarily. Something about that specific memory was frightening.

Why couldn't he remember?

Roads thick with ice and snow … his attention instead focused on the redheaded woman sitting next to him in the passenger seat …

His wife?

No … his wife had brown hair … someone else …

His attention snapped back to the present when he heard his wife ask for a final minute alone with him before they loaded the coffin into the hearse. She waited until the others left the room before reaching into the coffin to pluck off his sunglasses.

"I know you can hear me," she began, the distinct lack of pity in her eyes causing a shudder to ripple down his spine. "Curtis assures me that you're awake, you only look dead. The reason you can't move is because I drugged you with tetrodotoxin—an extract from pufferfish toxin. The proper dose can paralyze an adult man for hours, even though they're fully conscious.

"Since your condition wouldn't fool medical professionals, I needed to enlist my brothers to exact revenge. Curtis was the one who pronounced you dead at the hospital. Perry made sure that you weren't embalmed when they brought you to the funeral home—because I want you to be awake to experience what comes next.

"I'm going to bury you now," she continued, roughly stuffing the sunglasses back down onto his face. "But not in our family plot—I'm going to plant you next to where *she's* buried. The toxin won't wear off for another few hours, which will give you plenty of time to think about what you've done."

Her face tightened into a disgusted sneer as she threw a fluorescent, Halloween glow stick into the coffin. "Goodbye, Philip—may you rot in hell."

A shriek of claustrophobic terror echoed in his mind after she slammed the casket's lid shut, sealing him inside.

Jarring around inside the casket as the hearse traveled toward the cemetery, he tried to make understand what his wife had told him. Her chilling words echoed in his mind, but none of what she'd said made sense. Their marriage was far from perfect, but what could he have done to deserve such a fate? Surely, she wasn't capable of murder … if she went through with this, she'd have blood on her hands.

Blood on her hands …

Oh god …

All at once, the memory that had previously eluded him came back in full, vivid detail.

Red Porsche … snow covered roads … his fingers tapping on the steering wheel to the song blaring on the radio … wedding ring moved to the pinky finger of his left hand … the designer sunglasses he was wearing were a gift from the redheaded woman riding next to him … his gaze descended, stopping to admire the toned contour of her legs …

Not his wife … someone else … Bethany Milton, a co-worker with whom he'd been having an affair … the fling had started casually, but it hadn't been long before he

31

was spending late nights at the office and going out of town on 'business trips' in order to spend time with her ...

Making a quick stop for a clandestine encounter at a hotel one the way home from a sales conference ... distracted by the memory of what they'd done ... being startled when the windshield was illuminated by the headlights of an oncoming car ...

Slamming on the brakes ... skidding out of control on the icy roads ... Bethany's terrified scream before impact silenced by the sound of twisting metal and shattered glass ... upside down in a ditch ... his shock at seeing Bethany with shards of glass protruding from her face ... blood streaming down arms outstretched over her head, trickling down onto the tattered remnant of the Porsche's convertible top ...

The horrid recollection was chased away when he felt the coffin being lifted from the vehicle. He again tried to shout for help, but his paralyzed body betrayed him yet again, and he remained silent even as the coffin was lowered into the grave. Moments after the casket came to rest at the bottom of the hole, the first shovelful of dirt careened loudly against the coffin's lid. The noise eventually grew fainter as more and more dirt was piled on. When it faded entirely, he was left with the horrific realization that he'd been entombed.

I have to get out of this coffin! If I could somehow force the lid open ...

His panic gave way to hopefulness when he felt his face twitch. Now that he was thinking about it, he could also feel his chest now rising and falling as he breathed. He again tried to move his hand ... and finally succeeded. Whatever his wife had poisoned him seemed to be wearing off. But was it too late? Would he run out of air before the paralysis wore off?

This terrible notion was immeasurably worsened moments later when the glow stick his wife had placed in the coffin suddenly winked out. Surrounded by suffocating darkness, a primal scream rose in his throat, growing louder as the use of his vocal chords finally returned.

Fueled by adrenaline, he began to thrash, ineffectually smashing his uncooperative hands and feet against the interior of the coffin. Sobbing, he lay trapped for what seemed like an eternity, screaming for help—his pathetic cries dying in his throat only when he heard a noise coming from outside the coffin. Straining to listen, a wave of warm relief spread throughout his body—somebody was digging him out!

A few minutes later, he heard scraping on the outside of his coffin. Relieved anticipation gave way to astonishment when the top of the casket splintered above him, pouring dirt inside until the flow was choked off by something slithering through the opening. He knew at once that it was Bethany; not even the absolute blackness of being underground prevented him seeing how corpse-like her once beautiful face had become. The stench of decay overpowered the familiar scent of her lilac perfume, and he began to hyperventilate as the imaginary presence caused the few remaining strands of his sanity to fully unravel.

Gasping as the last of the oxygen in the casket was used up, the terrified man's dying scream was cut short when the hallucinatory revenant encircled skeletal hands around his throat and began to squeeze.

IT SLEEPS

STUART CONOVER

Deep beneath the great pyramids, it sleeps. Entombed in worship, in sacrifice, trapped within its own shattered mind.

Within the earth, beyond the tunnel, stairs, and abyss below. Buried in sand, darkness, and time.

It slumbers, a darkness held in check by dreams.

But all things that sleep eventually awaken. Slumbering in silence the drums beat once more. Calling to it, to them. The believers once more practicing the ancient rights. Some for power and some to awaken the sleepers.

Woe to the world when the great beast opens its eyes and births once more the creatures of the night.

TRYST

AMANDA BERGLOFF

The moon appeared red above the crypt. She picked black roses and sang a song to the dead. A song without words, yet it was full of despair. It was melancholy and macabre.

He listened as he stared at the dark stars. When she turned to look at him, he found meaning and purpose in her soulless eyes. He reached out his cold hand, and they shared black-hearted whispers until just before dawn.

When the sky began to lighten, they walked to the crypt for their final goodnight. Madness awaited them as they joined with the mist.

Morbid phantasm … eternal tryst.

TURNING TIDES

KC GRIFANT

The quivering masses bobbed above the shipwreck, trailing a plum-colored cloud.

Maggie tapped on her underwater camera. With the warming ocean temperatures, jellies were reproducing at unprecedented rates, spawning never before seen species.

It was beautiful until tentacles wrenched off her snorkeling mask. She kicked upwards but felt both electrified and numb. Neurotoxins, she thought. Her mind glommed around an emphatic declaration:

Ours.

Each flick of the buzzing tentacles onto her face imparted a new vision: massive jellies swallowed ships, clogged harbors, suffocated whole cities. Her throat gasped, desperate.

Ours.

The continents sparkled with purple dust, the seas liquid amethyst.

YOUNG LOVE

ROSE BLACKTHORN

"Mrs. Matthew Brentner. Kacey Brentner. Mrs. Brentner. Matthew and Kacey Brentner." Kacey doodled the different versions of the name that would (she hoped) one day be hers, tongue-tip protruding from her mouth without her noticing.

"Kacey," her mother called from downstairs. "Are you up there?"

"Yeah, Mom," she called back. She set her notebook aside as she rolled off her stomach and sat up on the bed.

"Come down here, please. The police have some questions for us about that missing boy from your school."

Kacey shushed the bound and gagged boy in her closet. "I'll be back soon, Matt."

FEBRUARY

HELLO MR. MAGPIE

ROSS BAXTER

Sophie looked at her watch again in frustration; Jim had kept her waiting for nearly twenty minutes now, even though he knew she needed to be home to collect her daughter from art class. She sighed heavily, bitterly regretting ever offering Jim a ride home from work. As she had to drive past his house on her daily commute she had offered to give her colleague a lift whilst he fixed his broken car, but over three weeks later it was still not on the road. She had not really known him before, but during the increasingly tedious rides to and from the office, she had learned more about him than she ever wanted to know. Just as she opened her car door to return inside to find him, she saw him stroll out of the front doors of the office and slowly made his way across the car park towards her.

"I told you I needed to leave at five!" she frowned.

"Yeah, but something came up," he explained casually. "I'm sure whatever you're going to do can wait a few minutes."

"My eight-year-old daughter and her teacher would probably disagree," she muttered, starting the engine.

Jim said nothing and unhurriedly climbed in. Sophie put the battered Ford into gear and roared off towards the outskirts of town. Luckily the traffic was light but she doubted she could get to the school in time. Another round of apologies to the teacher and to her daughter was not what she needed after a stressful day, and she started to think about what she was going to say.

"Just pull in at the shop on the left," said Jim. "I need some beers for the game tonight."

"You're kidding me?"

"I won't be long," said Jim.

"I've already told you how late I am! My daughter is already going to be really upset, as is her teacher."

"Oh, come on!" Jim cried, sounding more like a churlish teenager than the forty-year-old he was.

"Sorry," Sophie shot back. "Perhaps you can fix your car instead of watching the game?"

Jim shook his head and looked longingly at the off-licence as they drove past.

After a couple of roundabouts, they soon emerged on the country road which led towards where Jim lived, and she speeded up a little. Jim gave her a disapproving look.

"You know the limit is forty here?" he muttered.

"I'm late," she answered, looking at the empty road ahead.

Jim tutted to himself and then for the next five minutes kept openly glancing at the speedometer as they drove in silence. Suddenly he stared incredulously at his colleague as she appeared to salute and then mumble a few inaudible words behind her hand.

"What the hell did you just do?" he asked.

"Pardon?" Sophie asked back, keeping her eyes fixed on the road ahead as she steered the old Ford around a sharp bend.

"You just saluted and muttered something," said Jim accusingly.

"Oh, I saw a magpie," Sophie replied.

"And?"

Sophie sighed. Having to put up with the boorish and opinionated Jim for the twenty-minute ride was becoming more and more of a challenge every day.

"Why did you just salute a stupid bird?" Jim pushed.

"Because it's bad luck not to," she explained. "It is good luck to see two magpies together, but if you see a single one you're supposed to greet it and say 'Hello, Mr. Magpie'."

"Are you superstitious?"

"No," said Sophie.

"Then why does a grown woman openly salute and talk to a dumb bird?"

"My family have always done it. I suppose it's a bit of a tradition going back as long as we can remember."

"So, you are superstitious," Jim scoffed loudly. "That is so lame! I really expected more from you."

Sophie shrugged and returned her attention to the road.

"So, are you from a family of superstitious Leprechauns?" Jim continued. "Are your days ruled by avoiding black cats, not walking under ladders, and not getting out of bed on Halloween?"

"No," said Sophie flatly. "It's just the magpies. I've never given it much thought really."

"Obviously," sneered Jim. "I'm not sure if you realize but we do actually live in the twenty-first century and not the eighteenth. It's time to forget about stupid superstitions, especially nonsense about greeting magpies. I can't believe how some people still believe in such claptrap!"

Sophie said nothing, trying instead to control her anger at her boorish passenger. She had greeted magpies ever since she could remember; it was no big deal but she knew Jim was not going to let it drop.

"All superstitions are nonsense designed to frighten the weak and the ignorant; flesh and bone can't be harmed by old wives' tales," Jim ranted on.

"Whatever," Sophie said, trying to concentrate on driving.

"We've put a man on the moon; you'd think stupid superstitions would be a thing long consigned to the dustbin of history!"

Sophie ignored him; her attention drawn to a black-and-white bird pecking at roadkill on the narrow road ahead. She started to slow the car.

"You have got to be joking?" Jim sneered. "Just run it over!"

"Hello, Mr. Magpie," Sophie yelled loudly, flipping an extravagantly fancy salute as she slowed the car.

The magpie looked at the approaching vehicle and quickly flew off, but Sophie stopped the car anyway.

"Why the hell have you stopped?"

"Get out Jim; you can walk from here," she said calmly.

"But my house is over a mile away!" Jim spluttered in surprise. "I can't walk from here."

"You are the most self-opinionated and bigoted man I have ever met," said Sophie. "Instead of wasting energy on your constant lecturing, I suggest you spend it on fixing your car. Now get out!"

Shocked and for once speechless, Jim grudgingly unfastened his seat belt and opened the door. As soon as he was out Sophie gunned the engine of her elderly car and roared off, leaving him alone by the empty roadside. He could not understand what he had said to make her so angry and resolved to formally complain to her manager in the morning.

As he started to trudge up the deserted country lane the thought of making trouble for Sophie cheered him up. Dozens of possible stories flooded his mind, and after five minutes of walking he finally decided he would say that he had asked to get out of the car because Sophie had made a pass at him, that felt plausible, especially as he was sure that most of the women at work actually did want to make a pass at him. Spreading that story would not only get Sophie into trouble, but it would also remind his other female co-workers what an absolute catch he was. Maybe one of them would offer to give him a ride to and from the office; although he had actually fixed his car two weeks ago he did enjoy getting a free commute.

Thinking up the ultimate story to completely discredit Sophie in the eyes of her colleagues was fun, and by the time he reached the bend on the last rise it had completely absorbed him. He did not see the truck speeding over the rise, and in the failing afternoon light the truck driver failed to see Jim as he took the corner wide whilst retuning the radio. The loud music masked the thud as the lorry's offside mudguard glanced off the surprised Jim, and the trucker drove on oblivious.

The blow knocked Jim senseless for a few minutes. When he finally came too he found himself face-down in the dirt at the edge of the deserted road, confused as to how he got there. Then he remembered being thrown out of the car by Sophie, all because he told her it was stupid to believe in superstitions. With rage and indignation, he tried to clamber up but something was wrong.

Nothing would respond; he could not move his legs, arms or even his head. He felt no pain except for in his eyes which were full of grit, each blink causing him to cry out in agony. But his cries were silent.

Next, he saw the blur of a black-and-white shape hopping towards him. The magpie stopped inches from his face, coldly peering into Jim's bloodshot eyes.

Then it started to peck hungrily at flesh and bone.

GHOST OF A SMILE

KEN MACGREGOR

Ben had been haunting me for days. The moment he died, his ghost appeared. The apparition wore Ben's favorite shirt: the orange one with the ink-stain on the cuff. He was smiling.

My brother was always happy. Some people are impossible to depress.

I watched the undersize coffin lower into the ground. Mom tossed a handful of dirt; her eyes were red with constant tears.

Beside me, Ben began to fade, starting at the feet. As more dirt fell, more of Ben disappeared. Finally, like the Cheshire Cat, there was only his smile.

That faded, too and he was gone.

THE GREATEST LOVE

PAUL STARKEY

I fell in love the moment we met. How could I not? She was so young and vibrant. We went everywhere together, did everything together. I never thought it would last forever, only a fool imagines any romance ever does, but I thought we'd have many years together. Sadly, it was not to be.

She gave me her heart. Her other organs were placed in storage, eventually I'll need them too.

I loved her, but I'll love my next clone just as much. Hopefully we'll enjoy a much longer courtship before our love must be consummated on the operating table.

BATH TIME

STEPHANIE ELLIS

Every drip ate away at the rusted tub. Corrosion and time had done their worst. Nothing remained. And yet ears listened although they only heard blessed silence. Eyes watched, transfixed as they witnessed every flicker of disintegration.

On the wall hung the Waste Disposal outfit: the dirty yellow boiler suit, heavy gauge gloves and thick protective visor. He was very careful with the chemicals he handled, had a healthy respect—awe you could say—for what they could do.

Despair and resignation claimed her as he refilled the tub. She had given up trying to escape.

It was bath time.

MRS MARGOLIS

GREG MOSS

Mrs Margolis lived in the house across the street from me. Every night on the way home from school she was visible through her window, as she sat and knitted in front of the TV. One night she invited me round to help her with some chores, and I reluctantly accepted, she was going to pay me and I'd be able to afford the Spiderman graphic novel I'd been eyeing up.

Of course, I was surprised that evening, as after she called me into her house, I found her dead in front of the TV. Maggots crawling in her eyes.

KAMERADEN

RICHARD J. MELDRUM

The soldier slid into the shell crater, gasping with the exertion of running. Despite the stagnant water and the company of shattered corpses he was happy to be there, protected from the bullets and shells that clipped the earth above him. He had no gun; his Mauser had been discarded during the flight from the Russians. He cursed his luck.

His battalion had tried to push forward that morning, attempting to seize a nameless village on the Russian steppe. All they'd taken with them were a few Spandaus; the officers had only expected to encounter infantry, perhaps a few mortars at worst. Instead they'd met armoured resistance; T-34s. They were repulsed with heavy losses.

He'd got detached from his squad; somewhere in the scramble to escape, in the smoke, noise and dust, he'd taken the wrong turn and now he was behind the enemy advance. He was a dead man; the Russians would show him no mercy, just as he showed none to the Russians.

He daren't even peek out of the crater. He could hear shouts in Russian, the thump of boots and the squeak of tank treads. Sliding to the bottom, he feigned death, praying he would be overlooked. He fell into a deep sleep, despite the cold and fear.

It was night when he woke. The world around him was silent, foggy and pitch black. He assessed his situation. Clearly the war had moved on. He had no idea if the Germans had advanced or if he was behind the Russian lines. Stranded, his only option was to try to make his way towards his own troops. But which way to go? The wrong choice would be fatal.

A snuffling from the crater edge raised the hairs on his neck. Feral dogs would often eat corpses and sometimes, if they were hungry enough, they would kill wounded men. He wasn't wounded, but he had no weapon to defend himself with.

There was a familiar howl from above.

"Rudi?" he asked in amazement.

There was an answering bark, the sound of scrambling and then a dark shape jumped into his arms. He felt a warm tongue on his face.

"Rudi! It's you. You found me!"

He felt a huge sense of relief. Rudi was a stray dog the soldier had picked up about two months before. He'd been abandoned in a deserted village. Rudi loved his new master and followed him everywhere. Well, almost everywhere; the soldier always left Rudi with the battalion cook when the troops advanced, the soldier didn't want him in harm's way.

"Rudi, do know the way back to camp?"

There was a bark in response. It sounded like yes.

"Let's go, take me back!"

The pair left the crater and headed down the road. The soldier saw that the Russian advance had clearly faltered. The road was strewn with wrecked T-34s and corpses in brown uniforms. It made the soldier feel happy to see so many of the enemy dead; that meant his comrades had had the strength to counter attack. It meant they were probably still in the area. The soldier had a chance of surviving this night. He placed his hand onto Rudi's back, feeling fur and muscle. It was comforting, it gave him the courage to keep going.

Suddenly Rudi stopped, his hackles rising. He was looking in the direction they were travelling. The soldier strained to see what had alerted his companion, but it was just too dark. The silence was unnerving. There was a sudden clink of metal; the soldier recognised the sound, it was a rifle being loaded. Soldiers were moving in the darkness in front of him, but what uniform did they wear? Rudi bared his teeth. The soldier decided to trust him, moving off the road and into the undergrowth. He was just in time.

Only a minute or so later, two Russians crept past, their eyes nervously sweeping the road. Survivors, just like him. One clutched a rifle, the other a machine gun. The soldier backed further into the undergrowth, fearing he would be spotted. His boot knocked against something metallic. The Russian holding the machine gun uttered a guttural curse and spun round to stare into the bushes. For a second, he was clearly unsure about whether to fire, but then he lifted his weapon. Rudi, his body a blur, leapt from his hiding place and attacked. The Russian had no time to react before Rudi was at his throat, pulling and ripping. Huge spurts of arterial blood sprayed Rudi. The other Russian raised his rifle. He fired once, then again. Rudi fell to the ground. The soldier, still kneeling in the undergrowth, knew the Russian couldn't have missed at that range. Rudi was dead. He felt a huge surge of anger. Launching himself from the undergrowth, he smashed into the Russian, knocking him over. He grabbed a piece of metal and hit the Russian with all his might. It was over in seconds.

The soldier, his vengeance satisfied, turned to find Rudi; he deserved a decent burial. To his amazement, Rudi was standing, but his fur was covered in blood. Fearing the worst, the soldier knelt and held his companion, his hands running up and down the dog's body. There were no wounds and the soldier suddenly realised that the blood belonged to the Russian. Tears rolled down his face.

"I could have sworn he'd got you, Rudi. He was just so close. It's a miracle."

Rudi licked his face.

The rest of their journey was uneventful. The soldier found his comrades camped about four kilometres from the village. He called to the sentries and was allowed to enter, with Rudi at his side. He was greeted warmly, they thought he'd been killed. But the joy he felt at his safe return wasn't to last. His squad leader took him to one side, his face serious.

"I have bad news, kamerad."

"What?"

"I'm sorry. Your dog was killed just after we left this morning. A stray shell hit the camp kitchen."

"That can't be. He's with me now. He came and found me, just an hour ago. He protected me, saved my life. He brought me back to the camp."

The squad leader pointed to a small shape, covered with a burlap sheet. A paw stuck out from one side. It was Rudi. The soldier looked down, there was no longer a dog by his side. He knelt by the body of his friend, feeling a grief that can only be experienced when a beloved animal dies. The words sung over the graves of fallen comrades came into his head. *Ich hatte einen Kamerdan.* As he wept a wet nose touched his hand. He reached out and felt familiar soft fur. The soldier smiled, grieving no longer. Amidst this hellish conflict he felt a brief moment of joy. He hadn't lost his best friend. Rudi would be by his side forever.

THE REAL BOGEY MAN

LIZ BUTCHER

Quillon crouched in the darkest corner of the room, hidden from sight.

Though weak, he knew the boy still sensed his presence. He could see him trembling under the bed covers, too scared to tear his gaze from where the monster hid in the shadows.

Quillon welcomed the fear, it strengthened him and as it came to him in waves, he felt himself grow stronger, taller. The rapid pounding of the boy's heart was music to his ears as he stretched his arms out, scratching his nails against the walls.

With a guttural growl, he lunged, welcoming the boy's screams.

HUNGER MOON

JENNIFER CANAVERAL

The newlyweds sat against a spruce tree, the glow of lunar light shining down on their weakened bodies. A romantic romp in the Alaskan wilderness gone awry after fresh snow covered their tracks back to their cabin. Two days passed. Still lost.

Her husband snuck their last energy bar without her knowing. He forgot it had peanuts. He forgot his injectable epinephrine.

His agonal breathing echoed throughout the forest, drawing shadows into the moonlight. Sets of yellow eyes emerged from the trees and surrounded the couple. They don't eat humans, the wife thought, but they looked famished. They looked merciless.

GRANNY GWEN

HILLARY LYON

"Granny Gwen, who is the man in this picture?"

"Let me see, child. There's your brother Montgomery, and Mommy," Gwen said, tracing her finger along the old photo.

"But who's that man standing next to Mommy? Daddy?"

"No, hon. That gentleman is Mr. Scratch." Granny Gwen sighed and smiled knowingly. She returned the heavy silver frame to the gold-gilt Louis XV curio cabinet.

"Is he family?" The girl frowned. "And since when do I have a brother?"

"No, dear, he's the devil."

The little girl gasped.

"We made a deal and traded up. How do you think we got here?"

THE TENDER SPOT

ANDY BROWN

I'd been picking at it for a week when it really started to throb.

Just a spot on my leg … more a boil, really …

I had to do something about it so I squeezed it hard.

It just throbbed more.

I squeezed it again and it burst open. Pus squirted out and poured onto my leg, yellow and foul smelling …

I dabbed at it with an antiseptic tissue, mopping up the pus and the blood.

There was a moment of huge relief as the throbbing lessened.

Then I saw the eyeball …

It looked out from the open wound … at me …

LIFE AND LIMB

KEVIN HOLTON

I thought she was a rumor.

People never talked openly about The Surgeon. If she came up in conversation, it was in whispers behind closed doors. When Margorie first told me about her, I dismissed these discussions as rumors. Myths. Stories told to the desperate or fearful. Gullible people are why I spent my few scarce hours of free time at home, sitting around.

My couch was full of holes, but it was mine, and I was in my favorite spot, watching the Ultranet news feed on my holographic video screen. Beyond the couch and holovid, I didn't have much else, and my barren apartment showed it. Blank walls, a dirty floor I rarely got time to clean, and a bed that sagged in the middle were about all I owned.

On the news, another few people had been very brutally, very publicly, killed by Enforcers. Unity Government's official statement was, as always, "Obey the law, support your country, and do not resist arrest. Follow these rules, and you'll be fine."

A spasm ran down my arm. The left one, the Dynatech arm I had installed to replace my real one after the accident. Lately, it had been malfunctioning. I couldn't afford repairs, and UniGov ignored my appeals for assistance. I'd received an email of only two sentences. "We will not be able to help you. Bear in mind, a severe decrease in productivity may result in a punishment of a fifty thousand credit fine and ten years in prison."

Another harsh jerk, this one painful. All the new models were built to feel everything flesh and bone could, and that wasn't always a good thing. Frayed wiring sent electric bursts through my system, hurting both replicant and real tissues. Squinting my eyes shut, I massaged my shoulder, where the installation met muscle.

"Planned obsolescence," said a voice, and I jerked back, eyes wide. A woman stood against the wall, next to the news feed, where protesters were destroying a few bodegas to show how they disliked UniGov oversight.

"Who—how did you get in here?" The hammering in my chest overrode my pain. My door had been locked, and like every home, apartment, and business in Adonia, it had a complex combination lock. Only I knew the code. There were no windows.

"Wealth perpetuates. Design faulty goods, then design a way of life so you can't live without them. Buy, break, buy, break. Repeat, ad nauseum."

Her tone was cool, calculated, machine-like, but I couldn't tell who or even what she was. The woman wore a long black shirt and loose pants that flowed around her like an oil spill. On her face, she had a reflective mask, and a hood drawn to hide the rest of her head. When I tried to make eye contact, I only saw myself.

I stood up, ready for conflict. I didn't have much, but I had pride, and wasn't about to be intimidated in my own home, no matter how crappy a home it was. "What are you doing here?"

"Relax," she said, raising a hand, "I'm not your enemy. In fact, I'm here to help." Being around her made my head buzz with a faint static. My brain was caught between the channels of anger and curiosity. Darkness shifted, clinging to her frame as she levered herself off the wall, slowly approaching. "Let me see: a crushing accident. Hydraulic press came down in the center of your arm. Splintered bone. Torn muscle. Beyond repair. UniGov offered a new arm as compensation, but has no interest in upkeep."

All this was said as a statement of fact, and was completely accurate. She didn't need to ask questions. I was barely part of this—just an observer, not reacting, or sure how to, even as she reached out and began probing at my shoulder too, as I'd been doing moments earlier. Her fingers were cold. Real fingers, with skin and tendons, but long and pointed, almost sharp.

"Hm. Artificial supraspinatus and bicep tendons. Dynatech humerus head inserted into original glenoid. Easy." Despite her mask, I could sense a smile on her face, mouth stretching wide like she was ready to bite. "You're angry, aren't you? At this government, which treats you so poorly. At your ..." she rapped on my elbow, sending another jolt through me. "Limitations."

I'd had enough games. Hypnotic as her touch may have been, I fought myself to say, "Why are you here?"

"Because you want me here, David." Her reply, swift and rehearsed, told me she'd had this conversation many times before.

I swallowed, hard, feeling a tense knot in my throat. "You're ... The Surgeon, aren't you?"

She laughed. Just once, a short, rhythmic burst of melody that bore the memory of brighter times. "Is that what they call me now? Well, I suppose it's not wrong. That's what I offer you. Surgery. I'll remove this arm of yours."

That was downright unthinkable. No one offered Dynatech *removal*. I mean, even kids were getting Cosme-tech augmentations these days. Your wealth was literally measured in the price of your new 'parts'. Otherwise, you were just any old human. Or worse, Defective. "Why? What's in it for you? I don't have money."

"I know," she replied. It wasn't a condemnation, like it would've been from anyone else. I almost heard a note of sympathy. "I ask your service. I'll free you from the tyranny of cybernetics, and in return, you leave Adonia. Forever. Join my coalition back on Earth's surface, where the darkness of this floating nation is just a passing shadow. You'll tend fields, raise livestock, whatever the group needs. Whatever you can do with one arm."

It was an enticing offer. As it was, I was working to survive anyway. Having people around, actual companionship, and a job I could be proud of didn't sound too bad.

Another soft chuckle. "So, you accept my offer?"

That confirmed it. She really *could* read minds. The rumors I'd waved off as impossible held up. "I do."

"Then the first thing we have to do is fake your death, so no one gets suspicious."

A screeching filled my head and pain exploded behind my eyeballs, painting my vision red. I struggled to stay conscious, only faintly aware that I was crying out and kicking at the floor, my body reflexively fighting against this slow implosion. Then my limbs fell limp, refusing to respond to my primal urge to flee as she kneeled over me, holding up a scalpel.

"That involves a little screaming," she said, "and a whole lot of blood."

She held me down, and in truth, the operation didn't take long. True to her word, she let me scream; in my neighborhood, no one would bother investigating. Violent crimes were common. There'd been a news report later. Maybe. Plus, when you don't have to be careful or gentle, surgery isn't complicated.

I passed out from blood loss. When I awoke, for a moment, I thought I'd been having a nightmare. When I tried to sit-up, but could only push myself off the metal cot with my one remaining arm, I knew it'd been real.

My body shivered, but if I was cold, I didn't feel it. Shock, probably. Wouldn't be surprising. I'd been placed in an abandoned sickbay. There were a dozen or so beds, all like mine: rusted from neglect.

Voices caught my attention as I shook away the veil of unconsciousness. I followed them, passing a mirror in the hall. My left arm was gone. The stump of my shoulder had been branded, no doubt to stop me from bleeding out. In the center was an eye.

"… Just one of many recent deaths in this district," a voice said, drawing me out to a waiting area. This might've been a hospital. Now, it was just a waystation. A single holographic screen ran, projecting tonight's news. A woman I didn't recognize stood next to a picture of me. "A neighbor heard screaming. His landlord found the tenant's arm laying in a pool of blood. He has been declared deceased."

Deceased. She'd done it. I was officially dead. No one would be after me, or tracking me through the tech that'd given me an arm, but caused me so much pain and grief.

"You'll be escorted to a private vessel, and it'll take you to the surface. UniGov won't bother hunting for people there." Her voice echoed in my head, but she was nowhere to be found. Two men entered the room, eyeing me. "It will be a long, arduous life, but it will be yours, full of people who've made the same decisions. Try to enjoy it."

CONFECTIOUS

MATTHEW R. DAVIS

When a nurse comes down the hall, I show him the visible joins at my elbows, knees, shoulders, every joint weeping a pale putrescence—as if I'm a doll that some sullen child has stuffed with stale cream—and, fascinated, he dabs at my infection, this sickly confection, sniffs it … then licks his fingers clean and laughs, a hideous hunger swelling him, and he's all over me until my seeping hands grab a bedpan and pulp his face into sticky red jam, but he's not alone on duty tonight, and they're all laughing, licking their sweet teeth as they come.

MENTAL CHECK

PATRICK WINTERS

As I stow the last grocery bag, I still have that nagging feeling that I've forgotten something. I start taking stock of my trunk, just to be sure. Trash bags? Check. Extra duct tape? Double check. Disposable gloves? Yep. New axe head? Shining nicely in its package. Gagged and bound victim? Obviously. Kind of hard to forget him, especially with all the squirming and moaning he's been doing. He looks up at me, begging me to let him go with his puppy-dog eyes. Then it hits me; I finally realize what's wrong here: I forgot to get kibble for Rufus.

VALENTINE SURPRISES

BRENDAN O'DEA

A sadist refused to give his wife a divorce.

He did all in his power to make her life a living hell. On Valentine's Day, this cruel man made a present to her of a scarf that was the 'wrong colour'. He cooked her a meal that aggravated her food allergy. On her Valentine's card he inscribed the words: *My Love, we will be together till death do us part.'* Later, while driving, he laughed so hard tears ran down his face. He was caught unawares as a freak hailstone shattered the windscreen. He lost control, swerving towards his fate.

THE ADELPHI

ALYSON FAYE

It's not easy being the youngest. Becca was always being left out or left behind. It wasn't fair.

She so wanted to be in. Especially with them. So, when Jake and Joss had laughingly challenged everyone to the 'hugest dare ever,' Becca had been the first in the gang to leap up and accept. Now she was sorry. Sorry seven times over. Joss had nearly choked with amusement on her chewing gum, while Jake had smirked behind his usual fag.

"Ok, Titch," he'd said shrugging. "You're on."

Then he had bent down and whispered into Becca's ear. Her bones had melted and she'd had to hold onto her bladder.

"Bastards!" She thought, "you 100 per cent bastards!"

Two nights later Becca sneaked out of her family's tiny terraced house, with its clutchy curtains, and began hiking out of town along the main road towards the destination of the 'dare'.

"We'll know if you bottle it Titch." Jake had warned her, waving his lighted ciggy close to her face.

She'd spotted him spying on her from his bedroom window when she'd strolled past his foster parent's house. Keeping his beady on her. So, to show him, she'd waved carelessly. He'd laughed and given her the finger.

Ten minutes later Becca faced up to the old Adelphi; a once regal hotel, now derelict. Its state of decay didn't stop the local kids, druggies and the homeless creeping inside its rotten shell. Looking up Becca felt dwarfed. It had been such a grand old behemoth. She noticed the pair of stone lions still roosting on either side of what had been the main entrance.

"Bollocks," she thought.

"Don't forget Titch, you gotta go right inside. All the way down to the basement, take a photo and send it me," Jake had instructed, smiling all the time. As if he was her mate.

Becca knew how to get in; knew exactly where to lift the broken hoardings and slide through, leaving only a little bit of skin behind.

Once infiltrated in the Adelphi's innards, Becca found her way to the grand ballroom. Fifty years ago, with its marble floor and wall to wall mirrors, it had been the most glamorous venue in town. Now all Becca saw was a rubble strewn, filthy, echoey space.

Her phone bleeped. It was Joss. "U there yet girl?"

Becca frowned but obediently texted back, "Yeah. In ballroom. Stinks in here."

Joss sent an emoji of a smiley face. "Watch out 4 dead bodies."

"Cow," muttered Becca with great force. But she didn't text the thought back. She didn't have the nerve.

In the shattered spider webs of broken mirrors, Becca caught a glimpse of movement. Just a brief flicker. Heading for the door. She swung around.

"Who's there?" The glass shards crunched under her trainers.

She walked back into the foyer where a trapped sparrow was frantically beating its wings against the ceiling's fabulous plasterwork. The door leading to the basement was swinging slightly on its hinges. Just as if someone had passed that way. Becca gulped. Sweat was already breaking though under her armpits. Knowing she had to go through that same door didn't help either.

Reluctantly Becca pushed at the green baize and holding her breath because of the smell, she inched her way down the stairs. Past signs which read 'Kitchen' and 'Laundry.' Down, down several flights until the 'Basement' sign greeted her.

"OK. Let's do this," she tried to encourage herself. The carpet was mushy with mould. Some of the spores stuck to her trainers. The walls were splattered with green mouldy patches rather like a Pollock painting gone to seed.

Worst of all though Becca could feel an energy down here; a thrumming. It made her skin itch and the hairs on her arms lift up. Pushing open another swing door, she found herself staring at a room filled with floor to ceiling racks once used for storage. At last she'd got here. The basement. The bowel of the beast.

She could hear the skittering feet of rats. The air smelt of a blend of wood, damp and something metallic, which caught at the back of her throat.

"Just rats that's all girl. Chill." She tried to breathe steadily, calming herself. But her heart banged away at a quicker rhythm.

She knew if she didn't get this pic, she'd be out, ostracised, tormented, hounded. Right now, though Becca thought perhaps she could cope with that. Maybe being 'in' wasn't so big a deal.

Facing the racks Becca held up her iPhone at face height and took the shot. In the momentary flash she glimpsed a figure hanging from one of the top racks, its feet jerking, doing the death dance. She saw legions of dark things scuttling around on the ground feeding. She spied a stain creeping out from under the racks, dark and viscous. The air buzzed and hummed; she tasted iron in her mouth.

Becca turned and raced for the stairs. Heart thumping, bile in her throat, sweat pouring down her body. She had only one thought, to get up and out. What if they followed her? What if? She slipped on the mouldy carpet, fell face down and tasted the dirt. She heaved herself up. In her haste to escape, she ripped her hand on the barbed wire fence. She'd have to go to A&E with that the next day she knew. It looked deep it. Damn it!

Only when she was back on her own street, did she pause and take out her iPhone to check the image again. Surrounded by her neighbours' bins, gardens and under the street lamps she now felt calmer.

The image she'd clicked and sent to Joss and Jake showed only a cellar filled with tall wooden racks, stretching back into darkness. There was no hanging man, no scuttling insects, no pool of … fluid. Except when she peered closely at the top right corner of the screen there was a black spot there, a bit like a fly. Or a spore. Or something anyway.

Hearing a noise behind her Becca jerked around. No one was there. Except she couldn't help but think she'd just missed seeing something scuttle away, out of sight behind No 33's recycling bins. A rat, that's all it'll be, she told herself. Lots of rats round here. Armies of them.

Letting herself in quietly at the backdoor Becca made her plans. First up a shower. She felt disgusting. Those mould spores had got everywhere. Tomorrow she'd go to A&E, after that she'd tell Josh and Jake to count her out. Scary as those two made themselves out to be they weren't half as creepy as what had happened in the Adelphi.

"Sorted then," she muttered. "I'm all sorted."

Rubbing her arms, she headed for the bathroom. "Jesus, though I don't half itch."

Outside her bedroom window a black shape gripped the drainpipe and slithered up inside the tubing. Sucking in the damp and moist debris, drawn by Becca's scent. It had followed her trail of skin fragments, blood and sweat. It had been alone a long time, but now it had a new home.

THE PAPER CLIP

MATHIAS JANSSON

Do you remember the Commodore 64? Perhaps you also remember that you could use a paperclip on one of the ports on the backside to reset a game?

My friend I must warn you. Never try that trick on Friday the 13th at midnight as I did. I was playing a new text adventure called Inferno when the game froze and I tried to reset it with a paper clip. Suddenly an electric flash hit my hand. When I woke up it was dark and when I screamed for help a voice constantly was repeating: "I don't understand that command."

SWIFT RETRIBUTION

ROBERT ALLEN LUPTON

Carl slipped on a loose pile of gold coins and woke the dragon. It opened both eyes, spotted Carl, and knocked him over with one paw like a cat playing with a mouse. It tore open his backpack with a razor-sharp talon and raised its eyebrows at the gold and jewels that tumbled out.

"I can explain. I'm sorry, I won't ever steal from you again."

A wisp of smoke curled from the dragon's nostrils before it expelled a flash of fire and burned Carl to a crisp. "I know you won't," it said, smiled, and went back to sleep.

THE MONSTER FROM MOORSVILLE

ERIK BERGSTROM

The smell inside the old barn was always the first thing they noticed. Old and rotted and wet, it was almost a sweet smell.

Especially the newspapers—stacks of them on the floor, all forty, fifty years old or older. There's one story Polly showed Nell from 1965, talking about the "Monster from Moorsville", a name given to the man who stole kids from nearby farms and never got caught.

Nell was still reading the final paragraph when she and Polly first heard the footsteps and saw a large, dark shadow break away from the back wall of the barn.

MARCH

DOWN TO A SUNLESS SEA

DJ TYRER

Beneath the playhouse were passages deeper still than any the theatre folk made use of. They lay below the lowest of the property stores in which were held all the sets of costumes and sundry items necessary for the staging of their plays. They lay below even the foundations, stretching down through the earth till they reached the level where water pooled and they could go no deeper.

None had descended the stairs in years. There was no need. Besides, legend spoke of horrid things that flopped wetly in the darkness and of the tall, gaunt phantom that stalked those passageways. Yet, down he dared to go.

He didn't know why he went. Not exactly. Just felt a strange compulsion. It just felt right as he set foot on the damp steps and cautiously made his way down into the darkness, the wan yellow light of a candle stub his only companion.

The walls were carved with grotesque faces that seemed to turn and leer at him as he passed by, the candlelight flickering horribly across them. He shivered and crossed himself, although he wondered whether the sign had any power here, deep below the earth.

He followed twisting passageways that turned sinuously back upon themselves. He couldn't bear to halt. It was as if a force were pulling him onwards, downwards. Something flopped wetly past his feet, but he dared not crouch down to discover what made the sound. He knew better than that. Knew to press onward.

Somewhere in the darkness, he imagined he could hear the distant echo of soft footsteps, sometimes nearer, sometimes further away. Did another wander here in these dark tunnels or did he but hear the echo of his own footsteps? Somehow, he knew that was not the answer and that he was not alone. The phantom they spoke of walked here yet.

After many twists and turns and slimy stairs, he found himself in a cavern standing on the shore of a still and silent pool. Restricted to the narrow circle of candlelight, he couldn't tell if the water was of limited extent or not. For all he could tell, he might have been standing upon the shore of a sunless sea.

He stood there for some minutes as the candle flickered and died. He no longer feared the darkness.

Standing there, he gazed out across the water he could no more see, across that sunless sea. Above him, somewhere, the play would be beginning, but here, he was the lead in one all his own.

In the distance, somewhere far across the water, he could make out lights. At first, they were small and faint. But the longer he stared, the closer they came and the brighter they glowed. He was certain he gazed upon a city on the far side of an underground lake.

And, as he stood there, he became aware of another presence, not far off. Someone standing upon the shore and staring out at that same city. He barely turned his head, loath to look away from the lights of the city. He thought the figure was tall and gaunt and arrayed in rags, with a face as blank as the masks of drama and comedy.

He stood there beside the phantom of the lakeshore until the two of them were one, merged in their desire for the distant city. A city which seemed to grow ever closer, the longer he looked at it. It was his home, he knew that now. It was what had called him down here, calling him home. And, O! How he longed for it! His heart ached for it.

It was nearer now. So near …

He couldn't wait any longer, the pull was too strong.

He stepped into the water and waded out till it rose past his knees, his waist, his shoulders, his chin …

He would be home soon. Home, at last …

THE VERY BEST

BY CATHERINE BERRY

On Valentine's Day he gave Connie a bracelet that sparkled in the light, and she made him one her of her special dinners.

"That was delicious," he said, giving her a kiss.

"I wanted to give you the very best," she teased, delighted. "My favorite recipe for heart braised in wine; it seemed appropriate for the holiday."

"It was," he assured her after a moment, shrugging off the exotic choice.

Connie smiled. If he liked that, perhaps she'd cook him the liver or sweetbreads in the basement freezer. After she got rid of what was left of Roger, of course.

AWAKENING

KM ZAFARI

Drip … Drip … Drip …

The unsettling sound roused her from unconsciousness.

"Where am I?"

The utilitarian room was cold and dark, save for a thin strip of light peering beneath the door at the top of a wooden staircase.

Drip … Drip … Drip …

Large, metal hooks hung from the ceiling; from one dangled the body of an inverted man. Blood ran down in gullets from his grotesque, grinning throat, coalescing at the scalp before finding its way to the awaiting drain.

"Jeremy?"

Drip … Drip … Drip …

The door creaked open. "Oh, good," her captor said, a wry smile upon his lips. "You're awake."

KINDNESS IN THE AFTERMATH

ROB FRANCIS

Her mother's hands bore purple welts, and lesions rimmed her eyes. Her breathing came shallow as the ochre dust that lay on everything, the skin of a new world forming in the Aftermath.

Payal ran from the house, throat dry from the dead air, eyes stinging and wild.

Soldiers choked the village and blocked the road, a wall of men and machines. Masked and hooded faces turned towards her; then all was muted shouting and pointed guns. Payal raised her hands and saw the marks. She understood.

Amidst the cruelty of this new world, they were doing her a kindness.

RESURRECTION

CHANELLE PINA

The cream-colored ceiling greeted me when I woke up. The silence in my apartment complex was surprising, especially at this hour. I turned to my nightstand, and my small, red alarm clock blinked 8:20. I had work at 9:30 and the alarm had gone off, however, instead of the obnoxious blaring it was faint beeping noises. Swinging my short legs over the side of the bed, it didn't creak like usual. The hardwood floors felt warm despite it being December.

I bumped the bathroom door open with my bum and again, no creak. Meeting my own face in the mirror, I was confused. I squeezed my cheeks, lifted my eyelids, pushed my long, curly, black hair behind my ears for it to fall front again. For some reason, I couldn't recognize myself. I see that it's me but my skin looks gray and shallow. Blue lines of veins wiggle across my cheeks and forehead. The contrast of my dark hair to this zombified version of myself was chilling. I rushed the wet toothbrush across my teeth, scrubbed the minty foam along my tongue and spat. I didn't look back in the mirror.

I opened drawers in search for warm clothing, and every wooden knob I pulled did not make a sound. I shot a look over at the clock, 8:20. My heart leaped and released a pump of blood that made my fingers and toes tingle. My toes. I wiggled them, they prickled with pain and warmed as I pressed them firmly into the ground.

Is the clock broken?

I moved the white curtains, and bright light seeped through the blinds behind them. The cars in the street were parked and abandoned. All set in their lanes as if rushing through morning traffic, just still. The sky was grey, like my skin, not a cloud in sight. Was it just one big cloud? I pressed my hand to the glass, and they stung with painful pinpoints like my toes did. It felt heated as if it were a summer afternoon. But clearly, there was snow on the ground.

I pile on my black jeans, wool sweaters, and leather boots. The echoes of the thick heels on my shoes were just silence in the stairwell.

I stopped and dug my pinky finger into my ear.

Am I going deaf?

I heard the alarm clock, didn't I?

My fingernail had a thin layer of honey-colored wax on it. I stomped heavily as I ran to the bottom step but no noise emitted. My chest felt hot and my fingers prickled again. I pushed through the door to the outside and flashed my card at the reader.

Beep.

I stared at the green bulb of the scanner and flashed my card again.

Beep, and it turned red. Why am I only hearing these strange beeping noises?

My curls bounced in the corner of my eye. It was warm out, and the tight layers were making me lightheaded. I brought my hand to my armpit, and it felt warm but not moist. I'm not sweating, but I feel so hot.

Making my way down the sidewalk, the city was eerily silent, like the apartments.

The local coffee shop had a buzzing neon OPEN sign that flashed various patterns. I reached for the doorknob, and with every flash, a beep followed.

The tiny bell above the door did not ring.

It was dark on the inside with the grey light illuminating whatever was near the windows. The counter was darkest, momentarily being lit by the red and blue of the neon sign.

Muffled voices came from the door behind the counter.

I dashed for the door and jiggled the handle, but it was locked. I kicked the door with my boot, and it sent tingles up my leg. The voices were getting louder.

I tried the handle again, and it wouldn't budge. Punching the door, I tried to scream. My throat was warm and scratchy, but nothing came out. Bright light poured in from the bottom and side cracks in the door.

The voices were so loud it was like they were in my head. It was so overwhelming, I fell down onto my back.

Beep. Beep. Beep.

"Clear," a loud voice said.

The air was squeezed from my lungs and the heat returned to my chest.

The brightness turned to the faces of people in masks and blue gowns. Some of them clapped, and I heard it.

My breathing was heavy. I tried to speak, but my throat was sore and scratchy again.

"She's stable," a masked man said, followed by a high-pitched *beep, beep, beep.*

SEPARATED AGAIN

PATRICK WINTERS

I'm missing my wife already. She was beautiful. Perfect.

Those diamond eyes that could kiss you with a stare and those luscious lips that could give you the real thing; her tickling fingers and her tiny toes; that adorable nose; her cute little ears, which she'd wiggle to make me laugh; those warm arms that would hold me in the day and those long, lovely legs that she'd wrap around my waist at night.

There wasn't a single part of her that I didn't cherish.

I admire each for one last time before I toss them into a garbage bag.

STARTING OVER ... IN STYLE

ROSE BLACKTHORN

"Something old," she mused, looking down at James. He was certainly old, forty years her senior. He lay quietly, hands clasped together.

"Something new," she said, smiling at the five-carat diamond ring James had given her last night. It sparkled even with the curtains drawn.

"Something borrowed," she continued, glancing fondly at the last of her luggage. She'd packed all the jewelry and money she could find.

"Cassie, are you ready?" David—until yesterday just the sexy pool-boy—picked up the last suitcase.

She nodded, looking back. "Something blue," and yes, within the plastic bag, James' face was definitely blue.

THE SURVIVOR'S MUSEUM

ANDREA ALLISON

"Ladies and Gentlemen, my name is Devon. I'll be your guide for this evening. Welcome to The Survivor's Museum. Every person in our exhibits is the lone survivor of a serial killer. Learn the history of their tormentors as well as what they did right that granted them their life.

We arranged each display to honor a killer's specific tastes and it's interactive to make your experience more enjoyable. This is a one-time private showing. Under no circumstances are you to touch the exhibits. You paid a lot of money for this tour. We don't want any ... complications.

Let's begin."

BOUND

EMMA TAYLOR

Bound bodies were everywhere, unconscious or even alive, only God could have known. The bloodstained rope tore at my wrists. The knot at my feet was looser.

The grind of a garage door opening shattered the silence. An enormous shadowy figure emerged, moving as if he just woke up from a year-long nap. His massive teeth ripped into the first victim's stomach. Blood and intestines dripped from his scratchy beard as he moved from one body to the next. My stomach tensed.

I must have whimpered. He turned in my direction and caught my eye. Smiling, he moved toward me.

THE HAG OF THE MISTS

FRANK COFFMAN

A mist was rising o'er the lonely lea
As he approached a crossroads in the dark.
There, suddenly, an old hag, haggard, stark,
Was there before him standing silently.
Her cloak was green and hooded and half hid
Her face. But for some reason rising fear
Grew great within him as she drew full near.
Then she put back her hood and—God forbid!
Her hair was not just fiery gold, but flame!—
Real flames swirled like long locks around that head
Above that hideous face and glowing eyes!
Then she keened out—most shrill—a well-known name.
And he knew then that his true love was dead.
The banshee never errs and never lies.

THE HEART SONG

TIMOTHY ROCK

"I wanna stop, Mama. It hurts." Desiree said. She was bent over the family washbasin, her hands plunged deep into the ice-filled water.

"You'll do no such thing." Mama said "If you move those hands, I'll whip you good." There was the quick rapping of wood on wood; the spoon, Desiree thought, striking the table.

Mama marched across the room behind her. Desiree heard her heavy steps on the dirt, the opening and closing of cupboards, the rattling of jars and the clanging of pots; a frustrated grunt then a squeak of exaltation followed by the dry, scraping din of metal.

Desiree couldn't take it anymore. Her hands felt warm and tingly, alive with cold fire. She removed them from the icy water.

The pain was quick and sharp. Mama grasped Desiree's hands and submerged them back under the water. The wooden spoon was in her other hand. The pain on Desiree's neck brought tears to her eyes.

"I know it's hard, Dezzy." Mama said. "It's always hard the first time, but you need to do this. Only dead hands can find a dead heart. A few more minutes, then you can move."

Desiree nodded okay and Mama disappeared again. The minutes passed. The quiet ruffling of sheets as Mama finished setting up, then: "It's time, sweetheart. You can move, now."

Desiree got up, her legs stiff and her hands heavy. Her normally dark skin was ashen and lifeless.

Papa lay on the table, dead, and naked save for a washcloth over his eyes and a towel to hide his decency. Mama stood over him, the Special Knife gripped in both hands.

Mama beckoned to her, and Desiree went. She was scared, but everyone is scared at first. That's what Uncle Amos had told her. Uncle Jasper and Aunt Lily, too.

Mama placed the Special Knife on the table and pulled a small hammer from the inside of her smock. She gently stroked the gray stubble on Papa's cheek.

"Your Nana's Mama called it *The Heart Song*. The beat." Mama said, her fingers searching over Papa's ribs. "It's the strength of your life force. The first time I introduced Papa to your Nana, she was out of her skin with excitement. Said she could hear Papa's Heart Song through the walls.

Said he had good ribs. *Singing ribs.* Acoustics like a goshdarned opera house."

Mama's finger settled on a rib just below the sternum. When she was certain of her choice she brought the hammer down hard. The chosen rib snapped like dry wood.

"*The Heart Song* keeps on after you die. Like a band that continues to play even though its conductor has left." Mama smashed another rib.

"But it can't be found with living hands. No, only dead hands can find a dead heart."

Desiree watched as Mama made the incision between the smashed ribs, burying the Special Knife to the hilt and opening a glaring red mouth.

"Your father loved you, Dezzy. He would have wanted this."

Mama guided Desiree's cold hand into her father's broken ribcage. The heat was intense, like a vice. She pushed through it, glancing off tissue and broken bone until she found what she was looking for: a knot. Her fingers wrapped around her father's heart.

"I don't feel it." Desiree said, panicking. Had she done it wrong?

"Just wait, dear." Mama said.

Desiree waited, her hand gripping the soft tissue. Then, she felt it. A beat.

"I feel it, Mama." Desiree said. It was picking up, becoming stronger with each thrum.

"Pull." Mama ordered.

It only took one tug to pry the organ free. Desiree pulled it out into the open air. The heart beat in her hand like palmed thunder. It made her mouth water.

"Your father's heart was strong, dear. It has a lot to offer to you. Take it."

Desiree's hesitation evaporated. She tore into the heart greedily. The taste was intoxicating. Her father's heart seemed to beat on her tongue, between her teeth.

Mama said something, but Desiree couldn't hear her. All she could focus on was the taste, the hot blood, and in the back of her head, a high, singing chorus.

TILL YOU DO

P.J. KRYFKO

"Go to sleep. Please, go to sleep. I can't sleep till you do."

There's desperation in its voice.

"Go to sleep."

I hear the possible threat hidden in its speech, but I'm unconcerned. This ghost beseeches, but does not haunt.

"I can't sleep till you do."

Good! Stay with me! Explain your strange request! I need to understand.

I can't sleep till I do.

There's desperation in my voice.

I wait for a face to rise beside me, but nothing ever comes.

So we stay silent, neither of us able to explain the needs we wish the other would satisfy.

JUST A DREAM

ANDY BROWN

I dreamed about him again last night.

Every dream starts the same. I'm walking through thick forest. In the distance, someone is screaming. It's not a scream of fear … It's a scream of madness, from a mind totally unhinged.

I finally arrive at a clearing and see a man tied to a stake.

He's screaming and thrashing around, unable to escape. His eyes, his insane eyes, are darting about, scanning the tree line.

He turns towards me, and I wake up.

Last night the dream ended differently …

I recognized his face …

It was my face …

That's when I started screaming …

THE BLACK SPOT

BRENDAN O'DEA

"I judged our annual ghost story competition again today. Some of the villagers claim I am not capable enough, or sane enough, to do this competently anymore."

"I disagree. The third prize went to a story about a ship that disappears into the fog, second place to a tale about nocturnal comings and goings in a graveyard, while the winning entry featured the ghost of Blind Pew from Robert Louis Stevenson's *Treasure Island*."

"The latter story won because its main character came to me last night —tap, tap, tap—warning if it didn't win, I would receive the Black Spot."

APRIL

THE GIFT

PAUL WOOLDRIDGE

He shut the door, cutting himself off. Jeff was glad to be out of the board room. He closed his eyes, appreciating the relative quiet of his office. Stretching his shoulders, he sighed and ran a hand over his stomach. All bought and paid for, he thought. He walked around the desk and let the leather chair take his weight. He listened to the low rumble from the factory beneath him, all his machines whirring, busy producing for him. Each one operated by his employees, men who looked to him as their boss. The shareholders were happy, orders poured in and his company continued to grow. He sighed once more.

His office was decorated with images of himself shaking hands with other men in suits, or holding oversized cheques. There were framed newspaper clippings that praised his business successes or his charitable donations. *Local Lad Makes Good,'* read one headline. Jeff smiled.

The photographs that lined his walls were of businessmen, but on his desk, there were pictures of one particular woman. A number of years his junior, the woman displayed a highly polished smile. She stood in cocktail dresses, or lounged in swimwear, brandishing cocktails. She was slim, tanned and her blonde bob was well maintained. Jeff felt a flush of pride. He was a success, there couldn't be any doubt. He was closing in on his fiftieth birthday and there wasn't much he hadn't accomplished, there wasn't much he wanted that he didn't already have.

Jeff picked up a newspaper and began flicking through it. A local girl had gone missing, a single mother of seven bemoaned the cuts to her benefits, and youths had stripped the lead from a nearby church roof. The front page showed a photo of the missing girl, peering out from behind long ginger locks. Inside, the single mother held up her benefits letter, looking suitably miserable. Jeff tutted. Idiots, he thought, either incapable of looking after their own kids or unable to stop having them. The parents deserved to have their daughter go missing, and as for that bloated chav, she should be sterilised.

The other pages covered numerous prosecutions, a local stabbing and various ASBOs. Jeff was sickened by people's failures, and particularly their excuses. Hard work and intelligence had got him where he was, not shirking or whinging. It seemed everyone was always blaming others for their stupidity. Benefit scroungers, druggies, immigrants, criminals; they all had their sob stories, they all pleaded special circumstances and demanded handouts from the weak-minded liberals who indulged them, they couldn't just make something of themselves, like he had.

In the back pages he noticed an advert for a new car dealership. Sandwiched between shiny soft tops, a blonde girl caressed their paint work and beamed above an ample bust. Jeff briefly noted the cars but found his attention lingering on the girl. Blinking, he pulled his thoughts from her and smiled again at the pictures on his desk.

***

Jeff made his way to his car, parked in a named space closest to the entrance. He looked down at his BMW and wondered if an upgrade might be necessary. Once inside he ran his hands over the steering wheel and marvelled at the lights displaying the car's numerous high-tech capabilities. He turned on the radio and steered the vehicle out of the car park, out of the trading estate, and headed for home.

It wasn't long before he'd left the city's outskirts and was driving, speedily, through country lanes. The radio had offered some of his favourite tracks which raised his spirits. He'd sang along to Dire Straits but, as he drew nearer to the iron fence that ringed the estate, the radio news update began. The reporter summarised the headlines, the escalating refugee crisis near Calais, the missing girl—how she'd last been seen being approached by an unknown female—and the political turmoil surrounding Brexit. Jeff switched it off.

He entered the estate passing large homes, each surrounded by manicured lawns and sweeping driveways. He swung the car up, past the water feature, and brought it to rest outside his double garage. He got out and moved, as quickly as his large frame would allow, past the Grecian columns and up the steps to the front door. Inside, he removed his jacket and called out to his wife.

He moved through the reception room and entered the open plan kitchen, calling out once more,

"Kate?"

He poured himself a whiskey, a little perplexed as to why his wife had not responded. He was back at his usual time, she would normally be waiting for him, either in the kitchen preparing a meal, or in the bedroom, preparing herself. He removed his tie, undid his top button and felt the flesh of his neck spill forward. Then he heard something, or at least thought he did. A murmur, something faint. Jeff listening intently. There it was again, a brief intake of breath. He turned towards the basement door.

It was open. That door's never open, he thought. The sound came again, like a whimper. It was coming from the basement.

Jeff grabbed an empty wine bottle and approached the door, gently pushing it open. The steps stretched out, down into the darkness beneath him.

"Hello?" he called.

Immediately there was the sound of fumbling, as of something dragging itself across the floor. His heart jumped. He took a step back. There was something, or someone, down there, hiding beneath his home. Jeff gritted his teeth. How dare they break into my house. He adjusted his grip off the bottle and began his descent.

"You bastards, you're in for it now!" he barked.

Half way down he pulled a string and the room below light up in a faint glow.

"Come on then!" he bellowed as he turned into the basement.

Jeff gasped. He stopped dead with the bottle brandished above his head, his heart pounding. In the far corner, crouched against the cold stone of the basement, was a young girl. She turned away, scraping her bare feet on the floor and hiding herself behind her tattered dress. Her face was hidden but over her hands flowed long red hair.

"Wha?" he muttered.

Before he could process the scene, a high-pitched click came from the stairs behind him. He spun around.

Click, click, click.

Each sharp sound echoed off the walls as, gradually, a pair of high heels came into view. The figure stopped at the foot of the stairs. She was tall and her legs were crisscrossed by fishnet stockings. She wore a corset and her blonde hair hung in a perfect bob. She stood there staring at him, her dark red lips parting into a smile.

Jeff struggled to speak, "Wha ... What?" His words getting lost in his erratic breath.

"Happy Birthday, Honey," she said, "I thought you'd like a red head," nodding towards the young girl cowering in the corner.

Jeff looked at his wife, then, as the realisation dawned on him, stepped forward. He cradled her head in one hand, gripped her buttocks with the other, and greedily pushed his tongue into her mouth.

BATHTUB

MACI MILLS

You could hear the fireworks and smell the meat on the grill from a block away. Andre waited outside the bathroom for his sister to come out. *Knock, knock, knock,* that was Andre anxiously beating on the door.

"Hurry up Susan other people need to get in there."

Andre lost his patience and said, "I'm coming in if you aren't coming out."

Andre opened the door and he didn't see his sister, so he kept walking and he decided to look in the bathtub, so he pulled on the shower curtain and saw his sister lying in the bathtub motionless.

BURN

LIZ BUTCHER

Bound to the stake, she grimaced as the flames licked her bare feet; not from pain, but for the farce she'd endured for months. Now that it was over she saw no reason to pretend anymore. The heat from the fire caused the skin to split along her legs, and she glared down at the gathered crowd as the skin fell away in chunks, revealing red, molten flesh. They gasped in shock and horror as the fire danced up her body, igniting her true form to reveal itself. She laughed as her scalp fell away to reveal her monstrous horns.

NORMAN'S BUNNY

ALYSON FAYE

Norman took Archie with him everywhere. The pub, the bookies, the Social.

"He loves that bunny of his," the pub landlady said.

"Like his other half," intoned Mike who worked at BetzRUs.

No one saw Norman's wife much. Archie was cuter anyway. Flashing his winnings though cost Norman his benefits. Worried, Mike dropped by with some supplies. A huge pot sizzled on the hob. Beside it sat Norman. Alone. Stirring the stew. Shocked Mike exclaimed, "Not Archie?" Relieved he spotted the sleek rabbit snoozing nearby.

Norman laughed. "Course not mate. I'm not a savage. It's the wife in the pot."

PAYING THE BILLS

KEVIN HOLTON

We were about to lose our home, so naturally, I was distracting myself with the internet. I didn't have a job, though not for a lack of trying, so I couldn't help with the rent. Vacuuming, doing the dishes, folding laundry, that all fell to me, because Mom was busy working and my sis was always bogged down with homework. That's okay. I didn't mind jobs other people might've called 'womanly'. Mom and Dad split years ago; I had to pick up the slack he left behind. There's no gender involved with duty.

When the owner hiked up our rent, Mom begged him to reconsider. Didn't work. She made a decent salary, but not enough to support two kids, car payments, incidental bills, insurance, *and* a house. As always, she stayed positive, insisting we'd be okay. Abby stayed quiet and finished her AP work. I was scouting for boxes, ready to pack up and move.

I'm not a homebody, but most of my time has been spent at home, so I'm pretty tech savvy. Now, I almost wish I wasn't. Almost. Of course, I had a PayPal account, and I thought nothing of it when Abby asked me to explain how it worked, and what my email was. I could've explained so much—how proxy servers work, what's a VPN, how to use TOR. Anything, really. Her request was a simple one, easily obliged.

I always use TOR, because I don't like the idea of some shadowy government operative tracking my browsing history, or our internet provider selling that information off. I don't usually go on the deep web. That day, I felt drawn to these darker reaches of the internet, compelled to explore the fringes of virtual society. If anyone was likely to understand, and help with, my family's situation, they'd probably be there, on a secret message board, sharing secrets on how to dodge taxes and come into some quick, if illegal, money.

On one such thread were links to sites no one should visit. Places full of hackers, testing the realities of their cyberworld, and indigents, looking to celebrate all the parts of life mainstream society was too polite to even discuss. Some offered ways to make money doing it. Tons of links to prostitution. Organ farming. Martyrdom.

This last one pulled me in, its little, unassuming hyperlink glowing like a beacon, luring me to shore. I wound up on a page full of embedded videos, a note at the top saying that all content was free, but donations to the 'performers' was expected. Curious, I clicked on one at random.

A recording popped up, laid over the original page, with a note that said *'Streaming over: donations still accepted'*. On the footage, a tired-looking man with thick stubble and haunted eyes stared into the camera. He stared for so long I had to check and make sure it wasn't paused. Then he whispered, "Please. Make sure my brother gets the treatment he needs," and popped a pill. A few seconds later, he jerked, body beginning to shake. My stomach lurched. I'd seen enough movies to know what cyanide does: the seizure-like tremors, the foaming at the mouth. He collapsed, limp and unmoving, in his high-backed chair, head lolled to the side like a ragdoll cast into the corner of a child's bedroom. In the corner of the feed, a donation count steadily rose upward.

In movies, this is where someone would puke, but I've always had a strong stomach. I stared, open-mouthed, hands numb on my keyboard. A new box popped up over the video asking if I'd donate to the man who posted the video, titled *'Frank Hibbert's ALS Care'*.

I clicked the X in the corner, getting rid of the window. I closed the man's video and almost left the site when a new Live Streaming notice popped up, demanding my attention, blinking angrily as I tried to click the address bar. The video was titled *'For the People I Love'* and a thumbnail-sized feed displayed a blurry, fumbling hand adjusting the webcam's angle. I almost clicked "Not interested" when the hand pulled away. My heart stopped. I clicked *'View now'* to confirm what the tiny preview window suggested.

In the footage sat my sister, Abby. I didn't recognize the building behind her. It looked like an empty warehouse or factory of some kind. One emptied recently enough that the power company hadn't cut electricity yet.

"Sorry if the quality isn't great," she said, her voice shaking. "I don't really know what I'm doing. I've never live-streamed before."

Messages started popping up—comments from those watching. I was too shocked to type, not helped by what the other users were writing. *More like death-stream,* from Jax818, and *First time, last time,* from MariaAntwonet.

"So, I'm here because … well … my family needs money. We're broke. About to be homeless. Mom already works herself crazy. My brother … doesn't have a job, but he's sent out maybe fifty applications, didn't get a single interview. He does the chores, which is more than I can say for myself."

Economy's shit right now.
Get on with it!

I'm not here for your sob-story.

"Right, sorry," she sighed. "Just … figured you should know. They work really hard. They're good people. Me, I know I'm smart and all, but college is my only real option. If we don't have money *now,* how could I ask them to pay thirty grand a year so I can get a degree?"

Fumbling, I reached into my pocket to pull out my phone. Someone wrote, *College is worthless anyway.* I called her. *If your so smrt, y u gotta pay? Genuises go 4 free.* In the feed, her phone rang, buzzing along the table next to her. She glanced at it, then gave a sad chuckle. "That's him now. Calling me." Abby clicked the volume button, silencing the ringer.

I sent a text: I KNOW WHAT YOU'RE DOING. STOP. CALL ME.

An anonymous user wrote, *this might be the only time you're of use to the world.*

Another: *JUST DO IT! lmao*

Abby read the text message, looking confused, then her face scrunched up and she turned away. "Wow. That's … really? You're watching right now?"

I clicked the message bar at the bottom and typed, *Yes, it's me. Stop, now, please!*

She squinted at the screen, then gave a sad smile. "I … I wish I could. But I think this was a long time coming anyway."

Family bonding!

More like family bondage. Hehehehe giggity goo.

"Mom, Greg … I love you. Don't ever forget that." She picked up two power cables with clamps on the end, one red and one black, letting out a shuddering breath as I typed frantically, calling her phone, typing some more. I thought about 9-1-1, but even if they could get there in time, I didn't know where 'there' was. "For all you out there who want to know, these are hooked into a backup generator. The computer's on the main grid. All the extra electricity … well, that's just for me."

She crossed her arms and snapped the clamps down on her wrists. Electricity cracked and snapped as her body began to jerk. I screamed, looking away, but wouldn't mute it. I didn't have the strength to watch, but I refused to cut myself off from it entirely. I was the older brother. I should've been providing for us all, should've walked the streets with resumes and begged for a job if I had to—if it could've prevented this.

When the harsh cacophony of her death finally stopped, I looked up. A flood of comments rushed in, blurred through my tears as I stared at her blackened, smoking body. If I hadn't seen this footage, I never would've recognized her.

This just in: smart girl uses science for suicide! More at eleven.
And her brother watched? How … shocking.
DAMN. ZAP-DE-ZAP!
Shame. She wuz hot. Would've given $$$ for XXX.

A button popped up in the top-right corner, no doubt enabled by a moderator. It read *'Donate'* and an account labeled Admin posted, '*Suggested donations for electrocution start at two bitcoins. Double if underaged.'* I wept as my phone began to buzz with email notifications … *you've got money … you've got money … you've got money …'*

ODDWORTH'S SILENT PARTNER

MADISON MCSWEENEY

"Congratulations," said the hostess. "You've survived Oddworth's House of Horrors. Exit to your left."

The guest, still trembling from the experience, looked up. "It seemed so real," he moaned, recalling the sagging floorboards, the shaking walls, the apparitions.

The girl shrugged. "Amazing what you can do with trick wires and holograms."

As the guest left, an invisible presence slammed the door shut. The walls warped, and the framed certificate of poltergeist infestation fell to the floor and shattered.

The hostess braced herself as the air grew noxious. Then, an unearthly shriek:

"TRICK WIRES!? HOLOGRAMS!?"

Oddworth's benefactor, it seemed, was offended.

RAKING

S.C. CORNETT

Shay's fingers raked down his back, drawing blood.

Laughing at his whimper.

Last night he had said he liked it.

Telling her to hurt him.

Smiling she dug in deeper.

Last night he had been on top when this was happening.

Now he was strapped in, facing a mirror.

He couldn't see the blood running down his back.

She wrapped him in an embrace and dug into his chest as well.

Whispering in his ear that it wouldn't be long now.

Licking the blood from his back as her fangs extended.

Shay just couldn't help but play with her food.

WHAT FOLLOWS IN THE FOG

ERIK BERGSTROM

The fog was thick enough so that the rows of trees appeared like ghosts—there, but not quite. Thick enough that Jeff breathed vapor.

He'd just broken down camp, stalling afterwards with hopes the mist might clear. There was no way of telling from where he'd come, or where next to start out. Around him, echoes of clattering rock and snapping twigs unnerved him.

In three more minutes Jeff chose a direction and walked. Something was following. He turned, curious, and saw the children, dressed in virginal white, following him at a distance, fading in and out of the fog.

THE WATCHERS

JEFF DOSSER

It's been three years since I retired from Maverick Heat & Air and fulfilled our dreams of moving to the country. Alice and I were never wealthy, but we got by. We made do during hard times, tucked away what we could in the good. Once Kyle and Molly were grown, we'd even managed to save enough to buy some land and a trailer near the lake. Fishing had always been our shared passion and in our new home, we looked forward to years together along the water's edge.

But my Alice died of cancer the following spring.

After her illness, there wasn't much money left. I had little desire to fish. Then, last Christmas, the kids surprised me with the kayak.

"Dad, you should get out on the lake again," Kyle said as he and his sister carried in the blue plastic boat topped with a mammoth red ribbon. They set the gift beside the tree and Molly stared up her eyes wet with concern. "You'll get exercise while you're at it," she said. "I know Mom would want you to go on."

They'd both been right. Getting back to the lake had relieved much of my loneliness, and my strength grew as I ventured further and further along the shore. Then, in early June, I'd met Burt Grimes, Sid Meyers, and the enigmatic Hog's Leg Creek. Like me, both men were retired; Burt a gruff Army colonel from Ft. Sill, Sid a chatty software developer from Houston. Like me, they both loved to fish. Over the course of that spring, we grew to be friends.

Then, on an early-July morn I rowed to a meeting I didn't realize would be our last. Fog parted in silent gray curtains before the bow of my kayak as I rowed to that meeting. The metered dip of the paddle and the hollow thump on my boat's plastic hull were gulped down by the mists. Almost as if they hungered after any sound marring their uniform silence. I let the kayak drift and unhooked my rod. Then flicked the lure into the void; the unseen splash my only companion on the water.

I paddled along what I guessed to be the shoreline, throwing in the occasional lure. As the fog cleared, great stands of trees emerged along the banks, like the rough, bandy legs of giants. Burt was already anchored at the mouth of the murky Hog Leg tributary fishing rod in hand.

When he saw me, he glanced up and waved. "Bout time ya showed up," he called. "Thought I'd be fishin' alone."

I eased my kayak next to his fourteen-foot bass boat and dropped anchor. "Not all of us have years of experience navigating in this crap," I said.

"Speaking of which," Bert said. "Have you heard from Sid? Without his GPS that guy couldn't find his ass with a map and a flashlight."

"Hey, you old farts," Sid's disembodied voice hailed from the mists. His canoe emerged from a bank of fog his angular form hunched over the oar like some primeval savage. "I heard that."

Burt roared with laughter, pulling a cigar from his tackle box and lighting up. He filled the dense, morning air with its rich aroma. "So, where we headin'?" Burt keyed his boat's ignition, the throaty motor gurgling to life. "We goin' up the creek? Try an' catch The Watcher?"

"That's nothing more than an old wives' tale," I said. "There's no giant fish living up that creek. If there were, don't you think Sid here would have caught her?"

"Or been dragged to the bottom like legend tells," laughed Bert.

Sid's face grew serious. "I wouldn't poke fun," he said. "There's more to those old stories than people let on." He set his oar across his lap and drifted close, the metallic hull of his canoe bumped lightly against mine. "I've seen things along the Hog Leg, things watching from the water." He unscrewed the cap on a silver flash and took a long swallow. With a sigh, he lowered the container and wiped a hand across his lips. "Maybe someone released an alligator into the lake. I don't know what I saw, but I've been followed on this creek."

"Oh jeeezus," Bert drawled. "Not another one of those stories." His engine whined up in pitch and the boat pulled away." Hash out that bullshit later," he called over his shoulder. "It's time ta fish."

I watched him slip through the thinning mist and disappear around a bend in the creek.

"I'm not bullshitting," Sid said, his expression as flat as stone. "There's something living out there. Something that watches us." His eyes drifted to the fog-shrouded creek. "The fishing's good but you'll never find me out here after dark." His eyes caught mine. "Ever."

Five weeks later, the night of Sid's funeral, Bert and I sat alone at a table inside the Cold Nine Bar reminiscing on our friend's good nature and love of blarney.

"I never understood his affinity with that Watcher tale," I said, the memory of Sid's stoic expression while he spun his myth bringing a smile to my face. "He sure could pull your leg."

"He wasn't pulling your leg," Bert said. He set down his beer and leaned back in the chair. "He believed every word."

I laughed, but the set of Bert's eyes halted my mirth. "You're kidding, right?"

He shook his head, dropped his elbows to the table, looked me square in the eye. "I kid you not."

In the intervening silence, Bert pulled a cigar from his jacket and scratched a match across the table. The waitress shot him an angry glance as he puffed the stogie to life. "You know how he died?"

"His wife said a heart attack," I answered. I felt a pang of guilt that I'd not been with him that day. Maybe there was something I could have done.

"More than a heart attack," Bert said. "The ranger who found him said he had the look of a man who'd seen the devil himself." He blew a pillar of smoke waving it away with his hand. "Personally, I think he was stuck on that creek after dark; scared himself to death."

I eyed my friend with suspicion. "You're messing with me, right?"

He lifted his beer and took another languid puff. "No … I ain't. An' I'll tell ya another thing," he jabbed the cigar at me like a finger. "I've seen them Watchers. That's why I carry this whenever I go fishin'," he pulled aside the hem of his jacket revealing a holstered 1911 pistol. He drained his glass and rocked back in his chair. "I ain't sayin' I believe in none ah that shit, but I ain't runnin' into trouble without protection neither."

I stared at Bert in disbelief. Sid was a dreamer, a watcher of sci-fi movies and horror flicks, more terrified of the shadows in his front yard than real dangers presented by the modern world. But Bert; Bert was a no-nonsense warrior. He didn't believe in anything he couldn't rub between his calloused fingers.

"What do the Watchers look like?" I asked.

"Eyes," he said. "Eyes in the water." He drained the dregs of his beer then banged the glass on the table. When the waitress looked over, he swirled his finger above the table in a sign for another round. Then, leaning forward, he glanced left and right as if fearful someone might overhear.

"I seen em' on the shore. They got heads like toads but their bodies are … weird."

Just then the waitress arrived with our pints; the subject changed. I never figured if Bert was yanking my chain or not.

I didn't go fishing after that and I lost contact with Bert. The story of Sid's death and the Watcher had nothing to do with it. My son, Kyle, and his wife, Abby, had their first child. So I stayed with them for a few weeks; helping out with the baby. But eventually, I needed to return home.

When I got back, I began thinking about Alice; how much she would have loved to see our granddaughter. It was soon after that I began drinking. I didn't go out much or answer the phone. A week later, I was going through a stack of unread papers and spotted Bert's obituary.

My friend had died on a Thursday, buried the following Monday, three days before I discovered his passing. I searched the internet and learned he'd drowned at the lake. Right then and there, I promised I wouldn't shut myself away. I could picture Alice, arms crossed, her head tilted in her own jaunty fashion chiding me on self-pity. She'd want me back in the world, enjoying life.

The next afternoon, found me paddling along the overgrown banks of Hog Leg Creek, the September air alive with the call of cicada and buzz of grasshoppers. The sky a blue so intense the jays beat through the branches voicing their jealous protest.

I had some luck catching Crappie early on, adding three good sized fish to my stringer. Then, I paddled between the cattails to a spot Bert, Sid and I frequented for lunch. The creek was calm between the wide banks, the mirrored water deep. I sat munching my sandwich and staring absentmindedly at the far shore.

Then I saw it.

The first thing I noticed were the eyes. Two jet black orbs gleaming amongst the mossy twigs. When it blinked, I leapt to my feet, the thing disappearing into the depths with a heavy kerplunk. I could almost believe I'd been dreaming except for the wide ripples spreading across the flat green surface.

I continued my meal convincing myself I'd seen a frog. As a kid, I'd caught plenty of bullfrogs, some as long as your foot. I'd heard of Louisiana frogs as big as a newborn child. Although the eyes of this creature were the size of golf balls, I convinced myself a frog was what I'd seen.

Then I spotted two empty, brass casings glittering on the shore. They were .45s. The same caliber as Bert's 1911. I imagined him killing time plinking away at turtles. Then a more disturbing target came to mind.

I brushed away ridiculous ideas of lurking monsters and pushed off from shore, letting the current carry me deeper into the marsh. Until the sun dropped below the towering oaks, and I spotted them again. A pair of eyes bobbed alongside a half-submerged branch to my left. I caught the gleam of that malevolent stare and snapped my head around. The thing disappeared in a widening ring of fear that spread across the water's surface and set my boat to rocking.

Reeling in my bait, I plied the paddle towards the creek's mouth set on never returning. I hadn't taken but four strokes when, beneath my craft's hull, a rasping scrape brought me to a jolting halt. I'd been stranded on sunken limbs before but my efforts to break free were, this time, in vain. Images of submerged goblins ensnaring my craft beguiled the recesses of my mind, but I drove these thoughts away.

Although the water was deep, the muddy banks were a scant ten feet distant. An easy swim. I could even carry the anchor line and once relieved of my weight, might easily free the kayak from shore.

As I mulled these thoughts, my paddle dipped idly in the water, then was suddenly ripped from my grasp and dragged below.

It was then they came.

Creeping out of the woods like a plague of slime encrusted locusts. In snake like slithers and deformed, lumbering hops, they sidled across the leafy shore before plopping their disfigured bodies into the water, the brackish surface seething with their activity. Then, one by one eyes bobbed to the surface, surrounded me. A forest of ebony orbs lit with the malicious red glimmer of the westering sun.

THE UNREMARKED RETURN

KEN MACGREGOR

Jesus watched the six o'clock news on an immense flat-screen TV.

None of it was good.

He walked among the people, but no one saw him. They looked at their feet, their phones, at anywhere but others walking by.

He stopped before a church. It depicted, at the top, his own painful, drawn-out death. Seeing it took him back, made him relive the days he spent bleeding, aching, dying.

He came back to bring hope, to heal a broken world.

Shaking his head, he left the world the way it was. It was too much; he couldn't bear this burden.

KILL SHELTER

R.J. MELDRUM

The building was grey and anonymous. Inside, the doctor and tech set up the syringes and vials for the next batch. The doctor was an old hand, the tech was brand new.

"Doesn't this job give you nightmares?"

"Used to, when I first started. But someone has to do it, it's unpleasant but necessary. It's not our fault, it's the breeders. They just won't stop. The population is out of control."

The door opened and the guard brought in a fat toddler. The doctor sighed.

"To think they used to do this to dogs. Now, that's what I call cruel."

THE FART

MATHIAS JANSSON

His intestines screamed in pain after the great buffet. It was his first time in Paris and it sounded so great and funny. Eat all that you want and pay with a fart.

He couldn't hold it back any longer. He had to fart. The gas seeped out from his buttocks and was ignited by the candle. The flame burnt of the
string holding up the guillotine's blade that fell down with its heavy weight on his neck and decapitated him.

His head rolled over the floor and stopped by the sign which
translated into *The Exclusive Human Deli Store.*

THE IMPOSSIBLE VISITOR

CARL R. JENNINGS

Ellen stumped downstairs, running a hand through sleep—tousled hair. She saw her husband leaning against the wall. He stood with his arms crossed over his pajama clad chest and a look of contemplative concern on his face.

"Mark, honey," Ellen said, "What are you doing? Is everything alright?"

Mark nodded toward the wall opposite. "There's a knocking."

Ellen followed his gaze. *Where did that door go?* She thought. *Oh yes, that's right.* "The basement door," she said out loud, "Did an animal get in?"

Mark now looked at her with concern. "Ellen," he said, "We don't have a basement."

MAY

THE WORM TURNS

B.B. BLAZKOWICZ

The life of a bartender is an interesting one. The pay ain't great, but the stories you hear and the eccentric folk you see, are priceless. I bar-backed in a Gold Rush town at the foot of a mountain. It was colder than the kiss of death there, but the warm glow of gold kept the town alive. Found a few of the nuggets myself back when the boom first started. Although knowing what I know now, I would have taken that money and run until my legs were nothing but bloody stumps in the snow.

The morning started off well; the miners were in high spirits. One of them told me they found a cave deep under the mountain. The guy said it "was not natural, and looked to be made by hands other than mother nature." Another one chimed with excitement in his voice.

"Didn't go too far, but we saw some pictures on the floors. Like nothing I ever seen before. Looked like big coins with a mass of snakes in the center."

It didn't take a genius to assume they were all hoping to find the treasure of some lost civilization. I thought little of it, as long they were eating and drinking.

With the morning meal, and pint of drink in their stomachs the miners left for that cave under the mountain. It was not long after the miners that the rest of the town woke up. Cake bakers, bankers, cobblers and constables began pouring in. Most of them were relatively new. Once the word got out of the gold boom, people began showing up from all over. Almost overnight a whole town sprung to life. All was well, and all was good, until about mid-day.

A stranger walked in. He was dressed from head to toe in dark purple, silky robes, the likes of which I never saw before. Or ever again. His head was hung low and obscured by a large hood. Everyone fell silent and stared at him—if you could call it a him, or her. The figure strode silently up the bar and sat on a stool. I could feel myself start to tremble. Something was not right with this stranger. Still, I offered a drink. No need to make a tense situation worse. No reply came from the stranger. Instead, a long, ornate leather glove came out from the robes and pointed to a bottle of whiskey on the wall behind me. Not wanting to test the stranger's patience I grabbed a glass and quickly poured him three fingers of whiskey on the rocks. His hand then reached into the robes for what I hoped was money when a miner burst through the door.

"Cursed Beast!" he screamed at the stranger between heavy breaths. "That monster … that monster killed everyone!" He yelled, shaking all over. His eyes darted around like a cornered animal. He aimed the revolver at the stranger, cocking the hammer with a hand that looked like there was an earthquake in his elbow. I looked down at the stranger expecting him to produce a gun of his own. The stranger looked up slightly revealing an uncanny smoothness to the face. Before he could react further, a shot rang out. The bullet caught the stranger right through the chest and embedded itself into my counter. The robed figure did not even seem to notice, and there was no blood. What happened would make any man of faith deny their god, for what deity would let something so abhorrent run amok in their creation?

The robed figure slowly crumpled to the floor and out from under those flowing silk garments came thousands of sickly grey worms. Everyone at the bar got up from their chairs and pressed themselves up against the far walls. Their eyes were wide and fixated on those dreadful writhing … Things. All at once they bolted across the towards the miner, crashing into his legs like a tidal wave. He screamed out in pain as they wriggled their way up his body. He began thrashing about in vain trying to knock them free. Nobody moved. Nobody helped him.

"Maybe they would be appeased by the miner and let us be," they surely thought. Soon the worms covered every inch of his body and silenced his suffering wails. His body then went completely stiff. The worms continued wriggling and running their way up and down the body, and with a fluid motion the body stood.

The miner then calmly walked back across the bar and donned the dark silky robes. The gloves came next. The miner casually slid them over worm-infested hands. Then it bent down and picked up a white, pristine porcelain mask. A few people nearly fainted as it lifted the mask to its head. The worms slid back from the mask, revealing a freshly cleaned skull beneath. My blood ran cold at the sight of it. The miner had been picked clean. No eyes, no scalp, not a trace of tendon or hair. Even though there were no longer eyes in those sockets I could swear I could feel it staring at me.

It was at this point everyone vacated the bar. Tripping over one another trying furiously to get away from this thing. I could hear them screaming of demons beneath the dirt as they dispersed. I, on the other hand, was a little cornered the only way out was past *that*, unless I somehow jumped through a wall made of whiskey and solid bricks.

The thing then sat down, grabbed the glass of whiskey and slowly drank it in silence. After what felt like several lifetimes of screaming inside my own head, it sat the empty glass down. I smiled meekly and thanked it. The robed abomination nodded its head before reaching into robes like it tried to earlier. I backed up to the wall expecting to be the next one devoured as it did this. In its gloved hand were two gold coins which were then placed on the bar counter. The robed creature then stood up and strode out the door. I looked down at the coins. One was a mass of worms. The other was a skeleton in prayer.

Those two coins still sit on that counter to this day. As quickly as it sprang to life the town became abandoned. Stories of things that writhe and bend the bones of men drove anyone who was not at the bar that day from their homes. These days I hear little about that ghost town at the foot of the cold dead mountain. Sometimes though, I hear about some bumbling fool who claimed that they were going to recover the riches hidden beneath that dreadful place. That is also where the stories always end, because none of them return.

Yea the life of a bartender is an interesting one. Sometimes a story is just a story. Sometimes a story rings true. So, if one of those interesting people you meet have a porcelain face and are clothed in robes from time unknown. Then do yourself a favor and buy them a drink, lest you become food for the worms.

BURNT SOUP

STUART CONOVER

"Mommy! Dad burned the soup."

Closing her eyes, Linda took a deep breath. The kids didn't need to know how angry she was, again.

"That's okay Beth. Mom will fix it. Where's Dad?"

"In his office. He hasn't come out all afternoon."

Of course, he hadn't.

Walking up she tried the door. Locked. That was unusual.

Taking out a hair pin she easily opened the cheap locks they used.

Walking in, the anger rose in her voice.

"Richard!"

The anger turned to fear as whatever was feasting upon her husband turned to her.

Hunger filling its eyes.

NO FUNNY BUSINESS

S.C. CORNETT

Eyes wide open she awoke in darkness.

Emma tried to scream.

She couldn't.

Bound. Gagged. Blindfolded.

Terror set in.

She swallowed it down.

"I'll set you free if you promise to behave."

She knew the voice. *Bloody likely lecherous fool.*

She choked down the anger. Keeping it off her face, she nodded.

A blade traced down her cheek and pushed into her neck.

"No funny business sweetheart."

The blade cut the binding.

It cut the gag.

Finally, he leaned in to remove the blindfold.

"Big Mistake," was the last thing he heard before she sank her teeth into his neck.

A WALK IN SUNLIGHT

RICHARD J. MELDRUM

The sun was shining. There was a gentle breeze. The grass was green and the birds were singing. He could see the crest of the hill; he'd nearly reached the summit. That was where he'd rest and enjoy the view. He was surprised at himself, at his age he hadn't expected to find the climb so easy.

He reached the top. Suddenly, there was a high-pitched noise. Its penetrating pitch disturbed the peace. He grimaced, his head pounding. He felt sick.

The nurse switched off the machine and the flat-line alarm ceased. The doctor spoke.

"Time of death, 9:02 p.m."

SIGHT

LIZ BUTCHER

Megan squeezed her eyes shut, yet nothing could stop the images from flashing within her mind.

Since the car accident, the visions tormented her. Relentless, violent, horrific—awake or asleep—they came. With each day they'd increased in frequency and duration. She felt like she was losing her mind. The doctors answer to her pleas was a padded room and a myriad of pills that did nothing at all. Megan opened her eyes to find herself surrounded by decaying corpses. Their distended jaws mocked her with gaping smiles.

With a distraught howl, she ran headfirst into the door, praying for darkness.

THE GOOD SON

MATHIAS JANSSON

When we left her with our three-year-old son she smiled and with her strange foreign accent said:

"Your son look so good. I could eat him."

When we later returned home, the house was filled with the lovely smell of cooking.

"I have cooked your son," the babysitter explained.

"I have cooked for your son," my wife corrected.

"No," she said and dragged us into the kitchen. She showed us the pot on the stove and when the steam dissolved, I could see my son's face under a layer of vegetables and he surely looked good to me.

AGELESS

MARY JO FOX

Princess Samira locked herself in her bedchamber, then eagerly retrieved the empty oil lamp hidden in a wardrobe. She'd killed for this. Unable to wait a moment longer, she rubbed the vessel and recited the incantations she had read in the forbidden texts.

Mist arose out of the vessel, taking the shape of a man.

"Milady, I shall grant you three wishes," the djinn said.

"My only desire is to be young and beautiful forever," Samira said.

"Your wish is granted," the djinn replied, bowing with a flourish.

Samira froze in place, her youth and beauty forever cast in stone.

THE LIGHTS

MATTHEW GORMAN

"There's no such thing as monsters, Champ," Benji Friedman's father, Isaac, informed him from behind the *Sunday Times*.

The five-year-old was sure that there was something beneath his bed at night that meant to devour him and had just given a voice to his nocturnal concerns over Eggo waffles at the family breakfast table.

"They quite simply do not exist," the Friedman patriarch added, shaking his paper out flat to punctuate his point.

Unable to get a read on his father's face, hidden as it was behind a phalanx of newsprint, Benji looked to his mother for confirmation.

"It's true what your father says, Ben, under-the-bed-monsters don't really exist," she said.

Even Nana, present for her monthly visit from the Willow Glen retirement community, nodded her old head in agreement from across the table.

But Benji was far from convinced. He'd heard the sound of strange scratching noises coming from below him last night. Like sharpened claws scrabbling across the faux wood tiles. And the noise had carried too much weight behind it, too much heft, Benji knew, to be the mere scuttling of some tiny house mouse or even the largest of rats. Whatever it was, it was not small.

"The thing is, Champ," Mr. Friedman said as he folded up his paper and set it aside, barely missing his plate of syrupy remains. "You're five. And five-year-old boys have very active imaginations. I should know because I was one once."

"Oh, and it's not just the boys," Nana piped in with that croaky old voice of hers. "Why, this one here was so afraid of the ol' Boogey Man that she would weep like the prophet Jeremiah every time we sent her off to bed," she said, referring to Benji's mother.

"I *still* remember that!" Mrs. Friedman remarked with the muted half-chuckle of someone slightly embarrassed.

"And do you remember what I used to tell all of you kids whenever you were scared of something in your room at night?" Nana asked her.

"I do, I do," Benji's mother said, reaching across the table to wipe a dribble of maple syrup from Nana's furry chin. "You told us that all we had to do was to turn on the lights and that all of the monsters would go away."

"It was all we could do just to get you kids down for the night. You, and your brothers, all of you were quite the handful, oh yes you were ..." Nana said, trailing off into memory.

"Well, there you go, Ben," Mrs. Friedman said, turning her attention back to her son. "If you find yourself getting scared then all you have to do is go and turn on the overheads. And you just leave them on for as long as you need, sweetie."

"Sounds like sage advice to me," Mr. Friedman said, disappearing behind his paper once again. "You just go ahead and hit the lights next time you start to worry about monsters under the bed again, okay, Champ?"

Of course, he'd said it in a tone of voice that suggested he'd be more than a little ashamed if Benji were to do any such thing.

With breakfast finished, Benji's mother cleared the plates and then ushered him off to his room to get ready. They had a big day ahead of them. Nana wanted to stop by the farmers' market *and* the antique mall, and afterwards she had an appointment with the eye doctor. His mom had to drive her, and Benji was forced to accompany them because his dad had a football game to watch and didn't care to be disturbed.

But all throughout his boring day, sitting and waiting while his mother and his Nana cooed over shiny aubergines or vintage China patterns, Benji couldn't shake the feeling of impending doom. When the lights went out that night, he knew there'd be something waiting for him.

***

When bedtime rolled around at last—and after the area beneath his bed had been thoroughly inspected and deemed monsterless—Benji's mother tucked him in beneath his Boba Fett sheets and comforter and kissed him gently on the forehead.

"Now, you remember what to do if you start to get scared, honey? You just get yourself up and go turn on the lights, and then poof! No more monsters, just like that!" she said, smiling down at him in the dim light.

Benji nodded slowly in response, still incredulous as hell.

With that, his mother left his room and shut the door behind her. And once more, he found himself surrounded by darkness.

***

Terrified, Benji lay there completely still for what felt like well over an hour, listening only to the soft cycling of his own breath and the night wind rustling through the trees outside his window. He listened intently, waiting upon the horrible scratching noises to commence, but he couldn't hear a thing from under his bed.

After a while, his eyes began to adjust to the dark and Benji was soon able to make out the lumpy shapes of his bedroom furniture in silhouette all around him. But nothing seemed untoward or out of place.

In fact, he was starting to wonder if perhaps his father hadn't been right after all, and that this whole "monster business" was simply his imagination on overdrive.

Little by little, Benji began to relax, and soon his eyelids grew heavy as sleep's siren call beckoned him downward into its arms. But just as he was all but set to be spirited away to dreamland, he felt himself jostled from his somnolence by a familiar noise. A noise like the sound of a rusty nail being dragged down the side of a corrugated tin shack.

The scratching had returned.

Benji felt his blood run cold and panic set in. He didn't know what to do. He lay there frozen with fear, his tiny hands white-knuckled around two wadded clumps of bed sheet, too frightened even to call for help. Not that his parents, planted firmly, no doubt, before the blaring television downstairs would have heard him, anyway.

The scratching gave way to a low, slithering sound and then a sharp and violent hiss like water being poured into a pan of hot grease. And then something bumped up against the bottom of Benji's bed hard enough to lift it momentarily from the ground.

A wave of adrenaline surged through Benji's body and his heartbeat grew loud enough to hear. He remembered what his family had told him about the lights and wondered if it would actually work. If the darkness brought the monster, could the light really send it howling in defeat back to whatever nightmare world had spawned it? It had to work, he thought.

It was his only chance.

Summoning every ounce of courage inside him, Benji threw back the covers and bounded from bed, the soles of his bare feet touching down upon the cold tile. There wasn't much distance to cover and he was almost certain he could pull it off.

But as he ran for the light switch upon the far wall, a giant arm—impossibly long and almost skeletal in form but for a hideous layer of mottled flesh—shot out from beneath the bed and snatched him by the ankle. With a vice-like grasp, and its claws sinking deep into his tender flesh, the arm pulled Benji backwards, yanking him from his feet. He went down fast, his chin striking hard against the floor and pain blasting through his skull like a bolt of lightning. He attempted to scream only to find that the impact had caused him to bite his tongue nearly in two leaving his cries muffled by its mangled obstruction. And as his mouth filled with the copper taste of blood, and his fear reached a peak previously unknown, the monster began to pull him closer.

Benji thrashed about, his free leg kicking out into empty space, as he fought desperately to break the monster's hold. His fingernails squealed against the vinyl tiling, looking for purchase, as it dragged his flailing form across the floor. He twisted from his belly and looked towards the place where he was being pulled. There in the dark below the bed was a circle of even blacker darkness, and as his body slid towards it he realized that it was ringed by rows of razor sharp teeth. A stench far fouler than any he'd ever smelled issued forth from this gaping maw, and thick ropes of saliva dripped from every tooth. Once again, he tried to scream, and once again, he found that he could not.

And so, in the final moments of his all-too-short existence, while this monstrous dentition sunk deep into the marble white flesh of his naked thigh, Benji cursed his parents and their awful advice in the forefront of his screaming mind. He cursed his stupid Nana, too.

Why hadn't they believed him about the monster? And why, *WHY* hadn't they realized the simple flaw in their stupid, stupid plan?

Sometimes, you don't make it to the lights.

MOTHER KNOWS WORST

RUSCHELLE DILLON

Little Maisie was a bad seed. She was evil. That's what her mother said. And Maisie believed her. She came home bloody more than once, more than twice, with a skinned cat staining her lap. Hunks of flesh turned up often through her hair and between her teeth; sometimes belonging to an animal and sometimes … not. She was the neighborhood terror and a bane to the school bully. Her mother said she was bad to the bone. But which bone was it that made her bad? Curious, she took out a kitchen knife. And decided to start with her toes.

KAIDAN

PATRICK WINTERS

Yoshi awoke suddenly, unable to move, unable to scream. And scream he would've, for his wife hung above him—pale, moaning, and dripping wet.

She glared at him in mournful loathing, her mouth gaping, a choked gurgle coming out of her bloated throat. A torrent of frigid water came raging out of it, shooting across his face, down his nose, into his mouth.

Yoshi could not get out from under the horrid flow.

He died, drowned in the same waters that he had forced Akari under a month before, leaving her body to sink into the pond beside their hut.

NECROVORE

FRANK COFFMAN

We are the secret ones who haunt your lore.
Our kind has walked beside you from the first,
Spawning your legends of a race accurst
Who feed and thrive on Death and human gore.
Unlike our cousin vampires' sanguine thirst,
We crave the meat, the taste of human flesh,
The thrill of killing—and when kill is fresh—
The savor of the feast when blood has burst
Forth from the rend and bite of claw and tooth.
We roam your world, ne'er long in any place,
Looking enough like you that, face to face,
In passing, none can see the hidden truth:
Behind those lips that never smile, the fangs;
Inside those gloves, the curve of razor claws.
With many of your missing—we're the cause,
And take the greatest pleasure from your pangs.
At each new hunting ground, we find a spot,
Secret and dark, to have our grisly meals.
The bones are picked clean, and the blood congeals.
Then—to be sure our kind are never caught—
What's left is safely hidden in the ground
Of some deep nearby wood and buried deep,
Where Earth will long and long the secret keep.
And rarely—very rarely—are bones found.
We roam among you through this world of woe.
Few live who ever see us come or go.
When—if we meet—you see me bare my smile,
You have life left—for but a little while.

ALTARSTONE

ROBERT ALLEN LUPTON

The Yucatan is riddled with cenotes, sinkholes in the limestone making up most of the karst landscape. Many are partially filled with water, but some are dry. The Mayans used them for many things, some good and some bad.

I didn't know how many there were until my junior year. That summer, I joined a university sponsored mapping expedition. My motive wasn't anything as noble as archaeology, geology, or Mayan history. If Martina Crestada was going, so was I. We'd taken three semesters of Mayan culture and four language classes together.

The area is covered with rainforests and riddled with underground rivers. Wildlife is abundant, ocelots, jaguars, and wolves thrive on the armadillos, squirrels, rabbits, and peccaries.

I mentioned jaguars for a reason. We took a break after rigging an A-frame sling on the edge of an overgrown cenote. The pit appeared dry and there was a large flat stone in the center. There were carvings on the stone. Martina looked through her binoculars while I played the flashlight beam over the multicolored stone and she said, "Red veins. Could be iron oxide, or maybe blood. How exciting, Philip, do you think they're bloodstains? Is it an altar stone?"

A workman screamed before I answered. "B'alam! B'alam!" he shouted. B'alam is Mayan for jaguar. I turned and saw a jaguar slink closer to Martina and me. We were pinned against the pit's edge. I wasn't armed, I had a flashlight, a pocket knife, and a pith helmet, like an explorer in a Tarzan movie.

I threw my helmet like a Frisbee and hit the jaguar in the shoulder. It shrieked and charged. I pushed Martina to the side and unconsciously stepped backwards from the leaping cat. I fell into the cenote and the jaguar flew over my head and fell with me. We screamed all the way down.

I woke up on a pile of decayed leaves that the wind had deposited in the pit. My left arm was broken and I hurt all over. Martina called my name and I assured her I was alive.

"We'll be down for you as soon as we can. I've sent for a stretcher."

"I just need a harness. The air is pretty stale down here. It smells like rotten fruit."

"The jaguar fell with you. Make sure it's dead."

It hurt me to walk, but I found my flashlight. The jaguar was draped like a praying supplicant over the altar stone and the altar was decorated with carven images of cats, snakes, and wolves.

The jaguar appeared dead until I lifted its feet onto the altar. Its yellow eyes opened and it bit my forearm. It was a soft bite, almost a caress, but hard enough to make me bleed. I jerked my arm away and hit the cat repeatedly with my heavy flashlight.

Our blood mingled and flowed into the red stained cracks in the limestone altar. The stench of rotting fruit became overpowering and my head spun. I passed out and collapsed on the jaguar.

The pain in my arm woke me. The cenote was filled with flickering torchlight and smoke. Several men costumed in ancient Mayan ceremonial regalia filled the cavern. I looked for Martina. She wasn't there. The pit's edge was lined with women and children. The quiet was frightening.

It was like one of the silent moments in a horror film before all hell breaks loose. I wasn't the best judge of body language, but these folks weren't happy to see me.

I spoke in English. "I didn't know you were filming a movie. I'm sorry I messed up the take. I could use some help, my arm is broken. If it hurts any worse, I'll pass out."

A short ugly tattooed man with a snake headdress and bad teeth shook his obsidian knife and spoke in Mayan. His pronunciation and cadence were different than what we'd learned in class, but he said, "Who are you and what do you do here? You dare disturb this sacred ceremony. You have killed B'alam, the symbol of life, and you flaunt your misdeed by displaying his body on the gateway altar to Xibalba, the underworld."

I admired the multicolored snake tattoo on his forearm and said, "Where's the camera? I said that I'm sorry. I'll pay for damages to your set, but I'm really hurting here, I need a doctor. Stop with the Hollywood Mayan mumbo jumbo and help me. We'll sort this out later."

Snake Tattoo motioned to one of the other men, who pulled a war club from a leather sheath. He took two steps and punched me in the stomach with the club. It knocked the wind out of me. I bent over and he hit me in the neck with his fist.

I woke up in the cenote for the second time. Getting knocked out is no fun. I was tied to the altar. That's not a good thing. My audience was still visible through the smoke and fumes. A number of women with small pots and slivers of obsidian surrounded me. My arm throbbed and I was frightened for the first time. Who were these people?

Snake Tattoo said, "We must sacrifice this man with strange clothing. His sacrilege is an affront to Xibalba and his murder of the jaguar insults our gods. The gods say that the afterlife is closed to us until his death reopens the path."

"He is unclean and must be cleansed. He is ugly and must become pleasing in the sight of Itzamna, he who rules the gods."

The women forced a disgusting herbal mixture down my throat. They turned my head to one side and caught my vomit in bowls to ensure that I didn't foul the altar. They pinched my nose and filled my mouth with castor oil. The combination flushed my body from both ends. I'd envisioned that being clean would involve ritualistic bathing, but I was wrong.

Once I stopped spasming from both ends, the women washed me. I fought, but they held me and stabbed me repeatedly with sharp obsidian splinters. I was able to turn my head and see one arm and it was covered with blood and bruises. But it wasn't bruised. The little pots were filled with ink and dark spots on my skin were tattoos.

I'd read about the death by a thousand cuts in Fu Manchu novels, but I'd never considered death by a thousand tattoos. I'd fallen on a fire ant bed when I was a child, but this was worse. I was terrified. I couldn't stop the women and they worked as fast as a modern sewing machine. Dip the obsidian quill in ink, put it in place, tap the splinter with a block of wood to embed the ink below my skin, and repeat about thirty times a minute. It was excruciating. My body bled from a thousand cuts, my arm was broken, and I couldn't imagine what they had planned for me next.

Snake Tattoo twisted my broken arm and intoned, "His pain is nectar to the gods."

I screamed myself hoarse and passed out. I woke up dehydrated and weak from the forced bouts of diarrhea and vomiting. I had no idea how much blood I'd lost from the gang tattoo rape. Sometimes there was daylight visible above the cenote and sometimes there wasn't, but here were always people watching like the witnesses in an operating theater. I felt groggy, I was never really awake or asleep. I was only aware of the constant pain and my fear of whatever awaited me.

When the women tattooed my groin area, any residual hope I had that I'd fallen into a movie set was dispelled when the relentless obsidian needles moved from my upper thigh. I clenched my teeth so hard that I broke two of them.

Mercifully, the women finished. A ray of sunlight, like a tangible beam gleamed from the noonday sun. My audience waited, quiet and expectant. The sweet scent of rotten fruit filled the air.

The priest covered me with jaguar's skin and lifted an obsidian knife overhead. The smoke from the dried fruit incense made my head spin. I tried to move, but my muscles wouldn't respond. I couldn't scream. I felt my eyes lock open in terror when the knife descended.

***

I opened my eyes and Snake Tattoo was gone. Martina's face was above me. She screamed, "I found him. He's alive, but he's covered in tattoos." She waited with me while the workmen went for a stretcher. "I was so worried. I searched the cenote three times and you weren't there. Suddenly, you appeared on the altar stone. I was terrified."

"So was I. How long have I been in the pit?"

She hugged me and cried, "Only about ten minutes."

"It seemed longer to me."

***

A week later in a Houston hospital, my mind cleared. Hell of a dream. I suspected I'd been hallucinating until saw the IV in the snake tattoo that completely wrapped my arm. I sat up and a blue green jaguar face looked back from the mirror. My stomach clenched at the smell of the decaying fruit basket on the counter.

The doctor arrived and he was a small dark man with a snake tattoo on his right forearm. "Good, I glad you're awake. I've been waiting for you. We have unfinished business, you and I."

TIME WITH ETHAN

RYAN BENSON

The man played with his son, but his mind drifted miles away to his office. The four-year-old's words pulled him back to the yard.

"Dad, how do you spell 'stop'?" The boy sat on the concrete walkway, chalk in hand.

"Sound it out, Ethan." Would he make partner?

"Love you, Dad."

The man smiled. Had he neglected Ethan? Next weekend they'd get ice cream. Their time was precious.

A screen door slammed shut. A woman stood, hands on hips. "Ethan? Who are you talking to, honey?"

"Just talking to Dad, but he disappeared again."

She frowned. "Dad's in heaven, Ethan."

WORMS

DAVID TURTON

Veronica gasped as she entered her kitchen and saw several fat white worms slithering on the walls.

They smelt horrendous, like wet, rotting mushrooms. They fell onto her arms, biting her flesh. Veronica brushed them away but they kept coming. She grabbed a knife and slashed one, but it became two wriggling worms. She staggered forward and turned on all the gas knobs. As flesh fell from her body, eaten alive where she stood, she lit a cluster of matches. She was soon engulfed in flames, the air acrid with death and cooking flesh as she melted with the worms.

OUT OF TIME

KEVIN HOLTON

Grains filed through the pinch point, running down from the top of the hourglass. I'd warned her that time was short; she hadn't believed me. More than half the sand was gone.

"I love the symbolism," I told her. "Sand. Ground rocks. All that'll be left when everything—everyone—is dead."

She didn't reply.

"In a perfect world, the top wouldn't empty. Sorry, darling."

Looking down, I watched her thrash against the restraints. Her eyes were still open, blinking granules out, her nose and mouth covered by a small dune. The sand kept flowing into an hourglass with no bottom.

JUNE

WHAT THE DOG TELLS ME

S.L. EDWARDS

When Aunt Martha leaves, I watch Atlas.

Atlas is a Great Dane whose head reaches the middle of my chest when he is on four legs. He is slow and cautious, a shadow that lurks in the corner of my sight and watches me from behind corners and the backs of hallways. For a long time, Atlas does not approach me. Does not *trust* me. He does not make a sound. His growl is low and shaking, a rattling fear that crawls along my lower spine like spider-legged paradise. When I sleep I imagine I hear him outside my door, his heavy open-mouthed breathing an infernal, lingering pantomime.

But in the mornings Atlas is silent and impassive.

I know I am imagining things.

Aunt Martha's house is big and lonely, deep into suburbia where she has cut herself off from any relationship with her neighbors. Her house is full of photographs of a family that has grown old and apart; sons who speak only through email, daughters who send Christmas cards, pictures of grandchildren who she has only held once before. They stare out of their glossy two-dimensional lives and look into the vast now-emptied home that they left behind.

Atlas is in some of these pictures, but he always looks the same. No grey hairs, sagging jowls or sad eyes from the living shadow whose puppyhood is as ill-documented as the rest of his history. My cousins do not talk about the dog when I see them, nor do any of them have funny or cute stories which people so often ascribe to their animals. Instead they shrug, change the subject and say that Atlas has always been around.

I come under the impression that Atlas is not watching me out of suspicion but instead out of curiosity. As I water the plants and clean the shelves I feel his eyes on pressing on my shoulders, a physical weight which I can only take so long before my back is breaking. When I turn, I see a black silhouette retreat back into a place unseen. I cringe and whistle my fears of Atlas away. Increasingly I believe that he hates that I am here and am filled with the unnatural sensation that I am not the master in this house.

He watches me while I eat, sitting almost as tall as I stand, silently observing from across the room. I keep the television and radio off because the hair on the ridge of his back stands up when they speak. Atlas enjoys silence in his home, and in its totality, he watches me until I lock a door. From the other side of my sanctuary I sleep uneasy in the knowledge that he is awake, sitting laying silently on a couch with his eyes open; waiting for me to unlock the door so that he may continue his persecuting vigil.

In the hazy moments between sleep and waking up, I believe I see him peering over my bed. He is massive in the dark fog between dream and reality, reaching the ceiling and bearing down on me with burning red eyes. His breathing his hot and infernal against my face. I wake up in a sweat, and venture out to make sure Atlas is asleep.

But I cannot find him.

I do not sleep for the rest of the evening. It would be good, I imagine, if he were to leave. He is not a natural thing. But I know that he will be there in the morning, watching me as I reluctantly come out of the bedroom. I will need to eat.

And so will he.

On the fifth day, he finally speaks.

His eyes slide aside to reveal panels of shimmering white light. A horse moan issues from his long mouth, a tantric chant that begins with a guttural grown and crescendos in a man-like scream of rage. His meaty paws come down on my chest, and in a moment, I am paralyzed under him as his teeth come closer and closer to my nose.

"Leave."

And after that he is off of me. I wonder the house in a daze, splashing water on my face from the kitchen sink. I feel his stink still on me, and I wonder if he truly said anything at all. I wonder if Aunt Martha's hollow estate is really a good place for me. It is lonely here, and I am uncomfortable. I recall the words of one cousin who from the rim of their whiskey glass told me that he never wanted to go home. That there was a reason that his father left Aunt Martha.

That the house was haunted.

My breathing is heavy and labored, my hands shaking as stammering weeping comes out of my mouth. I am on the verge of real weeping, remembering that I had scheduled interviews for the week I was to return from Aunt Martha's. If this is not real, if I am so disturbed as to so vividly imagine the low, metal-on-metal grating of his voice, then I know I am in no shape for interviews.

Then I feel Atlas' stare, and I wonder if I have ever been anything *but* insane. In a delirious moment, I imagine the house is laughing with him. Then he shakes his head and leaves. I understand how hopeless I truly am. I clutch myself and cry on the kitchen floor.

When I wake up, he is peering over me.

He calls me horrible things, obscenities and slurs that are so foul that they cannot describe a human being. He tells me of the awful things he wants to do, the profane and abominable sins he wishes to unleash on me, on the world. He dips his head to my ear and begins to sing a song: He sings that the worm eats the man, that the worm grows the dirt and that all things walk on a bleeding planet. I begin to weep and he bites into my shoulder, telling me to stop my worthless screaming and that if I will do one thing right in my life it is to listen when he speaks.

Atlas tells me of the world that has been woven into ours, about the evil men that live under the clear surface of water, the twisting snakes that crawl under the gnarled bark of trees. He sings about the black planet that moves closer and closer into our solar system, carnivorous and wide he says it will swallow us all. I feel warm and Atlas roars with laughter.

Men, he says, are incapable of dealing with fear in a rational manner.

I open my eyes and Atlas is gone, the house is quiet.

Aunt Martha will be home tomorrow.

FLIGHT 666

LIZ BUTCHER

Charlie forced himself to breathe deeply.

He was grateful to have the row to himself. He hated flying with a passion, but it was unavoidable. He told himself the sense of foreboding sending chills down his spine was nothing more than his heightened nerves. As the plane ascended through the clouds, he thought he saw something. A face. He leaned into the window, searching. Again, he saw it in the distance—it was cloud-like, but darker, thunderous. He stared as the face opened its mouth wide and rushed towards the plane. Charlie screamed as the plane plummeted towards the ground.

THE ANGRY TREE

JACOB MIELKE

The tree stands at the center of the clearing. No other trees grow near it, they're too afraid.

It has no leaves and its bark is black and twisted. Axe scars are visible; they're ugly and cruel.

As I stare at it, I can feel the malevolence coming off the tree. Something dark has made it angry and vengeful. It wants to harm me.

As I stare at it, the tree bleeds. Dark blood flows from cracks in the bark. Red mist stains the air around the angry tree.

As I stare at it, I can feel it staring back.

THE POWER OF SUGGESTION

RICHARD J. MELDRUM

They were watching an Eighties film; the leading man was a famous actor.

"I wonder if he's still alive?" she asked.

"He must be dead by now," he replied.

The next day, a headline with a photo of the actor. He'd died in his sleep the night before.

That evening they were watching another classic film. It featured a different famous actor.

"He must be dead by now."

The next day, another headline. Another dead star.

"You should stop saying that," she said. "It's uncanny. Too much of a coincidence."

He looked at her.

"You must be dead by now."

FOOTPRINTS

JUDSON MICHAEL AGLA

I've been following the beast for days.

Armed with vanishing politics and torn flags.

I've got a can of gasoline and my monkey has the matches.

Ever since the war ended I've been delusional, it's the clearest I've ever felt and aside from walking into random government buildings screaming it's been quite beneficial.

The footprints were getting fresher; I was close on its tail, I could smell it, a stench of death, lavender and gunpowder.

They burned the books in the name of god, they burned the witches because they could, they burned the hopes that the new children would learn to burn.

The castles offered little history and even less poetry, the rivers shone with glistening rainbows of oil, and garbage filled the banks, rat heaven. The corpses piled so high children used them as forts playing war.

Me and my monkey found the fresh feces of the beast, it was here, I could hear the terra crackle under its feet, then its eyes, two bright yellow glowing eyes, and fangs, white, shining in the moonlight.

I won't kill for those greedy bastards anymore, I won't plant the seeds of ignorance and I won't slaughter for anyone.

Death comes as a cool breeze, a friendly tap on the shoulder, a black raven watching, waiting for its meal.

CARGO

ALEXANDER LLOYD KING

Virgil can't resist a good deed. Early in relationships, girlfriends always tease him about it.

"You'd throw yourself in a wood chipper to save a squirrel's nuts," the sweet gal from Georgia had said, her southern accent fumbling over a few drinks. This was during their first at-home date (his home) as he explained stories behind Peace Corps pictures.

"It's just who I am," he replied, bragging yet flirtatious. "It's just who I am," he repeats, staring at the back of the van a few car-lengths ahead of him. The doors are waves of fresh white over warped metal, paint splashed on patches of un-scraped rust. Obviously, the van is a throwaway intended for a few human trafficking trips, dressed up just nicely enough to pass for inconspicuous. Had it not been for one of the two back windows, he wouldn't have noticed. Greyish curtains hang down. They don't necessarily warrant suspicion, but what first caught his attention was the lower, left-hand corner of the right window. A solid substance—a board perhaps—is broken behind the glass in that section, and a piece of curtain was being tugged ever-so-slightly. He saw this at a stoplight and began following the van. Now he is sixty miles from home (his intended destination), in a town he vaguely recalls from the night he met the foul-mouthed girl from Nebraska. Finally, gas station ahead, the van's turn signal blinks. Virgil makes sure that the driver pulls in and commits to a pump before he drives into the side parking lot. He leaves his vehicle and peaks around the corner of the Go Mart to see a bald man with a handlebar mustache exit the van and step inside. He will pre-pay, obviously, in cash. There's a line of customers, so Virgil walks to the van and peers in the only open space of the back window. Four women, tied; they see him. Their throaty screams are barely muffled by ball gags. Sudden pain bites Virgil's bicep. The bald man has grabbed his arm.

"Thought you were tailing me, you son-bitch!"

With his free hand, Virgil points at the window. "Aluminum vinyl next time. One of your girls chipped off a corner of wood and was tugging at the curtain. Also, invest in better sound-proofing. Go to a music shop and tell them you're building a studio." The bald man releases Virgil's arm. His jaw drops the length of his mustache. Virgil checks his watch. "If you don't mind, I really should be going. I followed you far away from home. Safe travels, friend!" Back inside his car, he looks in the rear-view mirror and smiles at himself. He spots the reflection of groceries in the backseat. Georgia, Nebraska, Ohio, and Utah are probably very hungry (it's not like they can leave the basement to get food), but he's sure they'll understand when he tells them. He can't resist a good deed, and he wants to set the right example for their soon-to-be children.

THE GLOW IN THE MIRROR

AMANDA J EVANS

Looking at my reflection I noticed a slight glow at the back of the mirror. I wasn't sure at first and turned to see if I'd left a lamp on, I didn't. I peered closer, moving my face nearer the glass. The glow appeared brighter, glowing. A shape started to emerge in the light, moving, forming, solidifying. I moved closer, my nose almost touching the mirror, watching the shape appear. Two eyes, a nose, and a smile that turned sinister. I pulled back, not quick enough, as the shape emerged. A hand shot out dragging me into my glass prison.

FORMATIVE EXPERIENCE

KEVIN HOLTON

Mary had her hands around the grip, fingers near the trigger. Her glassy eyes didn't see much beyond the barrel.

"Hey now," Mike said. "Give it here. I know you don't want to hurt me, right?"

No response. Chrome gleamed in the flickering light of the bedroom's energy saver bulbs. Mike took a step closer. Another. Not sure if Mary saw him.

She turned, pointed, bumped the trigger. A flash broke his heart, each chamber neatly separated. Mary wailed, with no father left to comfort her. The evening news read, '*Toddler kills father. Up next: Live Coverage of Chili Cookoff.*'

POSTED: NO HUNTING

ROBERT ALLEN LUPTON

Margaret was kind, pleasant, and charming. Athlete, great grades, gorgeous. Everyone should've hated her, but she was so damn nice.

Her classmates began to turn up dead and butchered after Halloween. Margaret smelled the rancid stench of troll on the bodies. She searched until she found the trolls' bridge and pounded the railing with a baseball bat.

Her glamour vanished when the seven trolls approached. "Boys, you've been hunting in my territory. Mama was a hellhound and Daddy was an Imp. You are so screwed."

She took batting practice, caught the runners, and made it to homeroom the next morning.

MR. JACKSON

JUSTIN BOOTE

Darren Phoski lifted the blind and peered out the window. He was still there. Mr. Jackson; owner of the jewellery store across the street. Jackson had been watching him for over two hours now, and Darren was decidedly worried.

I shouldn't be worried, he thought, if we analyse the basics. There was absolutely no way that Jackson could have seen him during the robbery. He'd been wearing a mask, and hadn't said a single word that might have given away his eastern European accent. And besides …

So, what the hell was he doing out there?

And what the hell am I gonna do about it?

Darren sat back down at the table beside the window, and with a trembling hand picked up the litre bottle of beer he was drinking. The liquid swished and foamed. Pretty much like what his head was doing right now.

The initial shock and horror was now subsiding, to be replaced by unease. Uncertainty. He looked at the bottle as though it may hold the answer or a solution to the problem, and to a certain extent there could be a relation here, he mused. Certainly, after downing the fifth since seeing Jackson the first time, there was a chance he might be imagining it. Alcohol could play havoc with one's perceptions of things.

He decided to chance another peek. The seventh.

With the tips of his fingers, he lifted the blind, holding his breath without even realizing, and cast a wary eye out.

"Shit!" he hissed, and jumped back from the window as though it might explode at any minute.

Mr. Jackson stood across the road, dressed in his habitual three-piece black suit, arms by his side, and staring up directly into Phoski's second-floor window. The overhead street light cast an eerie shadow around Jackson that should not have been there either. And Phoski would have sworn that the shadow moved of its own accord, albeit slightly. Swirling, expanding and decreasing as though it were breathing. Partners in crime. A dark one. Very dark.

Darren slumped back into his chair; drunk, nervous, and alarmed. He mentally recalled the robbery. It had gone perfectly. Five minutes before closing time at eight, when Mr Jackson would have no customers, people would be busy rushing home from work, and Jackson no doubt thinking of dinner, and putting his weary feet up in front of the television. He was reasonably old-near retirement age presumed Phoski—thus should provide little or no threat. By simply removing the revolver he kept hidden in his jacket, no words would be necessary. The language of guns was universal.

Jackson had looked scared, as though he might suffer a heart attack even. Phoski didn't want that to happen. It was one thing going away for a couple of years for theft, another for fifteen for second-degree. So, he finished the job as quick as possible before anything nasty might happen, and left. The next day, he sold the jewels for a tidy eight thousand, and life seemed wonderful again.

And now this.

Somehow that old fucker had discovered that it had been him. How, he couldn't even begin to wonder, but then, considering that what was waiting, *lurking*, outside for him—and who knows what ideas Jackson might have in his head should they be re-united—it might be an idea to start looking at things in a new light

Because Mr. Jackson, owner of Jackson's Jewellery Shop, *should not fucking be there.*

All kinds of drunken thoughts passed through Darren's head. Maybe he'd read the article in the newspaper wrong? Perhaps he was shitfaced and imagining it? The guilt of what he'd done catching up with him. Could it be that…? No. Don't go there. Because that's impossible, right? He would be the first to accept that plenty of weird shit happened in the world—often tragic, occasionally amusing, sometimes downright bizarre—but that was the kind of shit you laughed and joked about in the bar with your buddies. The usual thing;

"Been smoking too much dope, have you?"

"Been watching too much X-Files, pal. It's getting to ya."

"Good idea to see a psychiatrist, don't you think, chum?"

On one occasion, during the robbery of a gas station on Halloween of all nights, the employee's girlfriend had startled him (scared him almost to fucking death actually) by appearing from the office wearing a zombie mask after hearing the ruckus out front. That had freaked him out, and for several days afterwards, had seriously considered a new career. An honest one. But this …

This bordered on abnormal. Beyond comprehension. Fucking neurotic.

Darren dropped the empty beer bottle. He couldn't stay here all night, on the verge of a mental breakdown, wondering if he had finally lost it, or there really was an explanation plausible, natural. It was time to confront Mr. Damn Jackson who should be somewhere else right now, somewhere specific that did not allow for doubt or certain questions about one's state of mind.

"Fuck it," he said and stood up, rapidly grabbing onto the edge of the table to avoid falling back down again.

Two things were about to happen. One: some guy impersonating Jackson was going to get very probably shot for freaking him out so much, or two: Darren was going to need lots of help very probably in the near future. If he survived.

He picked up his trusty revolver, thrust it into the back of his trousers, and before heading towards the door, looked once more at the newspaper article to confirm his suspicions;

JEWELLERY STORE OWNER DIES IN ROBBERY

Andrew Jackson, owner of Jackson's Jewellery Store, was found dead of a heart attack this morning following a robbery at his store. Police are currently investigating the robbery, but as yet have no leads ...

THE ITCH

S.C. CORNETT

There was a need she couldn't fill.
Sex, drugs, rock and roll, she'd tried it all.
It was always there, unfulfilled.
She wanted more. Needed more.
The boys couldn't help with lust and desire.
The girls couldn't help in the heat of the fire.
The highs lead to lows and turned happiness to woes.
The music was a reprieve but couldn't satiate her need.
But one day she found the solution to her pain.
An accident that happened while driving in the rain.
She'd killed her first in that dreary night.
It wouldn't be the last. It felt so right.

SOUL MATE

ALYSON FAYE

We gorge ourselves on the scents and sights of the street market. From behind the church, a lone flute pipes its melancholy notes. Lured in, we wander over to where the toppled tombstones hug the earth. A line of dancing children snakes out of the graveyard grass. One of them, a bedraggled girl, approaches with a pitiful smile showing rotted teeth.

"Rosemary?" She holds out her hand.

You cannot resist her call. The music tugs at your spirit. You are drifting away from me.

Selfishly I have kept you with me too long. It is time to let you go.

THE LONG ROAD TO IMMORTALITY

KEV HARRISON

It was dark. The road seemed to have been meandering forever. Her eyelids felt heavy and sleep was whispering sweet words in her ear that she'd already been half-seduced by. She'd passed through hill after valley, hamlet after village, and still her GPS pressed her to go on. The fuzzy white halos of light that were her headlights against the fog that surrounded the car had a comforting, relaxing aura about them, which only added to her wooziness.

Up ahead darkness loomed, somehow darker still. The car's engine continued its purr, pulling her toward it. Closer now, she could see skeletal fingers through the fog. Trees, barren with the burden of the frozen winter. She zipped through the forest, her GPS still silent, its long, slender blue line still urging her on. The road narrowed and the tips of branches began tapping at her windows intermittently.

"In four hundred metres, turn left," said the woman's voice on her GPS.

She squinted, peering in to the murk. Could see nothing. Still she drove on.

"In one hundred metres, turn left," the voice again. "Turn left."

She slowed almost to a stop and could just make out a dirt track veering off to the left. She turned, the car bumping off the smooth tarmac on to bumpy earth and stone.

"Your destination is in forty metres, on your right," came the voice of the GPS once more, the screen illuminated, clamouring for her attention to rate the directions she'd been given. She pulled in to the clearing on the right, swiped away the message on her screen and turned off the engine. She fastened her thick coat, pulled on her woollen gloves, tightened the scarf around her neck and stepped out of the car. She looked around. Nothing. No wait, a shape. She stepped towards it. Out of the gloom appeared a well. Old fashioned with a slate roof and a crank that could have been centuries old.

The wind blasted through the bones of trees that surrounded her as she approached the well. She looked back at her texts from him. *Meet me at these co-ordinates,'* the last one read. She looked around her again. Nothing. No-one.

She bit the middle finger of her right glove and tugged it off. Thumbed into the phone *'Here'* and pressed send. The light started to dim, then brightened, a tick next to message. Delivered. She stamped her feet to keep the blood flowing in her legs. It was a frigid night. Then her phone buzzed, the screen brightly coming to life. She swiped up.

'Do you still want to join the immortals?' read the message in her preview.

She took her gloveless right hand from her pocket, tried to stop it trembling as she typed. *'Of course. It's why I'm here.'* Send. Since the first message left on her voicemail. The anonymously delivered envelopes of money that had followed. The secrets that had been revealed to her in those cryptic emails. Her ego, massaged like it had never been in her utterly unremarkable life to date, would not let her off this train now.

Another minute passed. The silence was deafening. Nothing stirred, but for the icy blasts from the north every few minutes. She looked over her shoulder to her car. Plumes of steam were still rising from under the bonnet. Then another buzz. She brought her phone to life, another message. *'Coming,'* it read.

Then she waited. Paced. Reached out to touch the crank handle. Frozen, as she ought to have expected. She stepped backwards, almost tripping on an exposed root. Looked at her phone once again. Then she heard something. A cracking sound on the other side of the well. She tried to look, but could see nothing. *Why hadn't she brought a torch?* "Hello," she called out. No reply, but more cracking of branches. Closer. Then a figure—more of a shadow really—began to emerge from the woods.

"Hello, Emily," came the man's voice. "You've come a long way. Thank you. Are you ready?"

Emily nodded. Then realised it was almost certainly imperceptible in the darkness. "Y … yes. I am. I think I am." She shivered. She wasn't sure if it was the cold this time, or the anticipation.

The man stopped at the other side of the well. She could begin to make out some of his facial features. "Go to the well, Emily. Wind the crank."

She stepped forward, put her gloved right hand on the dull metal of the crank and pushed. It wouldn't budge. "It's stuck," she said, still trying to force it.

"It's not stuck, it's *heavy*. Two hands."

She lifted her left hand and pushed the crank harder, it began to budge. Her muscles screamed and she felt herself starting to sweat at the weight of the bucket on the chain. It slowly rose, the effort required seeming to multiply every with every revolution. She heard creaking of the wood, but could not see in the cylinder of darkness that was the well shaft.

"Almost there," he said in encouragement.

And then it rose up out of the darkness, that seemed to be broken like the surface of a liquid. In the wide wooden trough was a teenage boy. He was asleep. Possibly unconscious. It was difficult to see. He was wearing a filthy track suit, his hair was matted, his skin pale.

"Lock the crank, by pulling it down."

She did as he said.

"Look down by your feet."

She looked down. Could see nothing. Not even her feet.

"You'll have to get closer."

She looked at the man. His features, still out of focus in the shadows, remained impassive. She sighed and crouched, hearing her knees give off an arthritic click as she did so. She felt around with her hand, finding soil, leaves, twigs and then something solid. A knife. Her breath rushed from her. She tasted sick in her mouth. But she choked it back and stood, knife in hand.

"Now?" she asked, unable to form the rest of the question.

"Cut his throat."

There was silence. The wind had dropped. She could hear her heart drumming, double-time in her ears.

"What?"

"Cut his throat."

"And then I'll—"

"—and then you'll join the immortals. Do it."

She lifted her left hand to the boy's head, tipped it backward, exposing the neck. His sallow skin darkened under the pressure from her hand. She raised the blade so that the edge was pressed against his neck. Her hand trembled. She let out a breath and steadied herself. Then she pressed and slid the blade along the line of his throat. Dark blood, near-black in the pitch of the woodland, began to seep from the wound, then flow faster. The glove on her right hand began to get heavy and warm as it soaked up the blood, running over the blade. Emily looked up. He was still watching from behind the well. The boy shuddered, spluttered as his lungs gave out and then was still.

Emily released her hands from him, let them hang limp at her sides. Felt the blood already beginning to coagulate on the fingers of her cutting hand. She couldn't feel herself breathing. *Was she breathing?* Her mind was thrumming with what she had just done, but she managed to find a moment to focus. She looked directly at the man, or the shape of him, at least.

"And now?" She let her question hang in the icy air between them.

"Throw the knife into the well."

She tossed the knife down behind the trough, heard the metal clanging against the shaft once, twice, before any trace of it was swallowed up by the darkness.

"OK." She waited for a long moment.

"That's it," he said. "You're immortal now. You'll *live* forever."

"I ... I don't understand."

"Look up Emily, see your immortality."

She looked up. Saw nothing but the spindly branches of trees, criss-crossed over one another, hatching out every last speck of sky above. She looked back to him.

"Really *look*, woman," he said. It sounded like a taunt.

She leaned her head back again and then she saw it. Above and just behind her. A red light. A tiny LED. She felt the world enter a spin around her.

"Yes, it is," he said. She could hear him smiling. "It's a camera. Go-pro. Night vision. Why don't you wave to your public?" He chuckled at his own joke. First, I checked in to this location, then I started the live video broadcast, and then I tagged you. You're a social media star, Emily. There are, let me see—," he took his smart phone from the deep pocket of his long coat, "—two thousand-and-thirty-one viewers."

"But you—"

"Am not who I said I was. And an hour from now, will be someone else entirely. What's that?"

He turned his head slightly, his eyes darting upward.

"Sirens?" she asked, though to whom she wasn't sure. She looked back to the road. Nothing yet. She turned back in time to see the shape of the man melting into the shadows of the forest. She knelt. And waited. And wept.

JAGGED LITTLE TEETH

STUART CONOVER

They gleamed in the dark
Those jagged little teeth
Chomping at the bit
Nibbling at your feet
They're from under the bed
And scurry across the floor
Monsters in the shadows
Who live behind closed doors
They fuel our nightmares
And hide beneath the stairs
The knock at the windows
Scratching in the walls
Peace of mind is in the past
As soon as night falls
The clicking of their legs echo
As they approach their sleeping prey
A plague on the sanity
For those who've ended their day
They feed upon the happiness
On all who have dozed away

ROSES ARE RED: VOLUME 1

JUSTIN BOOTE

The baby's crying was coming from the garden. Strange, he thought, because they didn't have children. Joanne couldn't, she'd told him.

He donned his dressing-gown, and headed outside. The crying was faint, muffled. It was coming from the rose bush, but, he thought, *beneath* the roses.

Oh God. Could someone perhaps have buried …? A young mother perhaps?

He put his ear the ground. The sobs died away.

Frantic, he scraped away the earth until he came to a small bundle. Opening it, he saw a photo, and a child's skeleton. He looked at the photo. It was Joanne, heavily pregnant.

MONSTERS

PATRICK WINTERS

I never liked the well in our backyard. It scared me since the day we moved in. It smelled bad—like garbage and dead cats. The walls were covered in nasty moss, and it was in the water that mommy tried to pull up from the bottom.

And it was *so* dark down there. I knew there had to be a monster living in it.

I'm down here now, cold and waiting for the monster to get me. Mommy says that if I'm a good girl again, she'll let me out.

I think the monster will eat me by then …

JULY

SILVER & WHITE

JOSHUA SHIOSHITA

The man didn't want to be up here on these floors. It was too noisy, too busy, too loud. There were too many people, too many sensations. He tried to tune it out, worked hard to keep his gaze firmly lowered as he pushed past the nurses in their trim, white uniforms. He prayed they wouldn't stop him, wouldn't question him, and they didn't. They paid him no mind, just smiled and nodded as they wheeled the sick and decaying along faded linoleum on rattling, silver wheelchairs.

The elevators seemed to take an eternity to arrive. The man could do nothing but wait, his heartbeat thundering in his ears like a distant, late summer storm. It was during this eternity that he began to doubt himself, began to waiver. Yet despite the strong urge to run, as soon as the elevator finally dinged its hollow sound and the silver doors slid open with a shake, the man stepped inside without hesitation.

It was the air. That was the first thing he noticed upon exiting the elevator. The air was sterile. The smell of nothingness intermingled with an occasional whiff of ammonia or the sour stench of bleach. It filled the hallway. The man could almost feel it seeping into his pores, clinging to his clothes. He hurried on, not looking back.

The door handle was cold to the touch, as was the door, and when he opened it, he was met with more of the icy chill, like a tangible manifestation of his own inner soul.

He examined his surroundings. All was silver and white. Polished metal cabinets lined the walls. Trays with silver tools sat upon silver tables with clean white tablecloths draped about them. The room was utterly dead, and the man knew all who dwelt within were dead as well. As he turned to take in more of the still room, he was met with his own reflection in a thin silver mirror over a white porcelain sink. It was a startling sliver of life in an otherwise lifeless setting. He almost didn't recognize himself and started suddenly at the image staring back at him. He was thin and homely, with sunken in cheeks and eyebrows too bushy for his long, plain face. He was wearing plain clothes, plain shoes, had a plain haircut … in fact, his entire being was screaming out in plain. His manner suggested a shy, fragile man who probably had little contact with the outside world. He had never had a girlfriend, or even a true friend for that matter. He was the one picked on at school, the one always average but never above. He was the person everyone looked at on the bus but never really noticed. He was a tired, scared little man who had finally gone off the deep end but was afraid of drowning, and it showed in his every hesitant movement and gesture.

He maneuvered cautiously through the silver and white room, carefully winding his way around the metal tables until he arrived at the far wall. This far wall was silver like the rest of the room. Cold, metallic, lifeless, it had large drawers all along its face with numbers and letters scribbled above silver handles on pieces of white tape. Trembling, the man reached out and grabbed one of the handles. He gingerly pulled. It slid open without a sound, and the man gasped. The sudden intake of cold air made him cough, and as he coughed, he turned to see another man standing just a few yards away with another drawer from the long silver wall open in front of him.

As he turned, the other man turned as well, and their eyes locked. Immediately, a sheepish, embarrassed look crossed both men's faces. Ashamed, they reacted as if they wanted to turn away, but some force seemed to hold them locked in a helpless, awkward stare. The one was a fractured, mirror image of the other, as were the compulsions that led them both to this cold room in the dead of night. Slowly and deliberately, both men pushed the drawers back into the long wall and stepped away. Without a word, the stranger then quietly retreated into the shadows. A moment later, a door creaked, and he was gone.

The remaining man stood rigid and still, breathing in the silence. He looked down at his hands intently, held them in his gaze for a long moment, then reached over and picked up a silver tray from a nearby table. He watched as his reflection distorted and cascaded, morphing into hideous caricatures. Terrified, he dropped the tray, and for the first time in his adult life, unlocked the door hiding all of his innermost secrets, needs, desires, and emotions, screaming the scream of a dead man.

TIME OF DEATH

RICHARD J. MELDRUM

I wake to find myself in a nightmare. Instead of my bedroom, I'm in a white room with dozens of other people. A small man with a clipboard stares at me. On the wall there's a number. *10.38.*

"103. Below average."

"What?"

"The total should be closer to 107."

"What?"

"Deaths. 107 deaths per minute. That minute."

He points at the number.

"I'm dead?"

He nods.

"So, what's next? Judgement?"

"No. You spend eternity with those who died at the same time."

"What about heaven?"

"No heaven, no hell. Just this. It's the most efficient way."

I start to scream.

DARKNESS AND LIGHT

AMANDA J EVANS

The night was darker than usual.

No moon or stars lit her path. The heat from the sun had lingered. Carrying her coat in her arms she didn't hear him creep up behind her. There were no streetlights to cast a glimmer on the blade he raised and plunged it deep into her back. She crumpled to the ground. Her screams muffled by the pungent hand held firmly over her mouth. Piercing evil eyes met her panic as the knife sank through her flesh, stabbing her heart. A bright light caught her eyes as her last breath left her body.

145

DATE NIGHT

ALYSON FAYE

Watched by dead eyes, me and Billy crack open the crypt's padlocks.

Our bag tinkles with cans; this is as exciting as it comes in our little town.

"Ladies first," Billy sniggers.

We stretch out across the tombs. I'm lying on a Knight.

We drink, smoke and cuddle. I shouldn't do the first two though. Not in

my condition.

Behind me I hear a rustle. Turning I spot her—bloodstained dress, bashed in head, blue lips.

She looks familiar. I turn to Billy. "Is that …?"

No warning; his fists pulverise my skull.

Like trash, he stows me away. Smiling constantly.

THE ELEPHANT CURSE

L.S. ENGLER

Bianca was Mira's fifth elephant and hopefully her last, because any more would surely have the animal rights groups up in arms and waving their torches. None of us could figure out exactly why all of Mira's elephants were dying. She took exceptional care of each one of them and would be put out for entire weeks on end when it happened, each one more heartbreaking than the next. They had to practically peel her from the stomach of the last one as she clung to its still belly and wept into the dry folds of its rough skin as though her tears would revive it. If Bianca didn't survive, it might finally be time to wrap it up and develop some new act for Mira. She was young and talented, so it wouldn't be difficult, but she'd always wanted to work with the elephants, she was so fascinated by them, and she would never be the same if they were gone.

Everyone held their breath in the weeks where Mira got to know Bianca, who was a little smaller than the others but had this beautiful pale hide, almost white, that would look marvellous under sparkling dressings and spotlights. She was smart and clever and responsive, immediately taking a liking to Mira and constantly playing with her hair. Perhaps, we all though hopefully, though we were almost too afraid to hope, the previous ones had just been building up to this pairing, as if Mira had to experience the loss and heartbreak to truly appreciate the creature that was now in her care. It seemed a bit of a cruel method on the part of Fate, but we were eager to justify anything we couldn't quite explain.

The first show was a success, as well as the second, and the third. Every show after that was fraught with an undercurrent of nervousness. Is this the one where it will finally happen? What about this one? But night after night, the bond between Mira and Bianca grew, and they continued to perform well with no signs of sickness or injury or fatal accidents. After a steady month of shows, many of us around the camp were able to breathe easier again, confident that the fifth time had been a charge. But some of us still worried, Mira included, and we weren't about to let our guard down any time soon.

We were just outside of Louisville when Mira came to my wagon, so pale and drawn as to look like a skeleton in a spangled headdress, tears in her eye. I didn't need for her to speak to know what had happened, but she needed to say it, to let it out, which released a floodgate as I opened my arms and let her settle into them. "Something's not right with Bianca," she sobbed. "Something's wrong. It's happening again, Jeanette. It's all happening again."

I tried to hush her, tried to quiet her disturbed soul, but no amount of hair petting and tight squeezes could alleviate her despair. "There, there," I said, though a darkness was forming into a hard lump against my heart. The poor girl didn't know, but we had been discussing her strange and expensive predicament, realizing that we couldn't keep wasting so much time and money on the elephants, popular as they were. There just wasn't as much of a market for travelling circuses these days, and every set-back was enough to send us miles and miles behind where we needed to be.

We didn't want to believe it. Mira was such a sweet girl, talented, with a brilliant smile that charmed audiences into emptying their pockets. But she was clearly cursed. When I saw Bianca lying on her side in a matted bed of straw, her enormous stomach practically vibrating with the labor of her heavy breaths, I knew what had to be done.

"Mira," I said, my voice sticking in my throat, heavy and bitter on my tongue, "this isn't good. This isn't good at all. You know we can't keep replacing your elephants. We know you take good care of them. We know you're doing nothing wrong, so clearly you have to see what we see. It isn't the elephants, Mira; it's you. But there is one way to stop all this, and I think you can gather what it might be."

She looked up at me, her eyes as round as a full moon, thinking at first that I was going to suggest she pursue a new act. And then realization dawned on her, and her whole body seemed to melt in dismay. "No, Jeanette, no, please. It isn't true! I'm sure the curse seemed like a real thing back in the day, but you know it can't be real. Curses aren't real. They don't really exist, it's all just superstition. It's got to be something in the water, or maybe something we're feeding them. It's not *me*, Jeanette. It's not a *curse*."

"There's only one way to know for sure," I murmured. "I'm so sorry, Mira."

She saw the knife in my hand, opening her mouth to scream, but it was too late. With two swift movements, I stabbed the poor girl in her stomach, then pulled her head back to slit her throat. The blood I smeared onto Bianca's white belly, along with herbs and oils and incantations, left a faint pink stain on her skin, which lingered there to remind us, to help us never forget poor Mira. Her love for the elephants wasn't enough to overpower how toxic she was to them, but my magic was. We brought in a new elephant trainer, one who wasn't as charming or effervescent as Mira, but I'm fairly sure that Bianca will now outlive us all.

ROSES ARE RED: VOLUME 2

JUSTIN BOOTE

The rose bush was Sarah's pride. With reason, it had featured in many a gardening magazine, winning many prizes. Its petals were bright red, blood-red almost. The thorns; deadly. She smiled as she prepared the fertilizer. Her secret fertilizer. She mixed the ingredients, and added her special touch, leaving just a few drops for afterwards.

She stopped briefly to listen to the news; another child—Shaun—had gone missing.

"Terrible shame," she muttered.

Sprinkling the mix with the soil, she poured the drops she had saved over the petals.

The petals opened to receive them.

"Good-bye, Shaun. Thank you for helping."

JUST A TASTE

S.C. CORNETT

Lisa licked the blood from her fingers.

Metallic. Salty. A bit sweet. It was always strange when it tasted sweet. A flavor profile she had almost forgotten. Thankfully Diabetes was the new norm and those who cheated. They were a mouthful but she loved slurping them down. Humans. Dominant species of the planet. What a laugh.

Her kind roamed the stars long before these apes lost their hair. She would again once she could get off this backward planet. That's all she could get out the next day when they found her. Tripping, knee deep bathed in the hobo's blood.

THEY GLISTENED BLACK IN THE SUN

STUART CONOVER

The Clickers were everywhere.
 Thankfully Jesse had hidden.
 She knew if they saw her she was dead.
 They slept during the day.
 It should have been safe.
 Yet here they were.
 Each time they moved the clicking grew louder.
 Something had them agitated.
 They were hunting.
 The sound was drawing closer.
 She just had to be quiet.
 Not draw their attention.
 One of them passed where she hid.
 Its carapace glistening black in the sun.
 Closing her eyes, she tried not to whimper.
 Hours passed before they left.
 Hours more before she worked up the courage to try for home.

TO THE SEA, THE SORROW

DANIEL PIETERSEN

Leah sat on the edge of the pier and looked out to sea, salt tears welling in her wide grey eyes. She thought of her mother; the beautiful hair gone, oily sweat growing slick on pallid skin. She thought of the day she returned from school to find her mother's bed empty and her father stone-faced, teeth clenched.

"She has gone to the sea," he'd told his daughter who, old enough, dismissed the words as a well-meaning fable.

As Leah stood and left, a pale shape broke the water. Oil-slick and bald, it watched the girl with wide grey eyes.

THE COMPANION

CARL R. JENNINGS

I'm glad you're here.
I know.
I didn't know who else to turn to.
You can always come to me.
You're always there.
I'm always here.
It's beyond my endurance now; I can't sleep.
I know.
You always understand.
I do.
Everything's so dark.
I'll find you.
Something's moving around.
I know.
I can't see.
I can see you.
It hears me.
I know.
It smells putrid.
You'll get used to it.
I'm afraid. I don't know what's happening.
I can tell you.
It feels wrong.
You'll numb yourself to it.
I think it's coming for me.
I'm already here.

TO DIE FOR

STEPHANIE ELLIS

"Look, it's not even cooked." The diner poked at her food in disgust. "Ugh."

"You asked for rare," her companion reminded her.

"Rare does not mean raw." She looked around. "Waiter, I need to see the chef now!"

"But madam …"

"Forget it. I'll go."

She got up and marched into the kitchen, stepped over the bodies. She hacked another piece off the chef, flashed it under the grill.

"If you want anything doing properly," she said as she returned to her seat, "you've got to do it yourself."

She smiled happily. The food here really was to die for.

DIAO SI GUI

PATRICK WINTERS

Fan didn't know if it was the drink that had led him here, or some strange sense of fate.

He had not intended to venture out this far into the woods, his feet carrying him farther than his mind had bothered to realize. But hadn't he started drinking all those hours ago to keep his mind so very numb, to wash out the thoughts and the memories that always came creeping back this time of the year? To put this place far behind him?

And yet here he was, all the same, just barely standing on his feet, swaying and looking up at the old elm.

Gang had swayed, too, that night.

His body had danced beneath that one sturdy branch, the rope tight around his neck. Fan could still recall the creaking sound the motion had made.

Had nine years really passed since then? It'd felt like ages to Fan. He supposed the guilt contributed to that. Guilt could add hours to the days, days to the weeks, and so on, stretching the years out like taffy he didn't want to stomach.

They'd convinced themselves their actions were just, at the time. Now, though, such lies had long-since worn off.

When little Zhao Mei had gone missing that spring of 1988, all of the village had been dismayed. As she'd always been known for being the adventurous sort (and believing the people of the village were too close-knit to fathom a kidnapping), authorities assumed the girl had gotten herself lost in a jaunt through the forest.

One week and a day of fruitlessly searching the woods had passed by, though, and whatever hope there'd been of finding the eight-year-old had seemed to pass with it. But not for her father, Guang. He still had hope, and above all, suspicion.

He'd convinced himself that his baby had been taken, and that he'd determined the culprit: Gang, the hermit who lived quietly in the woods, and who was only ever seen on his occasional trips into the village.

Guang had brought his closest and oldest friends together one evening, sharing in his accusation with Sun Jian, Wu Yuan—and Fan.

"He's not a part of this place," Guang had spat. "He's a tick on the dog, living off of us when he needs to. We can't trust him. I swear, he took my girl, or at the least, he knows what happened to her!"

Hot blooded and seeking justice, the three had agreed to confront Gang and help their desperate friend. When Guang led them up into the woods, heading towards the outsider's hut, not one of them questioned the long length of rope he carried with him.

The hermit was asleep when they'd broken in his door. They'd shouted demands at him as they kicked and grabbed at him. He screamed and cried. They shouted more.

When he didn't give them the answers they sought, they'd dragged him out to the elm with the strong-looking limbs. Guang had given the old man a final chance to confess his guilt, threatening to string him up and let him hang until dead.

Still, Gang revealed nothing, and together the four of them tied the rope about his neck and hoisted him up high. They lashed the rope to a root and let the man kick—until he was past kicking.

Fan had since told himself that it was to be a scare tactic, one that had just gone too far. But he knew in his heart that they'd done exactly what they'd gone out there intending to do.

Mei's body was found a week later, several dozen miles from the village. Her body was frail from dehydration and hunger, but there were no other marks upon her. She had indeed gotten lost, searching for home in the wrong direction.

Zhao Guang committed suicide a few months later, becoming something of a ghost long before his passing. He'd ended it by a hanging. Wu Yuan moved to Hangzhou shortly after that; he died last year, run over in the street. And Sun Jian went two months back, a heart attack taking him in the night.

They'd kept their deed a secret in all that time, and now only Fan remained to tow their regret. He heaved a sigh, let loose his tears, and took another swig from his bottle. He nearly choked on it though, dropping the beer and falling to his knees as he went into a coughing fit.

As his breath returned to him, he heard the familiar sound of creaking overhead.

Fan slowly turned his eyes upward, knowing what he would see. Still, his gut went cold at the sight of Gang the hermit, who was swinging over him, his slack, dead gaze upon him.

He was dressed in the same rags he'd worn the night of his death, his white skin dirtied and showing signs of rot. An unnaturally long, red tongue jutted out from his mouth, lolling and twisted like a dead worm upon a hot street. There was as much demon about the specter as there was man—a twisted form born of the hell that Fan and the others had sent him to.

A hoarse whisper escaped the spirit's lips, a single, damning word spoken from beyond the grave:

"Innocent . . ."

Fan cried out in terror, feeling all of the forest and its arcane forces bearing down upon him. Whether he knelt under the dead man for a mere moment or an hour, he did not know, nor did it matter. For when he finally rose and stumbled away, the damage had already been done.

Crazed and forever blinded, Fan fled the place of his lasting sin, screaming for death as he went.

A week and a half later, a hiker happened across his body; it lay not so very far from where the young Zhao Mei had been discovered nine years earlier.

GLASS SLIPPER

ROBERT ALLEN LUPTON

The scullery maid wore the gown and glass slippers created by her fairy godmother to the royal ball. She arrived in a magic carriage pulled by enchanted livery.

The Prince stayed at her side and he never tired of gazing into her mirror like shoes.

At midnight, she ran and lost a shoe. The Prince caught her and knelt to replace it. He stared into the shoe and she realized that he'd been using the reflection to peek up her gown the entire night.

She screamed, "Pervert", ripped off her other shoe and shoved the high heel into his eye.

DABBLERS

SARAH DOEBEREINER

It was a day full of teeth marks and tears. Jerimiah pulled Bethany's hair: he stepped on the hem of her dress. She sunk her teeth into the flesh of his ankle. Instead of giving her a spanking, Momma sent her to church.

Now, Bethany watched gaunt townswomen encircle her. Melodious chanting lifted skyward as they fidgeted over loosely threaded beads.

The women's frantic breaths siphoned rolling smoke from the air. When they raised their heads, their eyes took an orange hue. It must have been the firelight reflected—a trick of the light.

Bethany would have much preferred that spanking.

THE SUMMON

MATHIAS JANSSON

To every teenage boy who stay up all night to invoke the devil and summon the dark one to come and collect their tormented souls. Drawing silly chalk lines on the floor, dropping blood on the carpet and reads ancient spells that they don't understand or cannot properly pronounce. When I finally arrives their faces always become pale and they shiver with fear. When they can see my face I always hear a terrifying scream.

—Mum?!

—Yes, my son, I reply, I am here, so clean up your fucking room before I drag your lazy soul back down to hell!

NOW I LAY ME DOWN

RUSCHELLE DILLON

Cali finished her last gulp of milk before climbing into bed. After downing a mug of her own, Evelyn slid under the covers next to her five-year-old daughter and blew out the candle on the nightstand.

The milk made Cali sleepy. But she wanted to talk.

"Mommy, when will the lights come back on?"

Evelyn could hear the tracks of the tanks in the distance chewing through the rubble.

Closing her eyes Evelyn whispered, "I don't know."

Cali reached under the blankets for her dirty but well-loved stuffed dog and kissed its frayed nose. She offered it to her mom.

"Candy wants a goodnight kiss."

Evelyn heaved open her eyes and gave the ragged dog a half-hearted kiss before tucking it between them both under the blankets.

Cali yawned but continued chatting, fighting the urge to sleep.

"Will daddy be home tonight? He said he'd be home soon."

Evelyn brushed a stray blonde hair from her daughter's forehead.

"I don't know," she sighed

The pillow under Evelyn's head was worn and flat. She attempted to fluff it anyway. Cali helped plump the broken feathers before pulling out a particular one that had poked through the threadbare cotton. She rubbed the down against her nose, followed by a playful move to tickle her mom's nose.

"Do you think I could play outside tomorrow?"

Evelyn snatched the feather from her tiny fingers and twirled it in her own.

"Just for a little bit," Cali pressed.

But before Evelyn could open her mouth to answer, the room shook from the mortar fire.

Covering her daughters head as a thin layer of dirt and dust gushed through the house's broken windows, Evelyn heard the men's voices and knew they would be on their street soon. She hoped the barricade against the door would hold for just a little while longer.

"Mommy, Candy's scared. It's really dark in here tonight." Cali whispered as she snuggled against her mom and kissed her cheek.

"Is this what it's like to be dead?" she whimpered.

"I don't know honey."

Evelyn fumbled under the covers for a small handgun she had tucked in the pocket of her nightgown.

As her daughter breathed soft and steady the milk finally taking effect, Evelyn fought through her own milk induced haze.

She could hear the men and war machines outside her door as she pulled back the hammer.

"But tonight, we're going to find out."

HUNTING HIM DOWN

MICHAEL A. ARNZEN

As you spot the lusty beast through your rifle scope, the wolf howls at the full moon. It's a wail of pain. You lift your finger from the trigger as its face contorts. Squinting through the lens, you see brown hair fall away like a porcupine shooting its quills, pointed ears curling down into lazy lobes. The creature tumbles in the soil and then stands erect, dirty, but bathed naked in moonlight. You wonder if the silver bullet you made from your ring will kill the monster or if you'd only be murdering the man.

Your prodigal fiancé waves hello.

THE DAY WAS HOT THE RIVER INVITING

CR SMITH

Joe was warned not to but the day was hot and the river inviting. He plunged straight in. Coolness quickly turned to tingling, followed by burning, and before he knew it his body was dissolving. His feet and lower half went first, then his torso, until only his head remained. It bobbed up and down on the water's surface, drifting with the current, eventually washing up on the riverbank joining the row of other heads. Some must have been there a while. All looked in various stages of decomposition, yet for some strange reason, they were all totally *compost mentis*.

EXIT

BART VAN GOETHEM

Now traffic news: there's been an accident on the A45.

Oh-oh, Jason mumbled to himself.

A truck crashed into a car right before the exit to Birmingham.

Great, that's my exit.

Witnesses say the car just stalled, as if it broke down suddenly. The truck behind it couldn't avoid the crash. The right lane is now temporarily closed.

That's strange. There's no traffic jam.

The driver of the car didn't survive the collision.

Okay, I'm nearing the exit. There's no sign that anything just happened here. It's—wait, why's my oil light blinking all of a sudden?

Oh, shit.

AUGUST

PORTRAIT IN BLOOD

STEVEN CARR

Durston stopped momentarily to wipe the perspiration from his face with his sweat-soaked handkerchief that he kept in the palm of his hand. He glanced up at the full white moon that shimmered in the early August sky, then continued on. An eddy of dust skimmed across the road in front of him and bits of blowing plant debris and grit battered his face and collected in his nostrils, ears and on his lips. By the time he reached the concrete pathway leading to the Pfrimmer house, huge sweat stains had formed on his shirt beneath his underarms. He pushed open the wrought iron gate and stepped through onto a narrow path blanketed with black pebbles.

At the bottom of the steps leading up to the wrap around porch he was able to form just enough spittle in his dry mouth to spit out the dirt. He looked up at the large, weather-beaten two-story white house and climbed the stairs, the steps creaking beneath his dust covered shoes.

After knocking on the door, he leaned his tripod against the door frame and brushed the dust from his shirt and shifted the strap of his camera bag. The bag wasn't heavy but in the heat the pressure of the strap on his skin felt as if he were carrying a lead weight. Rivulets of perspiration ran down his face and dripped from his stringy hair.

A little girl with long blonde hair and wearing a white summer dress and white shoes opened the door.

"Who are you?" she asked, her body half hidden in the shadows of the doorway, beyond the shining light of the moon.

"I'm Durston Hansen, the photographer," he said.

"You're late," the little girl said.

"My car broke down a little ways down the road," he said. "Who are you?"

"I'm Annabella," she said.

From a room further back in the house, a woman's voice called out. "Who's at the door, Annabella?"

Annabella turned and shouted, "The man is here to take our picture."

Behind Annabella a young woman also with long blonde hair and wearing a white floor length dress of a gauzy material appeared. She was holding a candle. The light from its flame flickered on her pale face and made her dark eyes glisten like black marbles. "I'm Mrs. Pfrimmer," she said. "We've been waiting on you."

"I'm so sorry," Durston said. "My car broke down. It's practically brand new. It just stopped and I couldn't get it running again."

"Walking that road at night can be dangerous," she said. "Wolves roam the countryside."

"Wolves?" Durston said with surprise.

"You're here now," she said. "Come in."

Durston lifted the tripod and went into the house and turned to see the door close on its own. He followed the woman and girl into a room with a small settee with red and black cloth upholstery in the middle of the room. Burning candles were on every table and lined the mantle place over a stone fireplace where logs snapped and crackled in an intense blaze. The room smelled of smoke, though none was present, and it was as hot and moist as a sauna.

"We wish to have our family portrait taken of us together on the settee," Mrs. Pfrimmer said. "Mr. Pfrimmer will be up from the basement momentarily."

Durston opened the tripod and set it up facing the settee. He took his Pentax 35mm camera from the bag and screwed it onto the tripod.

The woman and little girl were watching him very closely.

"Is that the camera you used to take the portraits in the flier that was left on our porch?" Mrs. Pfrimmer said.

"Yes, it is. It's not fancy but for the kind of portraits I like to take it works great," he said. "I don't use digital cameras. I prefer the older models and think of my portraits as art."

"Ours will be black and white?" she said.

"Yes, just as you requested in your letter," he said. "I've already loaded the film." He took the flash attachment out of the bag and started to slide it onto the top of the camera.

"What is that?" Mrs. Pfrimmer said.

"It's the flash unit," Durston said. "Even when you turn the lights on the flash may be needed. I prefer natural lighting and may not use the flash at all but I have it just in case I need it."

Mrs. Pfrimmer shook her bony index finger in his face. "Light other than from flames isn't allowed in this house at night," she said.

Durston looked around the room. Shadows of the flickering flames danced on every wall. "I guess there's enough light," he said. He put the flash attachment back into his bag and wiped his face with his sweat-drenched handkerchief. "Could I get a glass of water?"

"We have no running water," Mrs. Pfrimmer said.

"No running water?" Durston said.

A door at the end of the room burst open. A cloud of dust and the smell of sulfur billowed out making the candle flames quiver on the wicks. A tall man with a gaunt face and shoulder length black hair and wearing a tuxedo stepped out. He looked at Durston and smiled. "You're not married, you're twenty-six years of age and you spend many nights at the bar," he said.

A chill ran up Durston's spine. "How do you know that?"

"I know everything. I'm Jackson Pfrimmer," he said, crossing to Durston as if blown there by a breeze. He held out his hand for Durston to shake.

Durston took the man's hand and immediately pulled it away. He looked at the palm of his hand expecting to see it frozen.

"Shall we have our family portrait taken now?" Jackson said.

"Yes, please, if we can," Durston said nervously.

The husband and wife sat on the settee with Annabella sitting between them. They stared at the camera, their faces like stone.

"Say cheese," Durston said as he bent down and put his eye to the viewfinder.

"What is cheese?" Annabella said.

Durston began taking shots.

***

In his photo lab, Durston staggered backward against the enlarger. Clipped to a line above the table with the development trays were the enlargments of the portraits taken of the Pfrimmer family. In the black and white photographs, bright red blood dripped from two fangs bared by each of them. The white dresses of Mrs. Pfrimmer and Annabella were spotted with blood. These weren't the pictures he remembered taking at all.

He raised his hand and put it on the side of his neck and felt three separate pairs of puncture wounds.

JUST RIGHT

ROBERT ALLEN LUPTON

The three bears came home and found a golden-haired girl asleep in Baby Bear's bed. Someone had eaten their porridge and broken one of their chairs.

Mama Bear pulled a blonde hair from Papa Bear's whiskers. She shook the girl awake. "Is this that cheap hussy you've been seeing while I hibernate?"

The girl said, "Hi Papa", and the big bear smashed the girl's head before she could say another word.

"I swear I've never seen this one before."

Baby Bear thought she tasted too tough. Mama Bear thought she tasted too stringy. Papa Bear thought she was just right.

LIGHTNING NEED ONLY STRIKE ONCE

RICHARD J. MELDRUM

The storm closed in while Peter was cutting the grass in the back paddock. *When it roars, head indoors* echoed in his mind, so he made a beeline for the house. As Peter headed back, there was a crack and a flash from above. He flinched, but kept running. Reaching the house, Peter heard a scream from indoors. His wife. Alarmed, he reached for the door, amazed when his hand passed through the wood. The rest of his body followed. Peter didn't have to look back to see the crumpled shape lying the grass. He'd already guessed what had happened.

GUILTY

SARAH DOEBEREINER

Three rings to voicemail and an email response. A paper trail; that's all they'll get from me. That way I can choose my words carefully. I can answer those questions with the kind of precision it takes to stay one step ahead.

Paranoid? I don't think so. This is all submissible in court; every word, every passing conversation might be splayed open to scrutiny. It never hurts to be cautious. This watched pot will never boil.

What do I have to hide? I can't tell you that, out in the open where any passing dolt might hear, now can I?

ANYTHING STORAGE

G.E. SMITH

Rosalyn raised her open palm again. "Our customers' business is their business."

Ellis rubbed his cheek and didn't look up. "I know, but yesterday I smelled something around unit forty-one."

"You and your thoughts and notions and allergies." Rosalyn lowered her hand. "Wearin' a flannel long-sleeve shirt and straw hat in this heat is the stupidest thing I've ever seen. And you look more the fool wearing that faded yellow bandanna over your nose and mouth."

"The smell is like that of something dead," Ellis said. "I think we should at least speak to the person—"

Rosalyn backhanded Ellis. "People pay us to store stuff. It's our living. Not our business to ask questions."

Ellis raised his head and looked eye to eye with his older sibling, one of the few times he ever had. "But our business is our business."

Rosalyn flexed her fingers and glared at Ellis. They looked at each other for several moments, then she marched out of the room. She came back with what resembled a wooden spatula.

Ellis began to rock his upper body and rub the top of his legs. "I'm sorry, I'm sorry, please don't use that."

Rosalyn had named it the Thumper. It was a fourteen-inch long piece of hand-carved oak. The handle was as bit smaller than a paper towel tube, and it had notches in it for a good grip. The business end of the Thumper fanned out and was a half-inch thick. Ball bearings had been sunk halfway into the wood. "Your job, Ellis, is to clean the units after the renter has taken everything out. Not to snoop, not to play detective." Before he had a chance to even nod, Rosalyn went out.

Ellis grabbed his crutches, got to his feet, put his arms through the crutch cuffs, grabbed each handgrip, and made his way to the front door.

Rosalyn was in the golf cart. "Get in. A wonder you get anything at all done around here, slow as you are."

Ellis got in and the cart jerked forward. The bottom tips of his crutches bumped along the ground as they headed to unit forty-one.

The golf cart was the one decent thing Rosalyn had done for Ellis. He had several brooms in the back, a dustpan, and a box of garbage bags.

Rosalyn stopped and got out. Ellis crinkled his nose because of the smell and reached in his shirt pocket for his bandanna. Rosalyn slapped it out of his hand. "C'mon, I got end of the month bills to get ready."

Ellis got out.

Rosalyn stood next to a dark, gooey mass. "Get over here."

Ellis put a dab of sunscreen on his nose and made his way to his sister. "You don't have a hat on and the sun—"

Rosalyn snatched the tube of sunscreen and tossed it behind her in the tall grass. "First off, the renter wanted something smaller and in the shade so he's now got unit thirty-eight."

"Why didn't you tell me?"

Rosalyn shook her head. "If I spent all my time telling you every detail I'd get nothing done and we'd go broke." She gestured. "This is what's called a tree line." She pointed. "That is storage unit forty-one."

"Yes, but what about—"

"Shut up and listen. A trapper rented forty-one. That's why I had him rent near the tree line. That's why these guts are here. You do know what a trapper is, right?"

Ellis nodded.

Rosalyn huffed. "God help us. A wonder I've managed the business this long with the likes of you." She marched over to unit forty-one and unlocked the padlock. She put the padlock in a small plastic tray that all rental units had bolted near the door.

Two steps in and she lurched forward and fell.

Ellis flipped on the light. "Rosalyn, are you all right? Let me help you." He knelt down.

"Get away from me. I'm a grown woman." Rosalyn, face down, tried rolling over. When she got on her left side she screamed. "My hip! I've gone and broke my hip thanks to you." Her eyes fluttered shut. She moaned and went back on her stomach. "I wouldn't have ... wouldn't have fallen in the first place if ... if you'd not been so suspicious." Rosalyn swiped at her grey-streaked light brown hair that clung to her face.

Ellis noticed the Thumper laying several feet from Rosalyn. He pulled it away with the butt end of one crutch and picked it up. "I've done my best to not let things get me down. I've gotten along pretty good since the Polio. Even when Mom and Dad split up and ended up giving you this business instead of me." He looked at the Thumper. "Only two minutes younger than you and treated like a slave for as long as I can remember."

His sister grunted. Her lip was swollen and her chin was bleeding.

Ellis looked at a dark spot on the floor. "You slipped on blood. I've said before those shoes aren't fit for—"

Rosalyn turned her head and opened her eyes. "Shut your fool mouth! Always telling me what to do, what to wear. Damned cripples, wanting to give orders and watch everyone else do the work."

Ellis closed his eyes for a moment. After a measured breath, he looked at the posted laminated sheet on the inside of the door. All the units had one. "At least you fell inside, out of the direct sun."

He smiled, waited a moment, then put on his reading glasses. His smile grew wider and he began to read. "Rule one: Always turn the light out upon leaving any storage unit."

"You'll burn in Hell for this, Ellis!"

"Rule two: Always make sure you completely shut the storage unit door." He did, then reopened it. "This should keep you company." Ellis tossed the Thumper into unit forty-one. "Mind your fingers now." He closed the door.

Rosalyn hollered. She reached forward with nothing to grip but a rough concrete floor. She put her foot against the wall and tried to push herself toward the partially-open door. "Damn you to the darkest, hottest place in Hell!"

Ellis raised his voice. "Rule three: Under no circumstances are you to leave any storage unit for any time or for any reason without locking it." He closed the door, flipped the slotted latch over the U-bolt, slid the padlock through, and locked it.

Back home, Ellis went to his sister's office and turned on the radio.

"… and is expected to reach ninety-eight, with a heat index of one-o-five," the forecaster said.

"Whew, now that's hot." Ellis grabbed a pen and opened the daily logbook. "Storage unit forty-one occupied indefinitely."

NEST OF BONES

ALYSON FAYE

Up in the attic on the floorboards lies a brown feathery ball. Tattered and torn. Its blood spatters the dust. A fly lands on the bird's glassy eye. It does not blink. Sickened I turn away.

In the neglected fireplace rests a nest. An intricately woven tangle of twigs. Inside nestle white bones. Cuddled up. I hold them gently in the palm of my hand.

Thump! Turning I see bird after bird. An unkindness of ravens. A murder of crows. Target the windows. Some get in. They fly around, cocking their heads in unison. Surrounded, I wait for the attack.

THE TWINS

MATTHIEU CARTRON

The twins, Tom and Lawrence, were identical in every way, except that Tom bit his nails and Lawrence twiddled his thumbs. They existed in society as one person, and the school they attended only knew of that one person—Jim—and Jim would either be Tom or Lawrence, depending on the day. While one twin was at school the other got to do whatever he wanted.

But it became problematic when Tom started to murder. Eventually, the police apprehended him, and he was subsequently thrown into prison with a life sentence.

In class, Jim would now only bite his nails.

ROSES ARE RED: VOLUME 3

JUSTIN BOOTE

The rose bush was Sarah's pride. With reason, it had featured in many a gardening magazine, winning many prizes. Its petals were bright red, blood-red almost. The thorns; deadly. She smiled as she prepared the fertilizer. Her secret fertilizer. She mixed the ingredients, and added her special touch, leaving just a few drops for afterward.

She stopped briefly to listen to the news; another child—Shaun—had gone missing.

"Terrible shame," she muttered.

Sprinkling the mix with the soil, she poured the drops she had saved over the petals.

The petals opened to receive them.

"Good-bye Shaun. Thank you for helping."

ARROGANCE

BRYAN NICKELBERRY

My mind argues that I didn't know. How could I know that reading the book would actually end the world? But no. Let's not lie. I am a man of science. I have lived my entire life logically, and have made it a point to refuse being ruled by superstition or emotion. I have challenged and successfully debunked mystics, soothsayers, and all manner of supernatural mumbo jumbo without any real effort. So, when I saw the book on the shelf in the used bookstore, how could I not read it? How could I not challenge it? There has not been a single time in my life when I have not been able to disprove the proposed "truths" of the gullible and the foolish. I suppose this would be pride then, wouldn't it? Pride is listed among the seven deadly sins after all.

No! No. I will not give in to this. Even now. Even … at the end.

The book was sitting all by itself. No other copies. *The end of all that is*, the book's title read. And the author was listed simply as, *'I AM'*. Please.

I purchased the book, brought it home, and sat down in my study to read it. Opening the book, I was insulted. Ink dark enough to be the void of space, printed on a page so white that it seemed to glow; but as if it were written for children, only a single phrase was printed in the middle of that page. "A storm shall come."

I rolled my eyes. Storm season was already upon us, and we'd been promised a big storm this very evening. So I thought nothing of it as the wind began to blow. Each page that I turned revealed only another, single, solitary sentence. They described the storm covering the world, along with earthquakes, and flame. I live in Los Angeles.

The earthquake didn't surprise me, and we have wildfires of varying intensity every year. I was fairly certain there'd already been a wildfire burning when I began reading, so to smell its smoke did not overly bother me. I listened for sirens telling me to clear out of the area, and hearing none, I went back to reading. The fact that these things occurred while I was reading the book meant nothing more than coincidence. But as I continued reading about men on horses, and clashing forces of good or evil, I began hearing things I could neither explain, nor discount as coincidence. Horses are common enough in this area, but the screams of my neighbors are not.

I read on, determined to prove the book wrong, and I heard homes stripped from their foundations, saw the detritus which used to be the world I knew fly past my parlor windows; and all of it backlit by the flames of annihilation. I felt the tremors of giant footsteps, and heard things which do not sound or smell human enter my house. Part of me suspects that they may well be behind me as I speak; smiling, reading over my shoulder, waiting for me to turn. Stopped from taking their action only by the fact that I haven't read their actions yet.

There is nothing beyond my windows now. I hear a low wind whistling past the place where my stairs used to be. I've turned to the last page, but I won't read the last word. I can't. I know what it says, and can see its shape even through my tears.

"Die."

ROADKILL

RUSCHELLE DILLON

He waited on the side of the road for a ride back to college. For every car that sped past he hoped the next one would stop to pick him up.

As evening strong armed the light, his chances for a ride waned. He knew no one would pick up a stranger in the dark.

Who could blame them?

Scary people are out there.

With luck on his side, a car stuffed with college kids stopped.

He hopped inside but scrutinized each smiling face, making sure there wasn't a serial killer in the bunch.

There wasn't.

But there was now …

PICTURE PERFECT

CATHERINE BERRY

His photos were famous. Traveling anywhere he pleased, people rarely questioned a man with a camera and confidence. Most found it flattering to have a professional take their picture. They had no idea. No one ever did. He enjoyed immortalizing moments in his photos; keeping them safe from the passage of time. It was the dimming light in their eyes, as death claimed them, that he savored the most; even more exciting than finding, taking, and killing them. In every city he obsessively roamed the streets, looking for the next person to add to his collection. His picture perfect someone.

NOTES FROM THE GOD CHAIR

STEVE BEVILACQUA

Number 4 said she hated spiders. Fuck, will she regret that. He wondered how long. Probably by next shift. Maybe they'll wait. But she'll wish she hadn't let that slip.

Number 6 wanted something to drink. She begged. She raised her voice. He sent her into the antechamber and then had the grunts take away her stool.

Number 2 casually mentioned that he was born with 6 fingers on each hand. He'd had his extra fingers cut off. His ancestors were from the West Indies, he said, as if that explained it. He said the extra fingers were a sign of good luck. The man asked "Then why did you cut them off?" Number 2 had no answer. Per the ordinance, the temperature increased 30 degrees.

Number 3 asked him to talk to her, about anything.

***

The man was excited because this morning he'd tried a new way to work, and it had saved him 10 minutes. On the 705. Go figure, he thought. On the map, that route looked like it went far out of the way. The system never even suggested it. But he tried it and he beat the system. It made him feel good. Empowered.

At the beginning of every shift, the man checked the envelope that waited for him by the chair. Nothing out of the ordinary today.

He sat in the dark, watching the monitors. An entire wall of them. Different angles of the subjects crying and screaming. Having deep dark existential crises, and sometimes simply experiencing normal everyday crises. It was like having forty-eight windows into Hell.

While spending long hours in the dark room, at times he would begin to nod off. Then he'd snap awake, terrified that someone might discover he'd fallen asleep. Two curators had been removed for "inefficacy," never to be seen again. Thankfully, the screaming kept him awake.

The man watched Number 7 and Number 9 as they were forced to assemble furniture in their respective cells. At least they thought it was furniture. The one who finished first got a sandwich and the other one got the fog. As they nailed and screwed the bulky frustrating pieces together, they came to realize that they were building coffins.

He asked Number 8 if she had the chance, would she let Number 4 go. Number 8 asked why.

***

"If you press that button, someone gets hurt."

No response. Just the hollow eyes, not knowing where to look.

"If you press that button twice, someone gets seriously hurt. But you get ice cream."

"I don't want to press the button."

"Then no ice cream."

"I don't care. Fuck you."

Then there was Number 8 …

"If you press that button, someone gets hurt."

"Alright."

"If you press that button twice, someone gets seriously hurt. But you get ice cream."

"I don't like ice cream. What happens if I press it three times?"

"What would you like to happen?"

"Can I choose who gets hurt?"

The man had grown to like this Number 8. He wondered how long she would be around.

***

Number 3 is gone after an extended breakdown. She kept repeating that she wanted an apple. She screamed for the apple. When she was a girl, her mom used to give her an apple after school. All she wanted was an apple. An apple. The episode began before lunch and was still going on when he got back, only at a much shriller pitch. Number 3 was done. They carried her brain-fried remains from the cell.

The man found himself watching Number 8 more than the others. He knew he wasn't allowed to do that, but he couldn't help it. He was alarmed to discover that he was doing it without realizing it. He silently promised himself to correct that in the future. But he didn't. He was fascinated by Number 8 … what she did when she wasn't doing anything.

Number 1 isn't moving. The man wasn't sure if she was still responsive. Sometimes they just shut down for a time.

The man told Number 8 that she was the only one who never asked about the voice, and the person who spoke to them. The man asked her why. Number 8 simply shrugged. The man told her the rules stated that no answer meant a 30-degree temperature change, either hot or cold. Number 8 just grinned.

He didn't put in for the temperature change.

***

The veins on Number 2's forehead were bulging. It seemed like they'd been that way since this morning, and the man wasn't sure what to make of it. It looked bad, like his head might explode, or he was on the verge of experiencing some type of aneurism.

Number 2 didn't seem more agitated than his normal state of perpetual agitation. The man didn't think he'd ever seen Number 2 smile. The man asked Number 2 about the worst smell he had ever smelled. The brief from the envelope instructed this, in hopes of finding a smell even worse for the person.

Number 2 said that the worst smell he'd ever smelled was the fur of a manicou being burnt off. The man inquired further, and learned that a manicou is an animal like a possum. In Trinidad, people put manicous into a fire to burn off their fur after they're dead. Then they can cook and eat them. They say the manicou's fur being scorched off is the worst smell in the world.

There were alligators in the river where Number 2 played as a child. He had to dodge them while he played. Number 2 seems like the toughest one in this batch, the one who's lived the hardest life. This would probably lead most people to bet on Number 2 to outlast the others, but the man had been here long enough to know that things rarely worked out that way.

***

When they were begging, he almost wanted to inform them that there was very little he could do. He couldn't question what was in the envelope next to the chair. He followed the rules just like everyone else. He had to.

The man turned up the white noise so none of them would realize he was gone while he ran to the bathroom. It would be about 3 minutes. It had never been a problem.

Shit. Someone else has lost it. Every fucking time he leaves the goddamn chair. These screams had that distinctive last stage pitch. Number 5. But he's hitting his head against the wall, which sadly for him, is not a valid way out, according to the big book. The man put in for the sedation of Number 5. Someone needs a rest. Then the process will continue.

The room is dark, except for the small reading light by the God Chair, like a tiny beacon on the black sea.

Number 2 is making a stand. He's naked, and he's yelling. *Oh Number 2, that's so you*, the man smiled, watching Number 2 punch the mirror and walls while defiantly shouting.

***

The coffee was foul. This whole area was disgusting. The grunts never cleaned the area around the folding table with the horrible white powder that's supposed to be milk. They call it "hazelnut" to try to hide the fact that it tastes like freeze-dried human carcasses. It doesn't taste like hazelnut, and it doesn't seem anything like milk. Even if it did taste like hazelnut, like this world has seen an actual hazelnut in decades, the man didn't want any flavoring at all.

The girl was starting her shift. The man smiled at her with his eyes down and they made pleasant small talk in the dark corner. He liked the girl, but he only saw her in passing when their schedules sometimes crossed.

The girl smiled. Her eyes met his for a fleeting moment, "Sometimes I wonder if we're the ones they're really watching …"

Number 7 pulled off her own fingernail with her teeth.

***

He tried yet another new way to work this morning, a variation of his recent experiments. He took Cedar Road to a small street called Thorne which led him right onto the 705. Taking the 705 saved him almost 10 minutes, again. That was the third time this week.

The man was excited, because he thought he'd found his new way to work.

IN THE WOODS – ON THE HUNT

PERNELL ROGERS

The sound of the crunching leaves could wake the dead. Ken walked through the forest, at night, searching for it. He'd seen it earlier today. Its unmistakable dank, musky smell could make anyone puke. That smell would give it away at night. His rifle's strap dug into his shoulder.

Leaves rustled in the distance. Something else was out there. He pointed the flashlight in the direction of the sound. He detected the same smell. It's close. He readied his rifle. He heard a deep grunt from behind. He turned in time to see Sasquatch rear its arm back and swing.

SYMPATHY DISH

SARA TANTLINGER

The widow Lady Adrianna was a woman of exotic tastes. She liked organ meats. Fermented fish entrails in Thai curry, cervelle de veau for calf's brains, and sweetbreads of lamb pancreas. I ached to sample the mix of flesh and elixirs from her lips. Her husband's palate was too simple, but he was lean like well-bred swine. After he died, I brought the Lady a sympathy dish. "It's veal heart," I said as we dined together. My eyes focused on her pale throat as she ingested the meat, complimented its tenderness. She bit into her husband's heart again. Swallowed. Smiled.

BLOODLUST

KEVIN HOLTON

She was born a predator, easily catching mice and other pests. She had the skills, but spent most of her time playing, throwing them in the air and holding them in her teeth. There was a simple solution for that: starvation. Let the girl go hungry. Teach her that hunting wasn't about fun. Soon, our walls were mouse free. She'd even patrol the garden for squirrels. Once, she took down a groundhog.

I suppose I should've stopped her when neighborhood pets disappeared. Someone called the police. The police are coming, but the blood will never wash from my daughter's teeth.

SEPTEMBER

COMMANDER OF THE CLEW

NICK MANZOLILLO

I have found something and I am impressed. By diligently digging deeper and pushing myself further than I have intended, I have found something in the dirt. I am in love. Hunched over on my knees, I cast aside my gloves so I can feel my discovery as I pull it from the earth, cradling its limp white form in both hands. I raise my little treasure to the sky and it wriggles, ever so slightly. I am devoted. I will never go hungry again.

***

I was born and raised in a city of impenetrable concrete and tar. As a toddler, I was the first to find the bottom of the sandbox. When it snowed I would be the first to meet it, head on, while the accumulated drifts would chip away from the earth like dead skin from the clouds above. I would burrow into the frost and dig tunnels, scooping clumps of maneuverable frost with my hands until I was submerged and hidden. At the furthest reaches of every street block, I was the boy who lived in the slush pile; stained by dirt and hungry sunlight.

I didn't have my own backyard until I could afford my own home in a small college town, far from my un-crack-able city. I have grown old to the point that my joints are starting to tighten up, but I still have my inner list of pleasures to check off, the ones I first scribed in boyhood. I never quite got to play in the dirt the way I wanted to.

It's a Saturday. I'm free from the office. I have a new shovel that I bought along with a toolkit because I've never owned one of those before, either. I've picked up a pack of seeds, too. I think they are pumpkin. After I start digging, I realize the seeds were an excuse. A mock rationalization to sink my shovel into the ground.

I have already taken a solitary walk through the woods, running my fingertips along the heaving trunks of the trees. I've memorized all their names from the textbooks I used to receive for Christmas. The woods aren't new, surely, but it's easy to pretend they are. All of America, and all of New England especially, has been built over for too many centuries to be fresh. Old moss-covered walls of stacked stone scattered throughout the forest are the sole remnants of ancient property boundaries. I name the singing birds one by one and it is like déjà vu from an old dream.

When I sink my shovel into the dirt the two and a half decades of separation between the boy I once was and the man I now am is breached.

I choose a spot at the edge of my lawn, where the grass is yellowed and weakened as it meets the fold of the forest. As if it knew I was coming, the ground has been made soft by a recent spout of rainfall I at first despised for the unnecessary difficulty it caused when I moved in.

One of the gloves I wear has a hole in it that quickly fills with dirt as I clear the mound of earth around my crater with long swipes of my arm. Winter's memory keeps the air cool and the sweat along my brow never quite threatens to scorch my eyes. It's almost a lazy motion, chipping the shovel's blade into the ground. It's almost like softly stirring a brewing pot of soup. It's a gradual process before I'm standing in the hole that's grown with each soft jab until it's swallowed me up, gently. The smell of fresh earth is unlike nothing I've ever experienced. Flowers are pale, odorless weeds by comparison. I'm up to my waist when I notice the sun beginning to dip over the trees. I delicately lean the shovel against the side of my ground pocket and then head inside, for lunch.

I realize four hours have passed, without a sound, when I pass the clock in my kitchen. I'm surprised I didn't get deeper into the earth. My pace must have been more relaxed than I thought. What's the rush?

As I begin eating a hastily put together turkey sandwich, I notice a strange, crunchy sensation along my teeth. It takes me a while to realize I never washed my hands, and that the sandwich I'm feasting on is covered in dirt. You would have thought I was eating in the dark, oblivious with pleasure as I am. The whole experience reminds me of when I used to get stoned in high school and not even realize I was eating until my belly felt like it would burst.

As I lay in bed at night, listening to the owls signify their territory, the soreness creeps over my body as if some slivery black thing from the forest has suddenly decided to join me in bed.

Before the sun can beat back the morning murk, I find myself standing in the hole, barefoot. I'm craving the scent of fresh earth like one would a glass of water or bite of leftovers. I remember hearing that the urge for late night/early morning snacks relates back to primitive times when man would hunt at such hours. Before the sun can catch me, I start digging and whatever ache invaded me before bed is soon gone.

On Monday I decide to delay the start of my new job. I've done a lot already. I've made enough money to afford my own home with only a modest mortgage. At the university, there was a group of important people that greeted me on Friday when I went in for a meet and greet.

They were excited for me to start but, really, I can start on a Tuesday, a Wednesday, even. It's a relaxed job, I don't even have to call out. I just have to show up to my office and get in touch with certain professors and, well, I am an organizer, see. I'm an academic coach, I get things moving. I am important. I am a special employee, and I get to pick and choose my hours when they get to have me.

On Tuesday morning, I dig faster. I grunt with every thrust of the shovel, hacking into the dirt I now need to climb out from with an old stainless-steel ladder the previous homeowners left in my garage. If I were to take a break, I would have to run my hands along the walls of fresh earth forming a dome around me. I don't take a break. Not until I find it. I am beginning to believe the last frontier is not in the ocean like some say, nor is it really space, not until we really get out there. The very ground beneath us, there is so much to discover. It's where all the secrets are.

I am not sure what prompted it but at one point I begin attacking the ground, not even digging anymore just stabbing, spearing the earth until my arms fling the shovel away from me like a wildly swinging crane that's cables have been cut. On my knees, I begin plucking through the brown with just my hands. I've forgotten to wear gloves. My hands are raw; blood and pus soaked, yet they don't hurt. I tumble away the clumps of brown that grow darker and richer the deeper I dig. I pick through the bottom of my pit, and there I finally find the white worm.

Like a fat pinecone gone pale, I pick it up. I cradle it to the sky, and then bring it into the light. Cupped in one hand, held in front of my face, I don't let it leave my sight until I have left my hole behind. It is alive. It has been calling to me, all this time. It has decided to leave the soil and the dark behind. It has decided it wants to be found, and it chose me.

I set it on my dinner table and watch it come alive. There's a colony of black dots, eyes, along one fatter end of it. It slowly rolls and wriggles until it's facing me, as I lean close. I have not slept, I have not bathed. The flesh along my hands has been stripped and my feet are black and my toe and fingernails hang in shards. Dirt clogs my nostrils. Above all, though, I do feel, abruptly, one thing, as I stare into the worm's many eyes. It wants one last thing from me. I pick it up, and the thing is growing warm. There's a faint black slit below its eyes. A mouth, a little flickering blue tongue like that of a lizard. It wants more than a kiss. I raise my idol, and take a bite.

STORY'S END

SARA TANTLINGER

Momma's reading me a bedtime story about a princess again, but only because I begged.

The princess is beautiful like a summer day at the beach, or at least how I imagine those types of days. Momma doesn't allow what's left of my skin to bathe in the sun's glimmer. The princess falls in love. The prince destroys the monsters. The freaks. The couple lives happily ever after. I ask Momma why don't we ever get the happy ending? "Because," she says and closes her yellow eyes, "monsters don't get happy endings, child. You know this."

She closes the book.

BUGS

JUSTIN BOOTE

Christine swatted another spider with the newspaper. She hated them, feared them. She reckoned she'd killed thousands at her home over the years, and was proud of it.

She curled up in bed, confident she could sleep peacefully without another intruder frightening her.

The Human had killed its mate. It wanted revenge. It darted across the blanket, and dived underneath. It found the opening between her legs, and scurried inside. After a while, it delivered its package and left.

The next day, Christine felt stabbing pains below. She sat on the toilet. Screamed. Dozens of spiders ran down her legs.

LOVE'S LAST KISS

ROBERT ALLEN LUPTON

The dwarves dropped the cover to the stone sarcophagus when the handsome prince rode his charger into the clearing at sunset. His horse flinched at the sound and the prince bit his tongue.

The prince dismounted, wiped his mouth, strode to the stone coffin, admired the raven-haired beauty inside, and bent to wake her with a kiss.

His blood caressed her ruby lips, her eyes opened, and she smiled as her fangs extended. Her strong arms held him and her teeth slid smoothly into his neck.

He shuddered and three drops of his blood splattered her snow-white cheek.

YOU MUST NOT REMEMBER

JASON D. GRUNN

… Hi there.

… Um … can anyone here me?

… No. No one is answering, again. Maybe I shouldn't call out. I wish I knew better, I was taught that I *could* know better, but something told me to run and hide. I'm in the '*attic*', behind a large row of '*shelves*' against a '*wall*'. I can barely see in the '*dark*'.

This is miraculous, were the first words I ever heard. Was that when I was … '*born*'? I

want to learn more but—but, I guess I'm too '*afraid*'. I start playing with a '*spider*' underneath my '*feet*'. I don't think they know where I am yet. Not these spiders, but other things down below.

What am '*I*' anyways? I need to find a '*mirror*'. Please don't make noise feet, oh please oh please don't make any noise—

The floor creaks, making me cover my mouth. I have to sit down again. I'm shaking. As I curl up into a ball I try to force down my memories. They are bad, I don't know why they are

bad, but I *must* not remember them. I have to keep away no matter what …

My '*legs*' are hurting again. My '*wrists*' and '*neck*' feel sore when I feel them with my

'*hands*'.

My '*ear*' is pressed against the floor, I can hear them speaking … but not what they're

Saying …

I have to move—'*do not*'. I don't know what I should do. I feel like '*I'm crying*', but I'm

not, I'm not like them. I stroke my long '*hair*' to try and '*comfort*' myself. I learned a lot of new

words, and somehow know how to apply them. I was told that I was '*smart*', and that I was

meant to '*serve*' …

No! No! *No!* My memories stop right there. I still want to see a mirror, to see an '*image*'

of '*myself*'. If I move though, will they hear me? Will they *find* me? Will they—

"*Stop!*" I shout. I freeze. No, I shouldn't have done that. Did they hear–

"*I heard something*", a voice says from below. Movement. I have to move too. But I

can't. Oh no I can't make myself '*move*'. I listen to them talk some more. Again, I can't

understand what they're saying. Who are '*they*' anyways? I don't want to know anymore. I have

to get away. I must escape somehow.

I stand up quietly. Move silently. I think I saw a '*window*' up here somewhere. Then I

hear the words:

"*Upstairs, in the attic.*"

I start making a lot of noise trying to find a window. Oh please oh please oh please oh

Please—I find a knob and yank it open. I stare at the pale moonlight in front of me, and the long

way down. A pitch black '*forest*' is just beyond the '*yard*'. A noise comes from behind me, I

crouch down, and freeze in place. Please don't let it see me through the light.

"*Princess … where are you …*" it calls. What is '*it*' anyways? My memories again tell me

no, I must not *ever* remember them. But what happens if it finds me? Why do I have to be

so curious? I make a small yelp, it stops, then silence.

"*Time to come back.*" It rushes for me. I jump out the window.

I land hard and hear something break. I shriek '*in pain*'. Why, why do I have to feel pain?

But I have to move, somehow. They are coming for me again.

I can only '*hobble*' into the dark wilderness. I can't see, why can't I see in the dark? So

many questions, I feel as though my memories have become faded– but my '*escape*' is the only

thing that concerns me now.

I feel fear. It's the feeling of fear that forces me to run, even though I am in a lot of pain.

It is fear that keeps my memories away.

But I have to stop against a '*tree*', at least that's what it feels like using my '*fingers*'.

Maybe they won't find me, maybe they'll '*give up*'. Those two words make my fear increase,

and I'm afraid to ask why …

I listen. I stay very still. The '*door*' to the '*house*' just opened. They are moving. I

can hear them moving but they aren't calling for me.

I must move—if I don't they will find me.

I use the tree for support, then try to put one '*foot*' in front of the other—

"Ahh!" I yelp.

… did they hear? The only noise my ears pick up are the '*crickets*'. I '*wait*', and stand

still.

Something '*snaps*' nearby me, I begin running again.

And running and running and running—both of them are behind me—and running and

running and running and running—I stumble when my '*dress*' snags on a branch—and running

and running and running and running—I yelp in pain again—and running and running and

running—

It catches me by the '*waist*.' I '*freeze*', not from the grasp, but from the '*fear*.'

"*You poor thing, you damaged yourself …*" the one holding me says.

"*It doesn't matter, that's not the only thing wrong with her,*" the other one says.

"*Why did you run, Alayna?*" The holder asks. '*Alayna? Is that my name?*' My fear

deepens.

"No—*no!*" I shout. Not knowing why, just that I '*can't*' remember. No matter what …

"*Why is she so loud?*" The second one asks.

"*An issue among several. Such a shame too, she was going to make a wonderful edition*

at the café," the holder says.

Why is it talking like that? It's as if the holder is '*bored*' of my fear. Why does it—

Instant pain shoots through my '*head*', the repressed memories are starting to come back.

What is this … new feeling? It's called … '*panic*'. What I feel now—is panic. The holder

begins prodding my scalp, and then '*twists*' my leg a bit—

"*Stop it! Please!*" I shout. The holder only sighs.

"*No good, this leg is completely busted, beyond repair,*" the holder says.

"*Well then, we can at least salvage her for parts,*" The second one says.

I turn to look at them. My memories have blocked the images of what they once were.

All I see now are '*fuzzy*' and '*pixelated*' shapes. But I can still see their '*smiles*', their '*teeth*'.

A room full of '*computers*' and '*wiring*' appears in my head. No, no the fear says, you

must *not* remember anything else …

"*Time to go back inside Alayna,*" The holder says. I begin to '*struggle*'. The other one

grabs my legs, making me feel even more pain.

"Help! *Help!* Help, somebody, *anybody!*" I yell. The one holding me before smothers my

'*mouth*' shut with a '*hand*'.

"*No one can hear you, no one will come. Just accept it okay? It'll all be over soon.*" Sighing.

… '*Over soon*'? I focus internally, keep trying—no, try again—don't let it out! The block

on my memory breaks. Everything is coming back. *No …*

I scream as loud as I can, but the hand muffles it. Now I know why I hid, what I am, what

they tried to *do* to me before, what they'll do soon enough, what '*they*' are. I look up at that

'*face*' as they carry me back inside the house. I want to cry, but I'm not physically capable of

doing that. Not yet, please, not yet …

"Once you're completely disassembled, you won't feel *any* pain or suffering anymore, I promise." The '*human*' smiles.

ROSE RED

ALYSON FAYE

Booze soaked, head thumping, Rosie fled the nightclub into the streets of Valletta.

Thoughts of ice cold baths and all-night pharmacies propel her deeper into the old town's maze of ochre and vanilla houses. Lost, she halts by an ironwork gate. A man loiters there, smoking, sweating. Flirtatiously she takes his hand and sees red rose petals smeared on his palm.

"I'm Rose Red." She laughs. Meeting his eyes, she sees the foreignness in them. Inside his garden paradise he strokes her head with his hoe and harvests her. Bundled up under the hibiscus she is laid to rest.

MYSTERY

RICHARD J. MELDRUM

The deal was simple. Sign up online and receive a mystery package. Membership was free. *How can I resist that offer*, he thought? Eagerly, he signed up. The email confirmed he was now a member of the exclusive serial killer club. Open the box, investigate the crime. The package arrived a week later. Fake bloodstains adorned the exterior. Excitedly, he opened it in front of his wife. She looked dubiously into the box. "Look at that!" he exclaimed. "A fake severed head."

She stared at the blood oozing across the counter from the saturated cardboard. "I don't think it's fake."

EAT IT

BRIANNA M. FENTY

My shaking hand nearly drops the hunk of meat on its way to my mouth. I fight valiantly against my gag reflex as my tongue and teeth mash the fatty, globular slab of jiggling pink flesh against my gums. I swallow the macerated compote of raw protein, slimy and soft, down my throat. The taste is about as repugnant as you'd think. Pungent. Clammy. The tiniest bit salty.

The revolver's hammer cocks, the only sound in the otherwise silent chamber. Cold metal licks the side of my head, pressing through my sweat-laden curls, into my skin. The blood pulsing through my temples struggles against the pressure of the gun and the bullet promised in its barrel.

"Another."

His demand is husky. Vocals ravaged by a life of chain-smoking and barking orders.

My vision swims and swirls. The remnants of ketamine he'd stabbed into my veins blur my sight, corrupt my perception of reality. The restraints pinning my ankles to the fancifully carved mahogany seat at the head of the dazzlingly long, disturbingly empty dining room table seem to tighten. Their leather kiss is not gentle. I can feel the bruises blooming, sickening violet, putrid yellow.

I lift another chunk of brain from the gilded china platter. Meat oozes beneath my fingernails. Grease slathers my palms.

"Go on."

My sob is involuntary, muffled behind a mouthful of my sister's cranial contents. I chew slowly. Nausea churns my gut but the shame is a thousand times more potent, warping my mind, roiling my stomach, cinching my throat tight like a garrotte.

I splutter. Bits of grey matter and frothy saliva spray onto the immaculate tablecloth.

His revolver slams into my head, snapping my head to the left. I can't help the pathetic yelp and the effeminate whimper that escapes my lips in fear of the bullet inside.

"Eat it."

I am a coward.

I don't want to die.

So I force her brain down my throat, waging a grotesque war against my humanity with my will to survive, to flee this godforsaken place, and put as much distance between me and this cannibalistic monster of a man.

"Eat."

The gun is a frozen, undeniable force against my skull.

"Go ahead, Michael," he says. "It's okay to like it."

I shiver. I cry. Snot and tears do nothing to improve the taste.

I shovel quivering handfuls of my sister's brain into my mouth, murdered by the man's unforgiving axe just hours before.

I eat it. Piece by agonizing piece, I eat it.

Gobs of it lodge between my teeth. Drool slathers my face. My stomach moans in betrayal.

"Wasn't so bad, was it?" His laugh is deep, drawling, casual. "I've tried it every which way."

The revolver is icy.

"Sautéed. Baked. Grilled."

His breath is rank.

"But raw ..."

Goosebumps sting my skin.

"That's the way to go."

And then he shoots me.

Should've never gone to that damned dinner party.

THE GREENHOUSE

KEVIN HOLTON

Her ghost lurks in every corner. The shelf dust, the molding webs, even the corner shadows. I hadn't been home in years.

"She's obviously been here," Mark said, pointing to ivy, flowering plants, fresh blooms. "Who else would care for these?"

But I didn't reply. My brother's question hung in the silent gloom as I traced roots along the walls, thickening like fat fingers pointing to a secret.

"Do you think she's still living in this dump?" he yelled.

Vines wound their way into a back room, where they dug into Sarah's corpse—the best fertilizer around.

"No, I don't."

THE CHASE

PERNELL ROGERS

The intruder lunged, its claws grazed her arm. Clutching her cellphone, Helen burst from the house and scurried into the woods—her only escape. She could lose it in the woods.

No time for tears. Keep running. Breathe. Breath. Don't look back. Run.

She switched on the phone's flashlight. It helped a little.

Run. Run.

She tripped, but caught herself. She turned back. Nothing there.

Run. Breathe.

A sound came from the right. It reached for her. She dodged it.

Run. Run. I can't see.

She tripped, falling head-first into a thick tree trunk. Helen was scared no more.

A SIMPLE ACCIDENT

RICHARD J. MELDRUM

It was just a simple misstep on the stairs. She landed heavily, neatly snapping her ankle. There was no pain, unless she tried to move. She was stuck.

She was alone; her husband was away on business, the phone was out of reach and the nearest neighbor a mile away.

For three days she lay there. Their dog snuffled around trying to help, asking for food and water.

She realised she was going to die, not from the fracture, but from thirst. The dog was the same. She stared into its eyes.

"Help me."

She felt breath against her throat.

WEEDS

CHRISTINA DALCHER

We kill all the grass again on Monday.

We do this after throwing black fabric shrouds over the roses, which have begun to shoot new leaflets, red and webby, like witches' brooms on fire; after Father breaks his back digging trenches for the pachysandra; after Ma sets fire to the vegetable garden. The roses are the most tenacious—prickly thorns clawing and tearing at the blackout material. We don't need to worry about the trees anymore: they were the first to go. That was a job, felling those trees.

The Sandersons across the street work their yard in the same way—they've got almost an acre. We never see them sitting still, but all this weekend their house has stood dark and silent. Even the lone crow who used to hang out on their satellite dish hasn't appeared since Friday morning.

In the kitchen, Ma gets out the can-opener and slices the lids off our last five tins of beans and Vienna sausages, checking the production date before spooning the mess into a bowl. Black beans this time, flavored with rancid spices and the remaining dried herbs, now tasteless as dust. We complain about the herbs, but Father assures us they're edible—if you can call dust edible—since anything harvested before should be safe. The sausages are as flavorless as baby's fingers, which is a good thing if you're living on a diet of them. Also, this is the last real meat we'll have; all that's in the markets now are genetically-engineered cow and pig parts.

When Father says 'before,' he means when Sal and I were still in school, back when reading and writing and working our way through useless pre-algebra problems were all more important than covering up anything green. Did you ever wonder why poisons in fairy tales are always green? It's the plant matter, I think. Was. Is.

We tried goats, like everyone else. For a while, a real goat love-fest took over the neighborhood, thanks to news reports urging us on and a healthy—what a word—goat subsidy from the government. Golden Guernseys, Nigerian Dwarves, Belgian Fawns—you name a breed and some specimen would be chomping away in a yard on Sycamore Street. We had three at the beginning; the Sandersons maybe a dozen. The Sandersons are rich, or they used to be, back when they still had the organic produce chain of stores. Anyway, the goats lasted all of two months. When Ma found our last Golden Guernsey tits-up in a forest of rampant ivy, she set a blow torch on the entire backyard and then set to emptying out the crisper drawers in the fridge. Everything went onto the burn pile: lettuce, celery, carrots, a few onion halves in zip-lock baggies. And the goat, of course.

Sal told me that Mr. Sanderson told her that it was all Monsanto's fault, but Father blames the Miracle-Gro he and Ma used to pour on everything until the leaves dripped chem-blue. The old guy who ran the garden store (now he only stocks cordite and lighter fluid, and he's doing a hell of a business) swears it was the Round-Up. I don't believe a word of it; I think the plants just got smart. You know how they say there's a season for everything Why the hell not plants?

After dinner, Sal wants to take Dudley for a walk. She's allowed to go, as long as I go with her and we stay on the asphalt, avoiding cracks and potholes—anything where a resolute root might seek out the last remaining rays of sunlight. Dudley's seventy-five pounds of yellow lab, and dumb as a box of rocks, but he's smart enough to know not to root around in anything vegetal. Still, this dog's got a nose on him, and pulls at his lead, dragging us across a street named for the canopy of sycamores that shaded it, until we're at the edge of what used to be the Sanderson's lawn.

It's a sea of organic matter, burnt black. And it's moving.

"Come on, Duds," I say, fighting the pull until the lead is taut as a high wire. My effort's wasted; Dudley's retriever instinct—plus his seventy-five pounds—forces us deeper along the flagstone path toward the open front door. Sal and I navigate the gauntlet of crabgrass and weeds poking up through the gaps in the stone like football players doing that tire drill. Around us, the lawn roils as wickedly sharp blades push their way out of the earth, tiny green serpents' tongues of grass.

Dudley charges on, up the porch steps, and drags me into the Sanderson's living room, his nose quivering at the smell of raw flesh. An arm lies limp in one corner, webbed with the tendrils of a spider plant. The rest of Mr. Sanderson is scattered about, parts of him entwined with ivy, his hair threaded through a fern's feathery fronds. There's a stink in here, the kind of rot from the bottom of a flower vase that's been forgotten.

"Sal!"

There's no need to scream. Sal's already out the door, Mary Janes rattling the wooden boards of the porch. I hear a snap and a gasp, and turn in time to see her trip over a stray vine, its blackened stalk sprouting leaves like a time-elapse nature video. She falls face down into the lawn, now a writhing carpet of green, Dudley at her heels, ever faithful, ever stupid.

We bury Sal and Dudley in the charred earth of the burn pile, and we kill all the grass again on Tuesday.

LAST WILL AND TESTAMENT

STEPHANIE ELLIS

Will sat in his father's chair. Finally, the estate had come to him, just as his mother had promised. His elder siblings had been surprisingly relaxed about their disinheritance, betrayed no resentment. And James, usually so possessive of his beloved hounds, insisted Will inspect the pack.

"No time like the present," said James.

Will glanced out the window. It was late but a full moon was promised. They went out into the yard. Surprisingly, the huntsman was there but no dogs.

"Where are the hounds?" he asked.

"Oh, they'll come," said James as silver light washed over him. "They'll come."

THE DEAD OF NIGHT

CR SMITH

Hundreds of creatures hover around my bed, eyes glowing as they screech in stomach churning unison.

Half man, half bird, decaying lumps of flesh hang from their bones, a seeping trail dripping from the span of wings.

Wings consuming me in an amorphous mass while they peck at my exposed flesh with their razor-sharp beaks.

Petrified.

Silenced.

I am unable to muster a sound. Yet by morning's light the night's events are forgotten, leaving me puzzled as to where these weeping sores come from. Until darkness falls anew and I recall precisely why the dead of night terrifies me so.

METRONOME

PAUL ISAAC

"Sir, using the metronome's ticking we're able to manipulate the alien and control its heartbeat."

"It's safe to be in here?' Why not use a computer?"

"Only works with a localised, analogue sound. We've sedated it."

"So, we can finally kill them?"

"In theory. We have been awaiting your arrival."

The general pinched the pendulum and held it for a moment.

They weren't the only ones waiting. The alien burst free of its restraints, tearing them all to pieces. Its teeth punctured the human leader's flesh in time to the slow, swooping ticks of the redundant blood-stained metronome beside it.

CHOOSING

TIM J. FINN

Dr Samuels scanned the waiting patients through the two-way mirror in the clinic. Mrs. Douglas had gained more weight and some members of his club did so enjoy an order of robust dumplings. Young Johnson's sparkling blue eyes would make an appealing addition to the hors d'oeuvre plate. Laura's legs looked so tantalizing in their sheer nakedness. Decisions, decisions.

Samuels knew he needed an extra special entrée after Dr Tittle's near piece de resistance at last month's gathering. Samuels almost salivated at the delicious memory. He smiled and thought this month's menu could be a three-for dish. That would rule!

OCTOBER

ANUBIS

DIANA GROVE

"It was an amazing discovery," said Jordan with a huge smile, showing arctic white teeth. "Finally, we had indisputable proof that aliens exist and they have visited our planet."

"Great. Just take a few steps back Jordan and we'll get another shot of the big guy," the director said.

Jordan complied and Hannah, finding herself standing beside Jordan, breathed in the woody scent of his expensive cologne. A strange giddiness came over her. Hannah had watched every episode of *They're Coming*, the sci-fi series Jordan starred in. She kept telling herself she only had a crush on his character Max, not him. She didn't know Jordan Riley the actor; the celebrity who lived in Hollywood and had just been nominated for an Emmy. But when she was introduced to Jordan this afternoon she almost forgot her own name. He was so ridiculously good-looking. She found herself gazing up at his smiling, bronzed face and gaping like an imbecile.

They were in a research laboratory within the *Istituto Italiano di Scienze Umane* in Turin, Italy. The room was filled with half a dozen scientists in lab coats grinning like little kids about to open the best Christmas present ever and a documentary film crew. Never in her wildest dreams had Hannah imagined she would be part of a discovery like this. She, Hannah Kemble, forensic anthropologist and sci-fi aficionado, was going to see and touch an actual alien.

The wreckage of a spaceship was found recently in the Italian Alps and frozen inside was an alien–humanoid and about seven feet tall. The alien's face was completely covered by a metallic helmet and his neck and arms were decorated with gold jewelry. Harriet Bloomsbury, a British Egyptologist, was the first to point out the helmet looked more like the head of a jackal than that of a dog as people initially thought, and the strange weapon found with the alien resembled Anubis's Was Sceptre. After that, the media dubbed the alien Anubis.

Anubis had been entombed in his spaceship under tonnes of snow in the Alps for possibly thousands of years. Now he lay in a refrigerated capsule with little oxygen to replicate the high-altitude environment of the Alps and thereby ensure he stayed preserved. The scientists only had a short time to examine him.

Anubis was carefully removed and placed on a long, stainless steel table. Looking at his frozen body Hannah was pleased. *He appears to be in excellent condition.* Hannah carefully examined the helmet. It was tapered at the bottom, therefore, clearly not designed to be pulled off. If they attempted to do so it would seriously damage the alien's face. On one side of the helmet was a small round nub. Hannah pressed it with a gloved finger. Nothing happened.

"Try holding it down," said Pete, the English paleontologist standing next to her.

She tried again. This time pressing it for a few seconds. The helmet retracted with amazing speed and collapsed into a slim line at the base of the neck. Pete gasped and clamped his hands over his mouth. Someone swore. The alien's face was the stuff of nightmares. Hannah tried to appear calm, but like everyone else, she was shocked by the gaping wide mouth full of piranha-like teeth. The eyes were very small, like bat's eyes, and the nose was merely two slits. On the side of the head were protrusions that looked like curved fish gills. Hannah couldn't be sure if they were ears or something else.

"Wow, just incredible," said Jordan, coming closer.

"Close-ups. I want close-ups," called out the director.

Hannah stood aside as the tall Australian cameraman got his shots.

"Shit!" he yelled jumping back. "Its eye moved."

A few people laughed.

"I swear it moved!" he said looking around the room wild-eyed.

The director shook his head, his mouth a grim line.

"Hey, people! Only one minute before we've got to put this guy back in the freezer," said a perky biologist with a short bob and funky red framed glasses.

"I'm just going to take a tissue sample now," Hannah told Jordan moving closer to the table.

Aware of the camera trained on her, Hannah kept the scalpel poised just above the closest arm for a moment. She cut downwards, piercing firm skin, then suddenly stopped. A groan escaped her lips as her whole body seized up. The pain of her muscles and tendons spasming took her breath away. Suddenly everyone in the room began convulsing as though they had been electrocuted. Hannah hit the floor hard. She felt the sharp blade of the scalpel slice her arm but couldn't cry out. She was paralyzed. They all were.

What the hell happened? Why can't I move? Hannah and Jordan lay opposite each other on either side of the table. Hannah looked at Jordan and saw his gaze roam all over the room like he was following an erratic fly then settle on her. They stared into one another's eyes like locked-in patients who had no idea how to communicate.

Hannah wondered if Jordan's face was going to be the last thing she ever saw. She remembered the scene in *They're Coming* where Max was lying in a clover field with his girlfriend Rosie and they reach out for each other's hands just before the world as they knew it ended. Now here she was lying on the laboratory floor with him in the very same poses, but they couldn't reach out for each other and there was nothing romantic about this. Blood trickled down her arm, warm and syrupy. It seeped into her lab coat and the t-shirt underneath. The sodden fabric stuck to her stomach.

Hannah could see Anubis's right arm and a bit of his leg from where she lay. As she stared at him two of his fingers twitched. *Oh my God. He's defrosting. Did he do this to us?* Her heart thumped in her chest like a desperate creature seeking escape. Her fear was so overwhelming it eclipsed the pain of the knife wound.

According to the primitive part of Hannah's brain, it was fight or flight time but her body couldn't cooperate. Her mouth felt tight and dry, and her breath came out in short puffs. Adrenaline was coursing through her bloodstream, but she was as helpless as a beetle lying on its back. She was desperate to open the door and run screaming, not stopping for anything. But the only things going fast were her thoughts, ricocheting like bullets.

Yesterday someone left a newspaper behind on one of the tables in the hotel's breakfast room. Seeing it was in English Hannah swooped down on the newspaper like a seagull spying a chip and read it while she ate her toast. She remembered in one article Harriet Bloomsbury was quoted saying Anubis's Was Scepter represented rebirth and the resurrection from death. Hannah would have laughed if she could. *We'd been warned. We'd been warned and we didn't realize.*

The top floor of the building had been cleared because of filming, and everyone in the institute had been directed to stay away from that floor. No one was likely to find them anytime soon. Hannah was an anthropologist with medical training, not a biologist, but she knew that after hibernation there was only one thing animals wanted to do and that was eat. Anubis had been hibernating a very long time; he was bound to be ravenous.

The loss of so much blood left Hannah feeling dizzy, and her face had turned pale. She didn't pray; she wasn't religious. Hannah just desperately hoped that someone would find them. *Come to the laboratory. Please. Someone come to the laboratory.* It seemed like an hour had gone by to Hannah, but only ten minutes had passed when she heard footsteps.

A bowlegged Italian lady in her sixties with a bucket full of cleaning products in one hand and a cleaning cloth in the other stopped in front of the laboratory door. The heavy door had a small glass square in it. Maria was only 152cm tall, so she stood on her tiptoes and lifted her chin as high as she could to peer into the room. At first, she thought the room was empty then she noticed Anubis on the table. To Maria, he was just a mummy. She pulled a face and swiftly crossed herself. Working as a cleaner at the Institute for five years, Maria was used to strange sights but mummies always gave her the creeps. Taking a step back, she read the sign on the door that said in English and Italian, 'Filming underway – DO NOT DISTURB.' Relieved, Maria decided to start her cleaning on the floor below.

Wait! Come back! Hannah listened hard but she heard no more footsteps. Minutes passed and still, no one moved; they remained jumbled on the floor like discarded mannequins. Hannah stared into Jordan's eyes once more as the silence was broken by the jarring sound of fingernails scraping against metal.

BUGS #2

JUSTIN BOOTE

John screamed. The pain was intense and they were too many to fight. How could this have happened? Once again, government attempts at genetic mutation had failed disastrously. The idea had seemed great; at first. A natural and faster way to dispose of human waste. Now, another epidemic would threaten mankind. Created by the incompetent, suffered by the innocent.

They tore into every inch of skin and flesh, buzzing, feeding, swarming. As the life was drained from him, he remembered those fateful words; 'It's perfectly safe. Nothing can go wrong.'

The flies—the carnivorous flies—finished, then left in search of more.

REACTION TIME

KEVIN HOLTON

The rapport rings out, and all else stops. It's what they don't tell you about getting shot: the moment the bullet leaves the barrel, you get an eternity to yourself.

Trouble is, you can't move. Those last seconds stretch into years, and you can spend each one fighting to move, screaming, *Get out of the way, asshole!* Life doesn't work like that. Death, it seems, does.

I can see the bullet coming, point-blank shot, aimed at my forehead. Trust me: focus on what matters. Your parents. Your children. Your beloved, waiting at the altar, thinking you're just running a little—

TIME AND TIME AGAIN

RICHARD J. MELDRUM

The city lay in the shadow of the volcano. It bore the scars of numerous eruptions.

She sat at the entrance to a temple. She was a dishevelled creature, ignored by tourists and locals. She felt a rumble beneath her. She knew the volcano was waking once more. The city was doomed. She started screaming her warning to those around her. They ignored her, they always did. She felt an infinite darkness; she knew she wouldn't be released from her eternal curse until they listened to her, but it wasn't going to be this time.

It was never this time.

WASHED UP

MATTHIEU CARTRON

They will tell you about the calming sound of the ocean, or how the coastal wind waltzes with the waves and feels cool but not cold. They won't tell you though about the fetid, curdled sea foam, the scent given off from the dying, stranded algae.

The seaweed was thick that morning, lumped especially high in one spot, a six-foot-long crescent of red and green sludge. Nicky could see that, but it was the smell that bothered her. Her husband grimaced as he saw her nose contort and scrunch up into a tight stub.

He should've buried that body instead.

ACCEPTANCE

N.O.A. RAWLE

The Ouija board lay forgotten in the dusty basement. I knew it was there; it beckoned me in the depths of night. My parents didn't believe me when I told them; said God would punish my lies. When they sojourned to Dorset, I stayed home.

"No guests overnight, no imbibing spirits, no parties, okay?"

"Sure."

Down the dark steps I stumbled, following the summons I'd heard all my life.

"Finally, we are alone."

When the candle flickered and died, I broke every rule.

W-I-L-L Y-O-U L-E-T M-E E-N-T-E-R Y-O-U A-N-D S-T-A-Y A W-H-I-L-E? W-E C-A-N R-U-L-E T-H-E W-O-R-L-D!

"I will."

THE MONSTER

GUY ANTHONY DE MARCO

Billy Woods was tired but he couldn't fall asleep because of the monster under his bed. He curled up under his favorite Batman blanket, dark eyes open as he watched for signs of encroachment.

He yawned, left arm slipping over the edge of the mattress, fingers dangling into the abyss. When he heard a dragging noise as the monster began to unfold and creep up on the limb, the ends of Billy's mouth curled upwards in a cruel approximation of a smile. The monster below had taken the bait.

Sometimes the monster on top of the bed was far scarier.

YOU'RE JUST HIS TYPE

KRISTIN GARTH

On a break, the second day of his murder/rape trial, he notices you. Conferring with counsel, his over-the-shoulder peek into the gallery seeking friendly faces travels, lands far too long on yours. In your seat five safe rows away, his hard stare makes you shiver.

You do not know this hulking, bristly-faced rapist, jilted stabber of an ex-girlfriend. His case you choose at random, a court reporting course requirement: observe a week-long trial. "I'd choose a murder," your professor had suggested. "Most likely to be lengthy and engaging." You chose your murder straight from the front page of the News Journal, Law & Order style.

It's close to lunch, when it first happens. An entire morning devoted to the graphic, blood-spattered testimony of the brutal rape and murder of Jenna Wollack, 25. You look at poster-sized photographs of nineteen stab wounds inflicted on the victim on the concrete outside her apartment at 4:00 in the afternoon. This is when he looks at you, on this pre-lunch break—now that you've been acquainted with his handiwork. When he looks, his lips rub against each other in contemplation, and then the corners turn up.

The lawyer's eyes dart from the legal pad to his client. Noticing the contact, he scowls and nods towards the bench directing his client's eyes away. Released from his stare, your eyes drop to the floor, and you finally take a breath.

On the third day, you hear testimony from Jenna Wollack's male neighbor describing "female shrieks so shrill they penetrated my walls and my maxed-out Manson." He explains his decision both to race to open his door and then slam it shut as he saw the defendant, "Twenty feet away, soaked in blood, on top of Jenna still stabbing."

"She wasn't moving anymore. You see how big he is. He stopped and turned, was looking right at me. If I'd had a gun or something, but I—I just—I slammed my door and called the police."

Judging whispers of spectators in the gallery surround you as he leaves the stand, but you do not judge this witness. In this courtroom, surrounded by armed officers, he held you still with his eyes. You understand.

After lunch, before the jury comes in, he's brought into the courtroom. As he stands there being unshackled, he scans for faces, finds yours and freezes. Then his head tilts towards you, a playful nod. You look around you for any other possible targets, but none exist. As they turn him around to put him in his chair, you see a flirtatious smile.

The fourth day, his mother testifies about his fall, at two years old, from a kitchen counter. He'd landed on his head. After lunch, an expert medical witness testifies the fall severely damaged his prefrontal cortex, the part of the brain that governs impulse control.

The judge calls for a 15-minute recess. It's been a long time since a break. Most of the audience scurries out to hunt for bathrooms, water. You require no such relief, sit and process what you've just heard. The defendant's lawyers are arguing in animated whispers behind their legal pads next to him when he turns toward you again. Then his lips move, and you realize he's forming a word. It looks, to you, like "hi."

Grabbing your purse from the bench at your side, you race from the courtroom and the building. A monster has chosen you. You've heard the symptoms of his disease and seen photographic evidence of its fatal consequence. You can no longer sit and pretend you aren't aware.

Outside, requiring a drink, you wander a few blocks towards your favorite bar. It's only 3:45. They won't open until 5:00, but you're a cute, young regular, and your ex-boyfriend works there. You know they get there early to deal with the liquor deliveries. Someone will let you in; you know it.

When you look in the window, you see him, Peter, your ex, unloading liquor at the bar. You knock on the window. He smiles and blinks perpetually wounded brown eyes you crafted with carelessness at a party with a boy and some coke in a bedroom. He lets you in, though, as you know he would, even hugs you before he pours your favorite red wine you don't even have to request.

"You look pretty terrified. What's up?"

You tell him about school and the trial and the murderer's eyes all over you all the way to the "hi." He listens to your monologue, wide-eyed and attentive. Then bizarrely he laughs.

"Roger Farish, you went to his trial?"

"Yes?" His amusement irks you.

"He was a dishwasher at Rainbows, big-ass, creepy motherfucker. Called you Wednesday Addams."

"Wait. What?"

It's not Rainbows that confuses you. You remember the restaurant where Peter worked as a waiter while you were dating. Sometimes you

217

even ate there by yourself, to be close to him while he worked. You never saw this Roger Farish though apparently, he saw you.

"Almost fought that dude one day. Walked into the kitchen, him ranting about exactly what he wanted to do to Wednesday Addams. Good thing I didn't, though, right?"

He's smiling, but you're not.

"You never thought to warn me about this, Peter, a psychopath talking about me like this? I just spent a week at his murder trial."

Peter drops the smile.

"Oh, right, because you told me everything then, Jill. You kept no secrets."

You stand up to leave. You thought the wound you'd inflicted on this boy might one day heal, but now you're sure it never will. Walking out of the bar, you hear his angry truth.

"Of course, he would like you, Jill. You're just his type."

You don't look back and won't ever talk to Peter again. You'll go to Roger's trial tomorrow. It's personal now. You need to know how it ends.

SAVIOR

RICHARD J. MELDRUM

The castle sat on a high ridge. It was a cursed place. The villagers stormed the fortress, intent on finding the creature that dwelled within. They found the coffin. A man rose from the silk interior.

"You have come for me. In these modern times, with war, disease, famine, climate change and drought, you seek to destroy the smallest evil, yet you ignore the problems that will destroy your world."

The villager in front, ripped open his shirt to expose his throat.

"Master, that is why we are here. Make us immortal, save us from the end of the world."

ONE PERSON

ANDREA ALLISON

My life would be peaceful if I removed one person from it.

The one who whispers sinister words in my ear every day.

The one whose dark eyes sparkle as tears fall from mine.

The one that keeps me in good supply of bruises to coat my body.

The one who isolates me, forcing me to tell my loved ones to never come again someday.

The one no one believes exists.

His long bony fingers curl to rest over mine as I raise the gun to my head. Just remove one person. One shot and the devil welcomes a new monster.

THE BASEMENT

PATRICK WINTERS

It's in the basement.

It won't leave me be. I can hear it at all hours, moaning in the day and wailing at night. It's driving me crazy, scratching its fingers against the old trap-door in the kitchen floor, wanting to get out and take my life. I hate it. It scares me and I hate it.

It's scratching again, begging me to let it out.

I work up my courage and stomp on the door, shouting "Shut up! Just shut up!"

My son goes quiet again, at least for a while.

But it'll keep on trying to get out . . .

THE MARIONETTES

CAROLYN A. DRAKE

The humid summer air weighs heavy with the sound of my name.

Melanie … Melanie …

My kinfolk call for me as father's coach winds through endless dark copses. Near, I swing behind draping curtains of moss. Oaks groan and bend o're my body. Below, the brook gurgles.

The sweet voices draw near, but I cannot speak. Broken teeth splinter my lips and still my tongue.

Melanie … where are … you …?

A howl. A sorrowful call from one of the dogs unleashed into the woods echoes through the trees, but rain dampens the earth. The baying hounds can find no scent.

Swiftly, a man's voice rises in melody, calling for me. My body stiffens. Thomas.

Thomas's voice joins the wails of the hounds and cries of those who loved me, all of them drawing nearer and nearer.

Scalawag, I want to say. I want to tell them. I want to warn my sister, my pretty Dottie, who took a shine to my beau same as I when he came to town – a carpetbagger, true, but handsome and so charming that even father consented to his courtship of me. Dottie was hurt, but I was older, and father said there was time yet for her to meet a suitor … but now … now …

I want to scream. I cannot draw breath.

All I might do is sway … sway …

We all sway beneath the groaning bridge.

Dolls surround me. Once lavished with affection, their lips are frozen in an eternal yawn, parted and blue. Sparkling tokens adorn their fingers as their hands dangle limp by their sides. Cheeks sunken, bones pearly, skin weathered and worn, eyes fodder for the crows …

And I am now one of them. I am a part of the collection.

Tethered by ropes around our throats that silence our voices and still our limbs, we sway.

Wooden wheels clack. The voices are so near that I could extend a hand and touch one of the hounds as the creature bounds past, but I will never be found. The crows scatter, cawing and fleeing from beneath the bridge in a murder. Flesh clings to their beaks.

Dottie and Thomas call my name into the cavernous valley of foliage and dank mud below the bridge. The movement of my father's carriage o'er the wooden planks rocks our bones.

Below, we marionettes dance on our strings.

THE EYE

B.B. BLAZKOWICZ

I came to the darkest corner of the land looking for answers. The great well of knowledge, presided over by the shadowy beings, stands before me.

I ask for truth.

They respond in ephemeral voices that "Nothing in this life is free." A translucent appendage reaches out and tears my eye from me. For a moment, I can see myself in the void as I writhe in agony. I am now allowed to imbibe the well's secrets. I drink deeply, and hear their laughter at my irony. I have become the fool … some things are best left unknown by men.

HOST

SIAN BRIGHAL

Far too late.

You can scrub all you like, drown it in bleach until the fumes get you, but it's far too late. That black, oozing patch, isn't the mould growing. Not for this species. This is the decaying remains of its fruiting bodies; the spores long since expelled into the air. You sent your kids away for the weekend to a friend's house and moved you and hubby to sleep downstairs. You called in a specialist to clear it out. But it's wasted effort. You lean over it, with your face mask and Marigolds on, but you're already coughing.

CHARCUTIER

JAMES APPLEBY

November eleventh was once Peppero Day: after the thin stick candies. There were a lot of days in celebration of candy or fast food or carbonated drinks, back when conglomerates dictated such arbitrary things. And didn't the kids adore all those days filled with the sweetest of sweet things?

I should be grateful to them, given that it made the children easier to chase down, all jiggling bodies and softness.

I unshoulder my pack and unwrap a fleshy sliver like an ancient leather sole. It's not great—lean meat makes the best jerky—but it keeps me going.

HALLOWEEN EDITION

THE PUMPKIN CLUB

JUSTIN BOOTE

The kids ran around the street shouting, screaming, and singing. Harold Saggerbob smiled. He was in a good mood also. At Halloween, he always was. Another year, another chance to expand the pumpkin collection he had painstakingly built up over the years.

The doorbell rang. Harold put down the stained knife, and headed upstairs, whistling to himself. It was going to be a goodun this year, he thought. With a bit of luck, he might be able to fill the shelf above the workbench. That would make twenty; a nice round number, just like the pumpkins on the other shelves.

He answered the door to be confronted by Michael Myers, albeit a much smaller version, and accompanied by a very nasty looking witch.

"Trick or treat, trick or treat," they sang in unison.

"Oh my!" he replied. "You two sure look scary young folks. I guess it'd better be a treat. Wait just a moment, I'll be back," he said and closed the door.

"Little shits. The hell they think they're doing coming in pairs?" he grumbled, as he grabbed a handful of candy. Last year's candy was for those that came in pairs or more, fresh-baked chocolate cake for those alone.

He toyed with the idea of throwing the door wide open and bawling at them, just as a joke for ruining his hopes of it being some young kid alone, then thought better of it. The night was still young, plenty of time for another hapless little shit to come knocking.

"Okay, here you go. Now don't you come back and frighten me like that again," he said, trying his hardest to force a smile, and disguise the look of hate in his eyes.

The two youngsters took the candy greedily, yet Harold noticed they looked at him rather suspiciously, their smiles fading rapidly and backing away as they filled their bags.

Harold closed the door and returned to the basement, his voluminous body—almost as many kilos overweight as his fifty-five years—bouncing up and down on each step. He looked at the latest addition to his collection, recently acquired that afternoon. He'd already removed the top, and was busy removing the insides-not a simple or particularly clean task. The juices were already running onto the floor, and he'd inadvertently covered his plastic apron in the thick goo that made up most of the contents.

"Never ceases to amaze me the amount of crap that fits into one of the things," he mumbled, then chuckled as he turned it upside down to empty the last remnants, before working on the eyes. He wanted them to look particularly scary—it had after all cost him certain anguish obtaining this one; somebody had walked by just as he was claiming it for his own, and he had envisioned a heated discussion ensuing. Fortunately, the other person had ignored him, and left him with his new, grand prize.

Harold finally finished carving out new eyes, then looked at his creation. How to create the mouth? A nice, pretty smile, or a wicked, ghastly sneer? Or maybe a look of utter shock and horror? Would be fitting really, considering. He looked around the basement at the others. He'd painted many in almost war-like make-up, others he'd even put wigs on to heighten the effect, and the majority had small red or black candles sitting inside to give them a … cosier look as he liked to think. All good fun.

He decided on the shock effect. Taking the knife, and wiping it again (*so much damn sticky shit*), he began cutting out the mouth, when the doorbell rang again. Automatically, his heart began to thud a little harder and faster, while his intestines spun around inside. It was the anticipation which did it, of not knowing what to expect when he opened the door. Surprise and delight, or disappointment.

He took off his apron, put the knife in his back pocket, then headed back upstairs. Taking a deep breath, and wiping the sweat from his blotchy, round face, he opened the door.

"Trick or treat, trick or treat," said a voice. A single voice.

Harold's heart kicked into overdrive. The boy before him was alone. He quickly looked around to see if any friends might be hiding at the garden entrance, saw none, then faked his best smile.

"Oh my! What a scary little monster you are. You're going to give me nightmares scaring me like that!" he chuckled, and patted his heart exaggerating a potential heart-attack. Which, he silently thought, may not be too far from becoming reality. The excitement was almost overwhelming.

The boy beamed behind his painted face, evidently delighted at the effect his mask was having. "Trick or treat," he said again.

"Well, come on in! I've got just the thing for you. You deserve a special treat, young man. With that nasty-looking make-up you're wearing, you've just saved me a lot of work!"

The boy hesitated a moment, then entered. The man looked harmless enough with his round, red face, and goofy grin. He followed him into the house.

"I keep all the best cakes in the basement, young man. Nice and fresh. Follow me." He looked back at the boy. He appeared dubious, as though having some internal discussion with himself.

"I keep my pumpkin collection there as well. Unique in the world. I'll show it to you also. You never know; I might even let you join the club!"

The boy seemed to think about it for a while, then shrugged his shoulders, and followed him down the stairs.

Harold waited until the boy had entered the basement, closed the door behind him, and locked it.

"So, do you like my little collection?"

The boy looked around the room, frowned, his jaw dropped, then he began to tremble.

"I don't like this, sir. I want to go home," he said in a very quiet voice.

"But what's wrong? You don't like my pumpkins? I think they're very … cute. It's taken me a long time to build the collection."

"Please, sir. I don't like it. Can I go now?" He turned to leave, but Harold was standing in front of the door; a great, towering obstacle that suddenly reminded him of some of the monsters he'd seen in movies, and comic books. Like the trolls from Lord of the Rings. His bottom lip began to quiver, and tears fell copiously from terrified eyes. Not wanting to, but for some reason unable to prevent it, as though he hadn't believed his eyes the first time, he turned once more to look at the collection.

The walls were adorned with shelves, and upon them, sat row upon row of what Harold called his pumpkin collection. Children's heads in multitude of expressions; some grinning, smiling; others with looks of horror, surprise, terror. Many with their faces painted, some wearing wigs to highlight the realism. The tops of their heads had been cut off, and the insides meticulously scooped out to be replace by candles, and their features delicately carved to create new eyes and mouths.

"You know, didn't your mother ever tell you not to take candy from strangers? Even on Halloween?" he asked.

The boy didn't answer. Instead, he tried to run past Harold, but Harold's great bulk impeded him pass.

"Happy Halloween, young boy. I said I'd let you join the Pumpkin Club, and join it you will," he said, as he produced the knife from his back pocket.

THE COLD UNCERTAINTY OF LOVE OR REAL LOVE IN A COLD CLIMATE

MARTIN P. FULLER

I know they are talking about me again. Vicious whispers echoing along the tiled corridors. I ignore their gabble and instead carefully carry on rinsing and drying the dishes and jars. I bear the laughter as I wipe the surfaces dry, oblivious to the smirks and sly smiles. They prefer to ignore the customers at the tables to gossip about me.

I know what's next of course. The false offer of friendship to go for a drink after work which they know I'll decline. Now that the boss has sneaked off home early, it will be, '*Oh Davy boy, just finish up will you, we need to get off. Yes, thanks bye. See you tomorrow*'.

To be truthful I encourage it. I long for these quiet moments when I can clean up and set things right without the need to bear my co-workers.

I can freely chat with the customers before I finish my shift, delaying my dreary bus ride home to the flat where I am so alone.

I return to the main room and catch the eye of Sylvia. I overheard her name from Stan earlier when she arrived. She'd smiled at me as she came in and her eyes held me in their beautiful green gaze. She is absolutely stunning. I was surprised that she would even look at me but I sense an emotion in her, a connection. I smiled back but that fool Stan Dawson told me to get out as I was in his way. I was furious and embarrassed, but mollified when I saw that Sylvia understood and she gave me another wonderful smile of sympathy.

I carry on with my duties, trying hard to be professional. I'm above the sarcastic humour of those creatures who work with me. I respect our customers and try hard to maintain a high level of professional service. I care when nobody else does. Why can't they see that?

My prediction comes true as all the others leave early to go for drinks leaving me alone to finish clearing up. The moment they leave I turn up the radio and change the channel to the classical station. I love the classics and I hear a buzz of agreement from the few customers still here.

I suddenly notice that Stan has spilt fluids all over a table occupied by a lovely elderly lady. She reminds me so much of my mother.

I dash over and wipe up the mess, apologizing profusely at the oversight of my colleague. She thanks me with genuine sincerity. This is what makes my life worth living. Those simple *thank-yous*.

I smile back and notice that the rather dignified middle-aged gentleman on table two is nodding his approval. I'm sure I hear him comment to Sylvia about my helpfulness. I can't help sneaking another look at her again and see a sparkle of real interest in those eyes which shine from that white moon skin of her adorable face.

Totally out of the blue, she calls me over and thanks me for the care I take and for maintaining standards. We talk for an age, oblivious to the other customers and time itself. Decent people long to see the blossoming of love and I know their gracious hearts swell with pride at my achievement of having the courage to speak to this goddess.

An annoying thought reminds me I must clean the floor in the canteen and chapel. I make my excuses and dash to the store cupboard for my mop and bucket. It will take a full twenty minutes to wash the floors and put all the knives and instruments in the sterilizer. I quickly grab my sandwiches from the fridge as I'm famished. I work so hard that I sometimes forget to eat. After a few bites of sustenance, I get on with my tasks, my hands on the mop but my mind and heart with Sylvia.

Finally, I've finished. I am free. As I re-enter the room of cold steel and white tile I hear the welcome from the customers. I apologize to them informing them that it is late and I must turn off the lights and lock up now. They fully understand and thank me as I place them on the trolleys and move them into the fridges, ensuring the temperature is healthy and comfortable four degrees centigrade.

I am shocked to notice that Stan has done a sloppy job of stitching up the elderly lady's abdomen, and has even left the finger from a discarded rubber glove protruding through the stitching. Yet again am forced to apologize for the incompetence of my colleagues, who despite their doctorates and qualifications have the standards of the gutter. I unpick the stitching and gently tuck in the rubber finger, slightly uneasy about using her empty chest and abdominal cavity as a wastebasket for the detritus of the examination slab. I take great care in re-sealing her skin with precise stitches. Perfect. The lady giggles saying I tickled her, but thanks me all the same. I carefully zip up her bag and that of the distinguished gentleman as they indulge in a last bout of small talk. Then a final smile as I bid them goodnight and close the heavy fridge doors.

I now take Sylvia's cold smooth hand and say adieu. She softly whispers sweet words to me and smiles. I almost cry I'm so happy at her request. I gently close her fridge door blowing a gentle kiss and turn off the mortuary lights.

No long sad journey home for me tonight. Not for me the loneliness of any empty flat. After I finish up, Sylvia has asked me round to her place this evening. Life is good.

HUNGRY PIG

Jarrett Mazza

There were three more houses left before Frankie Kleetus felt ready to return to his home at the end of the block. So far, he had ventured down his main street, which was just north of his house and between homes that he was familiar with; those that were certain to give him a fair amount of candy and an even fairer amount of attention.

"Trick or treat."

"Wow. Don't you look ... *scary*," said the blonde-haired woman standing in the doorway.

She reached out and gave Frankie a handful of chocolate bars that she dropped into his opened bag. After five years of dressing in costumes and trying to be as scary as possible, Frankie wanted to do something different. Tonight, he decided to dress as a pig that had been slaughtered and to accomplish this, his mother bought him an old pig costume and some plastic knives that Frankie cut in half and pasted the handles onto his portly body. He painted red around the wounds and he did this until he believed he looked more grotesque and disgusting. Some people thought it was amusing while others saw it as ridiculous and weird. However, Frankie didn't give much thought to the people who disliked his costume. He didn't make it for them, he made it for himself, and so long as people shuddered or reacted to it in some way, then Frankie believed it was done well. He had lots of candy in his bag.

This year, he received more Halloween candy than he ever had before, and he believed it was a result of the houses he chose to visit. The one that Frankie wanted to visit next was the same one that he visited with his friends. An elderly woman resided there. She sat near the window and rarely came to the door, not even when Frankie and his friends threw eggs against the glass, and not even when they knocked on the door to irritate her. She was a quiet lady but she would shout and scream whenever Frankie and his friends trespassed onto her property. Some of Frankie's friends would make jokes about how she was a witch or some other sinister hag that tried to cast spells on them. It was a sensible assumption. When she chased them, she would talk funny and make weird gestures with her hands. Yet, Frankie didn't believe in witches, and neither did his friends, and if she did have candy, then Frankie would be sure to ask for it.

"Trick'r'Treat."

Frankie waited near the door but instead of being greeted by a person holding a bowl of candy, he was welcomed with a vacant, dark, and quiet hallway.

"Uhhh," said Frankie,

There was no one nearby and not a single sign of candy anywhere and if he had to guess, he'd say that the door opening was nothing more than a simple accident.

He peeked his hand inside and tried to see into the home.

"Hello?"

His voice echoed into the space before simmering and vanishing within.

"Hello?"

Frankie was standing in the hall and surveying the space with his bag of candy and waiting for someone to answer his call. He checked the rooms to see if they were like those he had ventured to before, with a sofa or television, if there were tables and chairs, but the space he was walking into was too dark, and he could not see anything other than what was in front of him, a space illuminated by scarce amount of light.

"Hello?"

Frankie proceeded into the house, passing by a table with a vase before he moved into the kitchen, one with a table and chairs. On the table was a tablecloth as red as the fake blood painted on Frankie's costume, and in the center, was a bowl of candy that Frankie rushed towards the second he spotted it.

"*Yesss*," he said. "More."

He plunged the candy into his sack and packed it in for as long as he could but stopped when he heard the basement door creak open behind him. Frankie's body became ridged and he could feel chills on his arms and shoulders. He didn't bother to speak. He didn't care if the old woman was home or not. She never did anything to him then, why would she do something to him now? He stood at the top of the stairs and looked down. His shoulders quivered and he could feel his heart beating. He listened closer, trying to hear where these noises were coming from and if they were really happening or just the result of his overly active imagination.

"Hee-hee-hee," a voice chuckled from beyond the stairs.

Frankie heard it, but when he heard it the second time, he noticed a full-sized chocolate bar sitting on the stop of the stairs.

"Whoa."

On Halloween, it was rare for houses to give full-sized chocolate bars, but if there ever was a house that did, kids would flock to it like vultures hovering over a rotting corpse. Frankie rushed to this candy and peeled off each wrapper and took in their scent. It was amazing. He had felt an impulse to gorge himself before but never like this. He felt as though the candy was calling to him, and as he shoved it into his mouth, he felt an instant craving for another as soon as he was done.

"Mmmm," he said. "Mmmm. Mmmm. Mmmm."

He swallowed the chocolate and licked his fingers.

"Heeee. Heeee. Heeee."

The snickering persisted and Frankie crunched the wrapper and threw it down onto the floor. He stepped down the first stair and making his way into the basement. He flicked the light switch on the wall and waited for the lights to turn on, but none did. All he saw was a light flickering at the bottom of the stairs.

He moved towards it.

He didn't think about the reasons why there was candy, or why the woman would place it at the base of the stairs. The light continued to flicker and yet Frankie couldn't stop thinking about the candy. It was better than anything he had tasted before. Frankie swallowed what he was still chewing while, lurking in the shadows, he saw the elderly lady, sitting on a rocking chair, and grinning ghoulishly at Frankie as he approached her.

He shuddered.

"Ah-huh."

The old lady glared and Frankie backed away.

"Shhhh," she said. "Don't be afraid. Don't be afraid."

Frankie was ready to run back up the steps and leave the house he knew he was trespassing upon.

"Don't be afraid."

The old lady raised her hand and smiled.

"I was down here when I heard you knock. I didn't know that I left my door open. I just thought … maybe you would like to come in and take what you wanted yourself. After all …," the lady lifted the blanket that was over her lap, "… I didn't want to be the one to stop you."

"Oh …," said Frankie.

"Yes," the old lady said with a sly grin, "do you want more?"

"Ummmm …"

Frankie was nervous to answer. He thought the old woman would recognize him but then he remembered his costume. He wanted to get back home. He didn't like it when he didn't obey his parents. His mother would yell and send him to his room, but this was Halloween and there was candy, lots of candy, and he wanted all of it.

"Come on," the elderly lady invited. "I know you want it. I know you want what I have."

Frankie gulped and tried to stay away, but couldn't help but feel entranced by this woman. And then, before Frankie moved to the door, he spotted another bowl of candy. It was filled with his favourites: Twix, Gummy Bears, and a bundle of black licorice. His hands were moist and his lips felt as though they hadn't touched chocolate in hours and yet it had only been mere minutes since the last time he ate it.

The old lady grinned at him.

"Do you want some more?"

Frankie's mouth was full as he waddled to the table and sat. He reached into the bowl and grabbed the candy.

"What's your name?" the lady asked Frankie.

Frankie swallowed and started to unwrap more candy.

"Frankie," he said, after he swallowed.

"Frankie," she said, smiling. "I like that name. I'm Gretel."

Frankie smiled back at her, but made sure to keep his distance.

"Good?" the woman asked.

"*Mmm-hmmm*," Frankie mumbled. His mouth was exploding with chocolate and cookie crumbs. "Great."

Gretel reached across the table and gently tapped the back of Frankie's steady hands.

"I have more, if you want more?"

"No," said Frankie, wiping his face. "I think I'm good." He marched towards the door and grabbed his bag, which was resting on the floor.

"Are you sure?"

"Yeah. Thank you."

"Wait," said Gretel. She stood up from her chair. "You can stay and eat more. I have so much more candy, more than any house on the block. You can have all the candy you want if you stay. I'll make sure of it."

Frankie lowered the bag from his shoulder and stared. His stomach ached and he felt an upsurge of vomit crawling up his throat. His instincts were telling him that this was all he was capable of consuming. The longer he stared at the lady's glistening green eyes, the emptier his stomach began to feel. He felt hungry and hypnotized by the woman's candid, unrelenting insistence, and the moment she placed another bowl of candy onto the table, Frankie's licked his lips and headed back to his chair.

"Okay," he said. "Okay." He ploughed his face full of chocolate and the lady watched him.

"Good?" she said.

Frankie was swallowing the last of his bar before he belched and wiped his face clean of the jelly that was accumulated around his lips. "Is this ... jelly?" he asked.

"Yes. Why, does it not taste *like* it is?"

Frankie was looking down at the back of his wrist and saw three red streaks that he assumed were from the candy bar, but then which was which, he didn't know. To his knowledge, there were no chocolate bars that contained jelly, let alone jelly so thick that it could stick to one's face, and appear in chunky globs around the hands. "I don't know of any candy bars that have jelly inside of them," said Frankie.

"Well, does it taste bad?"

Frankie shook his head. "No."

There were five wrappers on the table, all of them spaced apart and all made with the same silvery paper that appeared crinkled and covered by the shade of red that Frankie noticed from the beginning.

"More?" asked the woman.

Frankie looked down at the last two bars that he was holding in his hand. These were hard, so hard that they chipped a few of his teeth without realizing. They were like pebbles moving around his mouth and the reason why he could feel it was the same reason why he saw the red streaks at the back of his hand.

"Something wrong?"

Frankie was quiet. The hard ingredients inside the candy were now under his tongue and against the muscles below. They were stiffer than he thought they would be. "What are these candies made of?"

"Same things that all candies are made," the elderly lady said with a sly grin.

Frankie could hear her laughing but was focused on the plastic bag peeping from behind the door. He crept up to it and was immediately assaulted by the smells that were creeping through his nose and nestling in the back of his throat. The red stains on the plastic were familiar now, and as he spotted them, he drew his attention to his wrist. He could see the stains on his hands. It was the same as on the bag. It had a distinct and familiar smell.

"Hahahahaha!" He rubbed his hands and reached forward and touched the plastic. It was moist and there wasn't anything that he could see inside, not until he yanked and dragged it from the room.

The old hag laughed.

Frankie pulled it again and, from within, several bloody bundles rolled along the floor and into the sides of his feet. They were red; soaked like sponges and yet each one appeared different than the other. Some thick, others were lighter, but all of them acquired the same pungent smell. Frankie removed his hand from his nose and kicked the bag. More pieces fell out but then there was one that was larger than the others, and when it rolled it made a tumbling sound that was like a boulder sliding along until it hit something. It hit his foot. Frankie thought it was a rubber ball because of how it rolled, but he knew later that it was no such thing, because when it stopped, it turned over and there were two eyes staring up at him.

The old hag's cackle stopped and Frankie looked down at the severed head. It was then that it dawned on him; in his little premature, twelve-year-old mind, that in this bag was a body and those bloody stumps that hit him were all that was left of it.

He stopped and gawked.

"That candy was mighty tasty, wasn't it?"

Frankie pressed his hand against his stomach and stumbled out of the room. He could feel something rumbling from within and the taste that he once equated with chocolate had now radically shifted and all he could taste now was blood.

The elderly lady stood and opened her hand. In it was a bag of dust that Frankie didn't notice until now. She was carrying it with her as she crept forwards, her cackling carrying through the space, and her body shaking as she walked.

"Eat," she said. "Makes everything better. My favourite spice," she laughed. "My secret ingredient. Sprinkle it on and makes everything taste like chocolate. Hypnotizes the mind. Do you like it? Do you want to taste it some more?" She threw more at Frankie. "Here," she said, "there's plenty. Eat, fat boy! Eat!"

The dust spritzed Frankie's face and he could feel it changing his senses. It was now making him nauseous and dizzy. His vision was blurry and his footsteps became unsteady. He could fall if he did not find a way to stay balanced. Whatever the old lady was tossing it was forcing Frankie to wobble as he attempted to escape. He clutched the walls and hunched over and as he tried to puke out whatever was inside him, the old lady continued to laugh until she came right up to where he was and touched him on the shoulder.

"I killed him," she whispered into Frankie's ear. "Your friends. I killed them. I chopped them into tiny pieces and wrapped them up. Did you hear me, boy? I chopped them up into tiny pieces and wrapped them all up!"

Frankie vomited and watched as the liquid formed into a puddle around him.

"I didn't want to throw any of the pieces away," said the woman. "I couldn't, but I was willing to play tricks, and use some of my..." the old woman didn't finish her thought, "maybe I could find someone to do it for me," she said. "Maybe one of the many brats who steal from my garden, throws eggs at my house, and call me a witch, well maybe they could help. Maybe I could *make* them help me."

The lady threw the dust down on his face and it trickled into Frankie's nostrils as it did before. However, from this proximity, he could smell what he thought was a spice and it was similar to the smell of chocolate. It was what on the candy, which Frankie knew wasn't candy now, and it was how this woman was able to disguise the pieces of one of Frankie's friends. It was how she readied them for consumption.

It was how she made him eat it, how she made him eat *him*.

Frankie staggered up the stairs and into the door. He pushed it forward and raced down the path outside the porch, to the sidewalk. Although he was far, he could still hear the old woman laughing. He ran as quickly as he could while three more children walked up to the house. It took three rings before the door opened and once it did, the old lady answered; her face clean and carrying a fresh bowl of candy in her hands. "Trick or treat."

IN THE PUMPKIN PATCH

ROSS SMELTZER

The old ones broke open easiest. Their skin was but a thin membrane, nothing more. You needed only to dig your boot—or a sharp knife–into their puckered flesh and they would collapse upon themselves, disgorging their stewed guts onto the earth. Their guts smelled most foul, suitable only for pig slop. Zoraida was an expert in the preparation of pumpkins. She knew everything about them. She was famed for her stews. Her towering wedges of spiced pie delighted the children of Hampton. She painted empty pumpkins and sold them in the market. One could see her gaily-daubed gourds throughout the village all though the autumn. Zoraida knew there were other things one could make from pumpkins, however. She was a most ingenious woman. Zoraida tottered through the vine-choked pumpkin patch, her brittle limbs aching. She eventually came to an inflated pumpkin with a hide like a dried apricot. Tufted with white fur, she fancied it looked like a shrunken head. She would cook with it, she decided. It would delight her with its treacly over-sweetness. She would feast on stew for days. But this was a big pumpkin. It could have many uses. She kicked the pumpkin hard, smiled as it yielded to her piercing shoe. It buckled like a corpse. Its innards, liquefied by rot but still stringy as seaweed, oozed onto the ground. She then took a rusted knife from her belt and plunged it into the pumpkin, hacking off misshapen hunks and collecting them in her hand. Zoraida had not been to this pumpkin patch in many years, more than she could reckon. It was her favorite, for it marked the spot where imprudent old Goodman Bosworth had once tried to farm. He hadn't heeded the warnings of the elders, the ones who knew that the Wessagusset had once interred their spirit-women here. That had been his last mistake. He had been a most foolish sort of man. Now, she had come to punish another man, equally unwise. She chuckled to herself. Her laugh sounded like the shrill cry of a crow. She returned her knife to her belt and began to form and knead the cold pumpkin slurry in her hand, idly giggling as she did so, exercising great care. Eventually, she made for herself a globular, jolly-looking sculpture, a doll, mucoid as a newborn. She had limited gifts as a sculptor.

The keen-eyed observer would observe that this doll possessed a bulbous head, stumpy legs, and a big belly, full and swollen like a gravid crone's. An inhabitant of Hampton might chortle and exclaim: "'Tis

Goodman Colby! Oh, Zoraida, you are most wicked to mock him so!" Perhaps this person would laugh and indulge Zoraida's unkind wit. Indeed, the poppet was an imperfect approximation of her neighbor, Goodman Colby, a reckless youth, given to sloth and—evidently—to stealing. Zoraida hoped very much that he had enjoyed feasting on her beloved he-goat, Buer, the beast of the fortunate conjunction, born when the darkling sigils burned brightest on the skin of the moon. She had doted upon him for many years, filling his barrel belly with rotten apples and sweet corn, stroking his long beard and caressing his spiraling horns. She had followed him as he revealed to her the secret paths in the deep woods. Young Colby's denials had been most unconvincing. Tears had spattered his cheeks like raindrops as he protested his innocence. Indeed, he was correct, animals often wandered into the woods and were never seen again. Indeed, the wolves had grown lean and hungry this year. She had assured him he had nothing to fear. "I do not tarry in the wood any longer," she had told him. Zoraida was nearly as good a liar as she was a cook. "You are a silly boy," she tittered, her words scraping against each other like rusty nails. "You will pay a high price for the gristly meat of that poor beast." Zoraida's smile fell away as she gingerly implanted a strand of Colby's straw-colored hair into the poppet's spheroid chest.

Silent now, her eyes hard and black, Zoraida dug deep in her apron for a pin. She found it among yellow knobs of ginger and sprigs of blackened wormwood and hag-tree fetishes. It was sharp yet. With a ferocious motion, she stabbed the knife into the unformed, notional man-shape in her outstretched hand. She sought the place where the man's belly would be.

The poppet might have squirmed, thought that could have been nothing more than a trick of the gathering dusk. And it might have shrieked too, though that could have been nothing more than a distant crow. One thing is certain, though: fluid, thick as old molasses but red when it should have been brown, dribbled from Zoraida's hand and pooled at her feet.

And Zoraida, the hag of Hampton, laughed as she had not laughed in many years. She then began to gather up chunks of pumpkin for her stew. Her work had made her hungry.

OUR ONE NIGHT A YEAR

CHRIS CAMPEAU

I couldn't tell if Rhea was still mad at me for scaring away her crush. She hadn't spoken until we got home. Then, as were about to start up the steps to the front door, she grabbed my arm and suggested we detour to the backyard to play one of our old games. So, high on Twix bars and Tootsie Rolls, Rhea and I did the 'tornado' 'til we were warm again, twirling in our Halloween costumes under the arm of the giant maple in our yard. She was a yellow Crayola crayon and I was the same thing I'd been the previous three years: black jeans, black long-sleeved turtleneck, blue spray-in hair, and a featureless white mask. I called it a "freak," and I was quite the treat. After 10 seconds of whirling like spin-tops, we threw our bodies to the grass. We closed our eyes and let the world swim around us. After a minute, Rhea stood up and attempted to walk. She stumbled here and there, a drunk crayon colouring the yard. "Whoa, mama," she said. She tossed her black hair out of her face, then tucked it into the little hole below the crayon's tip where her pink face peeked out. "So dizzy. Going to hurl." "Gross," I replied from the ground. A cold wind stirred around us. The arms of the maple loosened their remaining leaves with a bone-rattle shake, sending dark shapes dancing into a bruised sky. I reached for the candy bag at the base of the tree trunk. It was a dirty old pillowcase, off white and pregnant. I sat up cross-legged, spilling a few bags of Ruffles as I dragged the sack into my lap. "Looks like you lucked out this year." I tossed a shiny chip bag at Rhea, hitting her mid-crayon. "Hey!" She bent over to pick it up. "Ooo— Ruffles!" She crayon-waddled over and handed me the tiny bag so I could open it for her.

"Don't know how you like these things," I said, handing her back the chips. "They're stale before they leave the store, ya know."

"It changes the taste. They're just … better." Rhea sat beside me and turned her pillow case upside down, spilling its contents onto the darkening grass. Her hands spread the goods thin, fingers smoothing a giant heap of rocket rolls, fizz strips, gumballs. She sorted the candy into small piles: chocolates, gums, caramels, sugar candies; then into sub-piles: bite-sized bars, full-sized, Nestlé brand, Cadbury. Her hands moved with the sure speed of a veteran trick-or-treater, tossing aside the odd can of club soda as they went.

"Listen, Rhea. About Jordy." My voice sounded muted, as if underwater, from behind my mask. "I know. It's not your fault … Well, it is, but it doesn't matter." "I was only doing what any brother would have done." "I know. Really. It's fine." I waited for her to burst into an angry assault, and when she didn't, I raised my head. "Yeah? You mean it?" Rhea looked up from her work. "Braxton, it's O.K. Besides, I don't even really like him anymore."

Though she couldn't see it, my face had lifted in surprise. I couldn't believe Rhea would give up that quickly on a boy, not after having allocated a dime a week of her allowance for the past two years to the bottom of the town fountain, in a wishful toss to secure a boyfriend. For an 11-year-old, she was abnormally invested in romance. "I saw him pick his nose at Mrs. Rady's," she confessed. "He's ultra-gross now."

"I see."

"He did it when she made us sign her stupid guestbook before she gave us candy," Rhea said. "While Sarah Taylor was signing, Jordy took off one of his claws and stuck his finger in the nose hole of his wolf mask. It was big-time disgusting." I chuckled. "What did he do with it?"

"What—the snot?" she said.

"No…the wolf claw." I grinned under my mask. Rhea rolled her eyes and flicked my forearm.

"I dunno. Ate it?"

I laughed at that, and then she laughed, and then I was coughing, deep and watery. Rhea looked at me and fell quiet. She drew her knees up to her body and wrapped her arms around them. The breeze came at us again, colder this time. I shivered in my damp clothes. "How come you scared Jordy by showing him your face, but you won't show me?" she said.

"Rhea…"

"How come?" She tore her eyes from me and went back to fidgeting with her candy.

I listened under the wind, hoping I wouldn't hear our parent's Volkswagen pulling into the driveway around front. We never had enough time. "He was calling you names. That's why. I don't know if addressing you as 'Crayon Crud' means he likes you, but he was being a bully." I reached over and touched her legging-covered knee. "So, I bullied back." And did I ever. I had Jordy by the fuzzy chest of his wool sweater. I'll never forget the boy's eyes. They doubled in size in his grease-painted face when I lifted the chin of my mask, exposing the water-logged flesh of my face. I hadn't gotten it any higher than my mouth before he broke my hold and tore off down South Street. He howled like a wolf cub split from its pack, and his clip-on tail wagged below his butt as he ran. Rhea looked at me. She sat in a line of warm light spilling over the hedges from the neighbour's back porch. It carved half her face out from the darkness around us. She really was growing up.

"You're leaking again," she said.

I brought my hand up to my jawline.

"No, here." Rhea raised the corner of her pillowcase and dabbed at the liquid escaping my mask at the chin. The fabric was soft, though I hardly felt it. She set the linen down and returned to sorting her candy. She got faster every year.

"Braxton?" she said, after a minute.

"Yeah?"

"How did it feel when you drowned?" Rhea turned her eyes on me. The darkening sky behind her had lost its purple hue. It was all black now. I buried my hands in the grass, wet around me. I didn't tell her about the panic, or my first desperate lungful of water. I didn't tell her about the pressure—all that weight on my chest—or how the river grew darker as it took me under, and even darker as it carried me toward the dam. I didn't even tell her about the warmth that somehow stole the cold from my body when I finally gave in. I grabbed another bag of Ruffles. "Maybe when you've outgrown trick-or-treating," I said.

"So never?"

I smiled under my mask, and opened her a bag of chips.

TRICK OR TARANTULA

KEVIN FOLLIARD

Last Halloween, Dr Mason distributed jarred tarantulas. Little children screamed and ran. But some older boys accepted the creatures with wide-eyed fascination.

"Feed them a mouse—once a week," Mason instructed. "They'll soon outgrow the jar."

Spiders grew, in shoeboxes and terrariums, under heat lamps in closets. The most dedicated boys returned for further instruction:

"A pigeon—once a week—until he outgrows the tank."

"A cat—once a week—until he outgrows the shed."

Come spring, the doctor congratulated his new apprentice: "Excellent, Timmy. Release Fang in the woods. Once a week, he'll treat himself to a scrumptious hiker."

I REMEMBER SAMHAIN

CHAD VINCENT

There is no boogey man. No, but I am real.

I write this across my cell walls in dirty, bloody graffiti. A diary entry. Mouth dry.

Junior high was rough, long ago. They teased, mistook a small body for weakness. Fools.

Remember the eighties, when kids trick-or-treated in their neighborhood? Without parents? A graveyard pack bound by sugary euphoria, the oldest no more than ten?

My first taste of blood.

I hid among the bushes behind a plastic mask, clutching my daddy's straight razor. Laughing their way towards me, Miller and Lisowski. Sidewalk idiots. I hated them enough to smile.

GOOD CARVING DEPENDS ON THE PUMPKIN

CR SMITH

You smile in anticipation. A knife's hidden beneath your costume, you're squeezing the handle ready to pounce when this year's victim moves close enough.

There's resistance as you first push against flesh, your razor-sharp blade slicing straight through their throat. They scream silently. You love the way blood splatters outwards releasing its tang—it's what makes Halloween so special.

Licking away blood specks from your hand, you move round, gazing triumphantly into shocked eyes, before artfully carving shapes in skin, awaiting that final exhale as life slips away. They always seem taken aback to see the pumpkin wielding the knife.

NOVEMBER

JUST A LITTLE BLOOB

G.A. MILLER

Kathy couldn't remember exactly when it progressed to hatred. She had a hazy recollection of the slide from young lust to something *resembling* love to begrudging acceptance, and then bored indifference, but when it finally crossed the line into hate somehow escaped her.

Joe wasn't mean or abusive, nothing like that, but he was indifferent to her, to her wants or needs or feelings. They'd evolved into a dead-end couple working dead-end jobs to maintain their dead-end house in their dead end neighborhood.

Not the fairy tale she'd often imagined as a little girl, no, not at all, much more like a reflection of her mother's life when she looked in her mirror, becoming more clear and distinct by the day.

And she hated it. She hated her life, she hated Joe for his casual indifference, and she had to admit, she hated herself for just going along with it, day after day.

It had become worse lately, though. She began making an effort to eat better, more salads, more vegetables, leaner proteins, and Joe would have nothing to do with it.

"You can do what you want, but *I'm* not eating that goddamn rabbit food. I'll pick something up on the way home from work for myself."

And he did. He tried a few of the usual fast food places, and finally settled on a new place in town, the 'Taco Tower'. He'd bring home spicy smelling bags and eat their contents while she had her salad, neither of them talking much at all during their meals any more.

The worst part for her wasn't what he ate, not by a long shot. It was the aftermath.

He'd begun farting regularly, producing the most obscene, vile odors she'd ever had to endure. She'd worked in a nursing home as a teen, and tending to the bed pans was nothing compared to the repugnant smells he produced.

She soon learned that the loud ones, the ones that sounded like thick leather being torn, weren't so bad at all. It seemed most of their energy went into producing the loud, wet noises.

No, the worst ones were what Joe came to call "a little Bloob."

The tiniest popping sound, followed by a poof that reminded Kathy of actors blowing out candles in the old black and white movies. That was the 'Bloob'.

And those produced the most hideous, rank odors imaginable. She'd be lying on the couch, he in his recliner, and as soon as she heard the little pop, she'd pull up the comforter and cover her nose and mouth with it. Even their little Jack Russell Terrier would hear that sound, jump off the couch, and trot outside through his doggie door to the fresh air out back.

With his sensitive little sniffer, she didn't blame him. Even dogs had their limits, it seemed.

As time went on, Joe stopped there more frequently, and it got worse. She'd taken to keeping a can of air freshener at her side at all times, like a Sheriff's six-gun in a lawless town, to try and offset the revolting odors emanating from his chair.

The arguments got worse, more bitter as time passed. One day, he made an extremely rude comment as she was in the kitchen, and she stopped her work, not believing what she just heard.

She finally lost it. She'd had enough. She raced in from the kitchen, her chef's knife in hand from slicing vegetables, and told him she couldn't take it any longer. She wanted out.

And he laughed. He actually laughed in her face, laughing so hard, he produced one of his room clearing "Bloobs".

She shrieked, gripped the handle of the knife in both hands, and plunged it deep into his gut.

Even before he howled in pain, she heard the hissing, *wooshing* sound. The sound of a broken air line, or perhaps escaping compressed air.

She understood immediately that she'd made a critical mistake. She'd hit the stomach, possibly the intestines.

Her eyes widened to comical proportions, realizing what she'd done. She began backpedalling, waving her arms frantically, but the stench hit her hard, a noxious cloud straight from the very bowels of Hell itself.

Decomposing bodies floating in raw sewage would be spring roses in a field of lavender compared to the malodorous effluvium quickly filling the room. The back of her legs hit the couch, and she went down hard, choking and gagging. She leaned to the side and vomited profusely, trying to get it all out and not choke on it, completely ignoring Joe's frenzied cries for help.

The Jack Russell was already out in the yard, howling instead of barking.

She rolled off the couch onto the floor, praying the stench would rise, like stifling air does. She began crawling toward the door to the kitchen, to try and get away, and as she passed the wall vent, she heard the click of the heat coming on downstairs.

And they heated their home with natural gas.

The resulting explosion shattered the windows in seventeen houses nearby, causing severe structural damage to the ones closest. A Desert Storm veteran who lived down the street was quoted on TV as saying it looked worse to him than direct hits by missile strikes from air support in the desert. He was not at all surprised to hear that the governor had mobilized the National Guard.

Neighboring towns had to lend support, tending to the wounded, and transporting the worst cases to nearby hospitals.

Neighbors first thought an aircraft fell from the sky, hitting the house directly, the fuel exploding on impact. The damage was too severe, too total to have been caused by anything inside. Kathy and Joe were normal people, they said, not criminals or terrorists.

Arson and bomb squad investigators ran every forensic test in their arsenal, looking for trace evidence. They suspected a meth lab, a hidden cache of explosives and weapons, but every test came back negative for those elements.

The only unusual result was an exceptionally high trace of natural methane, which they could not explain. There were no signs of accelerants, and the trigger seemed to be the pilot in the furnace going on as it should, nothing more than that. Even the FBI, once called in, had no meaningful results from their labs at Langley.

The medical examiner couldn't shed much light, as there just wasn't enough left of Joe or Kathy to autopsy.

The mystery remained front page news for a couple days, only to be replaced by the latest wave of scandal and accusations making the rounds in the Capital.

Locals looked forward to the new coffee house being built on the grounds of the former 'Taco Tower', which had been shuttered and abandoned by its owners without explanation.

Life moves on.

BUGS #3

JUSTIN BOOTE

Doctor Henson ran to the injured girl, laying in the rain by the roadside. He decided on mouth to mouth. As he breathed, movement to his left caught his eye. A puddle was forming rapidly around them. He had to reanimate her quickly or the puddle would cover them both. The water covered his ankles, then his legs. As he breathed into her mouth, something tickled his tongue. My God! Is she kissing me? Then, it ran down his throat. Shocked, he spat it out. The thing ran to join its companions that were the puddle. The cockroaches engulfed him.

LET DOWN YOUR HAIR

ROBERT ALLEN LUPTON

The old tower was covered with moss and ancient vines. The doorway was bricked with dry crumbling mortar. The Prince called to the turret high above and a woman answered. "Thank goodness. Help, A wicked witch chained me here years ago."

"The doorway's bricked shut."

"I'll let down my long hair. Climb it." Her golden hair cascaded downward like a waterfall. The Prince caught the first strands, but the hairy deluge continued until he was trapped and the weight suffocated him. Rapunzel pulled up her hair. Damn, I've killed another one. Not to worry, the wolves will eat him tonight.

BREAK HER BACK

RICHARD J. MELDRUM

He first heard the rhyme when he was eight years old. He believed it absolutely. He couldn't imagine hurting his mother. That was when he started avoiding the cracks on the sidewalk. His mother chided him for staring at his feet, but he couldn't stop. For forty years he followed his own rule, but the inevitable happened. He was at an intersection. He stepped off the kerb without checking. Looking down he saw his foot, sitting neatly on a crack between two pavers. He prayed the gods would forgive him. His phone rang. It was father. It was bad news.

CHARLA NASH

AGNES MARTON

I used to tease my school buddy, Sandra: she would never be brave enough to keep a monkey.

She proved me wrong.

It was Friday the 13th when Travis arrived. We felt damn lucky. That weekend we, best friends forever, neither slept nor had meals.

In some weeks Sandra let the chimpanzee out of his cage.

The Herolds, Sandra's family, ran a tow-truck business. When Travis got to ride in the truck, we asked: "Steak?" Nod. "Cupcakes, pretzels?" Nod. "Lemon tea?" Nod.

On his birthday, pink champagne.

Once, not himself, he stormed out and roamed. Sandra called me to interfere.

The chunklets of my fingers reminded a witness of minced meat. Most of my scalp went, my eyelids got bitten, my nose and lips were ripped off.

Not my ears.

Everyone talks about my ears, noble like ivory. Nobody mentions my removed eyes and the hole in my face to drink through.

Whenever I have visitors from hell, I try to chase them away by touching my forehead—but I have only one thumb left, and it is numb. And there's nothing to feel, only a polished yet raw bust to represent I'm able to chin up.

I made it to the Oprah show, I was wearing a veil.

Sandra? We are not on speaking terms. What words could we exchange?

I might look shattered but I remained the same.

Travis was shot dead.

If I had my eyes, they could still talk to him, offering relief.

TEA PARTY

ALYSON FAYE

Edward hands his guests china cups. Several pairs of glassy eyes stare back. It's a quiet gathering. Edward is the centre of attention. Just as he likes it. He combs Lillian's blonde tresses. Silky soft and real. Shorn from her dead scalp. He remembers the girl vividly. Her wide pink mouth and lolling tongue.

A knock makes him jump. "Put your dolls away. It's dinner time," his wife announces. Guiltily Edward drops his hand. Red faced he stands up knocking Josephine who falls into Lillian's lap.

"They're historical artefacts," he whispers.

Edward kisses each doll's cheek. His silent adoring girls.

PINK POODLE

KEVIN M. FOLLIARD

Amy found a pink poodle buried halfway into their lawn. "Amy! Come play!"

"You're a talking, doggie?"

"Yes!" The poodle's eyes shined. "Pet me!"

She reached for it.

"Amy!" her mother called. "Lunchtime!"

The poodle yipped as she hurried inside. She ate PB&J on the porch and watched the poodle emerge. The top was a fluffy dog, but the bottom was a huge pink crab with orange tiger stripes, scissor-shaped claws, and gnashing teeth hidden under the dog's torso. It crawled to the neighbor's lawn and burrowed back down. Davey Chen came skipping outside. "Davey!" the poodle said. "Come play!"

IN THE WOODS

STEPPEN SAWICKI

You've gotten all tied up in how dark and mysterious everyone says the woods are. There's nothing here but the trees and squirrels. Come on, I'll show you.

Don't jump at that rustling. It's just a mouse in the grass. See, there's an owl diving to catch it.

Hush. Those aren't fingers in your hair. It's just the branches brushing against you.

Don't worry about the fog. It's not entirely out of reason for the weather to turn hazy at this time of year … I think.

That snarling? It's probably … Look, maybe we should go back.

… Which way is back?

THE SCUTTERINGS

MARTIN P. FULLER

I know they are out hunting again. I hear their scampering's and scuttering's as they sneak ever nearer, waiting in the dark. Stalking. Watching.

It's at this time of year that they hatch. They travel with the blowing leaves, a twitch in the corner of your eye, a blur across your vision, masking the sound of their clawed feet under the rustle of the leaf.

It sounds insane to those who do not know: who have not been blessed or perhaps cursed, with the sight. The ugly realisation that we are not alone in our cruel intelligence.

They bide their time as summer dies and look for an opportunity.

Let me ask you a question. How many of society's outsiders vanish?

The homeless, the tramp, the vagrant. All of those we try to avoid thinking about. Those living in the dark, lonely places away from our sight.

Some are fated to become the feast of the Autumn born.

We hardly notice their sudden disappearance. Who cares that the unsightly in our society just ... vanish. We don't bother to ask where they go.

Only when our own beloved pets go missing and homemade posters adorn lampposts in the neighbourhood, do we ever begin to wonder.

Food. The creatures of the falling foliage regard us and our furry pets, as food. Clever food. Intelligent food. Dangerous food even.

That's why they hunt in packs, letting the windblown leaf, cover their stealthy advance till they are near. Till they can pounce. Until they can kill and feed.

You must ... must ... have seen something. The faded shape suddenly speeding across the road in front of your car. A sudden scrape sound around your feet. Remember the shock of fear before you rationalise that it's just the breeze and a few dead leaves idly tumbling across the ground.

You are so easily tricked by the dark creatures, in their seasonal migration from the tree tops in Autumn. They journey to breed in the winter months of long darkness as they have for millennia, this ancient nemesis of humanity.

You will never see them directly. You will fail to describe their small jaws, sharp needle teeth, mouldy green eyes. You will not be able to relate their colour or number of limbs. Nor could you know of their instinct to secrete themselves in the soggy piles of detritus, waiting for a gust of wind. The same piles of leaves you allow your children to kick with such happy abandon, under the predatory gaze of the pre-winter killers.

Be warned and learn from one who knows. Listen for the breathing of the wind, the touch of decaying greenery, and try not to walk alone as the nights draw in.

NO ORDINARY GAME

N.O.A. RAWLE

The film hadn't scared them so much as intrigued them.

"Let's make a Ouija board—there must be a DIY on YouTube," Joy suggested.

"Wouldn't work," Bill dismissed.

"Let's ask Mr. Vincent in the toyshop—he'll order one—knows nothing about toys!" The kids slapped a high five.

Mr. Vincent frowned, "Ouija board? Why of course." He shuffled behind the curtain hiding the back of the shop.

"I told you he knows nothing about toys," Bill whispered.

In the darkness Mr. Vincent lit a black candle then blew out the match.

"So true, so true. But about the occult …"

CRIMES OF PASSION

MICHAEL PARKER

Antoni sat in his car and gaped at the statement for the joint credit card. Her affair was itemised.

The bedroom light was on as he pulled up. His key wouldn't work in the front door. He hammered on it. No reply.

The key wouldn't open the back door, either.

There was a half house brick in his hand, edges rough, corner jutting.

The back door jerked open. His cuckold leapt out, shirtless, brazen and cursing. Antoni quietened him with the brick, and went after the woman.

He'd need to find a new woman. One of them would be faithful.

HIS COUSIN'S TALE

ETHAN HEDMAN

"You've gotta be kiddin' me." The dwarf took a deep gulp of ale. A bit of froth dripped from his moustache to his beard. "Tryin' to terrify ol' Galbur, eh? Well, it didn't work. That story's the dumbest thing I've heard in years, boy."

"Think what you will," replied Ernoth, the tavern's bartender, "but Alret was shaken. I've never seen him so upset." Ernoth was in his twenties, but was hardly offended by his aged patron's use of the word boy. Dwarves age into the hundreds, and Galbur, a traveling merchant who often spent a night in the tavern while passing through, had more than a few gray hairs wrapped in his auburn braids. "You know as well as I do that my cousin has no reason to lie about his travels."

"Aye, no reason, apart from impressin' you and anyone else fool enough to listen. This whole adventurin' craze with young'uns is nonsense. It's just a bunch of travel and trouble mixed together." Galbur snorted, downing the last of his drink. "Still, I suppose it's better to have your cousin forge his path as a travelin' storyteller of sorts than hang around here as a farmer or some such, even if he is tryin' to make you deathly afraid of a bloody box." The dwarf chuckled. "Now, then, be a good lad. Give us another, and spare me your kin's mistruths."

Ernoth reclaimed the tavern's mug and placed it below a tap. "He did mention something that might interest you. There's been an awful harvest in a few villages just east of here."

"Is that right? See now, that's a bit more handy than a woeful tale for children. Have they got enough to get by?"

"They might have enough for themselves, but they wouldn't sell Alret so much as a scrap when he passed through. He was glad to have a proper meal when he arrived here." Ernoth passed the refilled mug back across the bar. "You often head east when you leave, don't you? If I were you I'd take some food to sell along with your usual stock."

Galbur bellowed a laugh, shaking in his stool. "Forget all the damn junk I've got loaded now. If they're hungry I'll leave the lot out back—if you don't mind, of course, lad—and load the cart full with salted meats, onions, potatoes, and bread first thing in the mornin'. I'd not likely sell anything else if they're all starvin', anyway." He took another deep drink, belching afterwards. "Well, thank Albert for me. And you, as well, for bein' the messenger."

Ernoth grinned as his cousin's name was misspoken. The dwarf had a tendency for ignoring names as he was always hearing more of them on the road. The fact that he was able to remember that of a humble bartender was an unspoken compliment. "Paying your tab regularly is thanks enough for me. It's not as though I could load a cart and go there myself. Someone has to tend the tavern while the sun is up."

"Aye, and regale the midday patrons with fairytales while we wait for the servin' wenches to come at sunset." Galbur laughed again, the floorboards groaning beneath his bouncing seat. "I guess your cousin's folly's good for somethin'."

"Alret was here?" called a voice from the entrance. Variel, the town's blacksmith, made her way to the bar, taking the stool to the left of the dwarf. "Did I miss him?"

"You did," Ernoth replied. "He headed north with his companions. They're searching for another ancient ruin. I hope his journey will be safer than the last."

"Aye, it'll make for another fine story, to be sure," Galbur said with a wink. "Say now, let's have a second opinion, eh, lad? Tell her what you told me. See what she makes of your cousin's bloody fable."

Ernoth sighed. "My dwarven friend refuses to believe that there could be unknown dangers in the world. While Alret was adventuring, he and his cohorts came across a chest—"

"Hold there, lad," Galbur interrupted, scratching at his damp chin. "Don't rush right to the end. Tell the lady just what sort of *adventurin'* it was that they were up to."

"The same as he hopes to do now. He was scavenging a ruin with his colleagues."

"They were robbin' a crypt, the way you told it earlier. Dark, dismal, rancid with the smell of death and decay. Seems you're leavin' out all the flavorful details."

"That's hardly how he described it, or what I told you, for that matter. A ruin strewn with ancient corpses is hardly a crypt. It was likely a besieged castle that had been broken and battered long ago, having been reclaimed by nature since."

Galbur shrugged. "I reckon a stinking, miserable crypt'd be more likely to hold treasures than some wreckage of an old fort left to rot. Albert's smart enough to know that, too."

"Let Ernoth tell his cousin's tale," Variel said, resting a hand on the old dwarf's shoulder. "So, he came across a chest?"

"Yes. It appeared ordinary enough, so, naturally, one of Alret's companions went to open the chest. When he did—"

"You said it was a man with giant's blood, might have been twice as tall as me, didn't you, lad?"

"My cousin said so. A hardened warrior from the mountains in the north. When he approached the chest and began to open it ..." Ernoth took a deep breath. "Well, the chest attacked."

Variel nodded. "Trapped chests aren't unheard of."

"It wasn't a trap. The chest itself put up a fight. It sprang to life, thrashing about the room, flapping its lid back and forth. There were dozens of sharpened teeth in its maw. This chest flailed this way and that, trying to slaughter the group."

"There you are, lass. The dumbest thing I've heard in years."

"It killed the giant man! It bit into him as though his bone was soft as butter."

"The only thing that chest killed was your common sense when you decided to believe in it, boy. I've sold every damn sort of chest and box you can imagine. Not a single one has flapped around or nipped at so much as a mouse."

"If the ruin *was* a castle, it could have had a mage. The chest may have been enchanted."

"Magic, is it?" Galbur scoffed. "Come now, you know better than that."

"I admit, it does seem somewhat far-fetched," Variel said, leaning back in her stool.

"Yes, but Alret's reputation is ironclad. He wouldn't lie about such things."

Variel nodded again. "Of course, but when it comes to that chest, who are we to say? Alret saw what he saw. Perhaps it really was a trapped chest. In a moment of panic, we might've seen it the same way."

"Fine, fine, to each their own. Me, I say it's a tall tale. The first of many, most like. Maybe next time he'll come back talkin' about townsfolk turnin' into wolves or drinkin' blood." Galbur slid his mug back across the counter. "Time'll tell, eh? In the meantime, keep fillin' me up, lad."

Variel left shortly thereafter, and Ernoth returned to his home once the barmaids arrived to take his place. Galbur, however, stayed long into the night, having far too much to drink and entertaining his fellow patrons with Alret's ridiculous second-hand story.

The inebriated crowd found the tale as absurd as Galbur had, causing scattered bouts of raucous laughter each time it was told. Eventually the patrons stirred enough of an uproar that none of them took notice as the tavern itself began to creak and sway. It chortled at the naivety of the mortals inside. The structure had sat idle for decades, but determined that tonight would be a truly poetic occasion for the townsfolk to learn about the unending hunger that a wooden creature can possess and the savage wrath it can unleash.

TWO IF BY SEA

JENNIFER CANAVERAL

The evening sky was clear over Waikiki and the moonlight danced on the steady ocean waves. Miranda and Tommy sat on their straw mat and dug their toes into the cool sand, watching a young couple bodysurf nearby. Miranda hiked up her sundress and pulled a flask out of her garter. She took a swig then offered some to Tommy but he declined.

"Drink, baby," Miranda said. "It could be hours before they come to shore."

"I'll wait," Tommy responded. "Let 'em bask in that lovely mixture of salt water and oblivion, just as we had. Before they turned us."

THE PARASITE

H.B. DIAZ

It will damage the optic nerve en route to your sinus cavity, but you will not be blinded. It needs your eyes. You will see it, amorphous and dark, always at the edges of your vision, writhing. Growing. The incubation will end by the dawn, when it will crawl across the dry tongue of your corpse and begin to feed. And when you are nothing but a suit of soulless flesh, it will take your form and go home to your family. Your mother will sit beside it at the dinner table. They'll drink coffee together and it will laugh.

HOW TO PREPARE ROADKILL

CR SMITH

During a quiet spell at work I searched the internet for tried and tested ways of jointing and cooking a human. On the way home I drove to the supermarket, purchasing a meat cleaver, a plastic sheet and an extra-large wok. I timed it perfectly. As my prey stepped off the pavement I put my foot down, stopping only to collect his carcass. There was a fair amount of meat on the man. My mouth watered imagining ways I'd cook him. Stir-fried. Poached. Braised ...

What I wasn't prepared for were the bloodcurdling screams when I began to dismember him.

DECEMBER

THE LAST ENGLISH SPEAKER

JAMES BURR

Dr Ndosi crossed the well-manicured lawns of the clinic on her way to conduct yet another interview with the last lunatic on Earth. Coming towards her was Dr Zahirovic, his tie loose, sweat dripping from his forehead.

"Sawubona," she said and smiled.

"Zdravo. Vreli dan, zar ne?" he replied, as he glanced at the blue sky above and fanned his face with his hand.

Of course, she had no idea what he was going on about, probably something to do with the weather judging from his actions and his exaggerated puffing as he wiped the sweat from his brow. So, she smiled again and despite knowing that he couldn't understand a word she was saying, replied, "Noma kunjalo, ngifanele manje ngikhulume ngenyanga yokugcina. Hamba kahle."

Despite knowing better, she still hoped that one day the faces of her colleagues would light up in recognition, that they would understand that she had said she was going to interview the last lunatic on Earth, and they would then excitedly respond in fluent Zulu. But instead, Zahirovic smiled at her vacantly, looked again at the sky as if seeking further conversational inspiration before obviously thinking better of it and saying, "Zbogom. Vidimo se kasnije" and scurrying off up the path. She did not speak Bosnian but she had heard Zahirovic and his wife say it so often she took it to be some kind of valediction.

She entered the main Clinic building, pausing briefly to show her pass to the Japanese guard on the door. Dr Mueller was sat waiting for her in the cool reception and as he saw her he raised his hand to get her attention before getting up, straightening his jacket and making his way over to her. "Guten tag," he said and nodded. Ndosi had never had a proper conversation with Mueller for obvious reasons, their interactions limited solely to purely functional interactions clumsily facilitated by whatever translation software they tapped their thoughts into. Mueller was a pragmatic man however, so made no attempt at further niceties knowing that such interactions were futile. Instead, he beckoned Ndosi to come with him to the secure quarantine ward where the last lunatic on Earth was now living.

Ndosi hated having to interview the crazy man. Despite not knowing what he was saying, the way he would scream and wail and spit at her was upsetting and frightening and a depressing reminder of the international genocide/suicide that had killed one billion in a frenzy of violence and gore. She braced herself for a moment before opening the door. The lunatic, known only as Dave, any family name being long forgotten by the maniac himself or anyone who had ever known him, was shackled to the bed, thick leather straps across his knees and chest, his wrists and ankles restrained with thick, leather manacles. He saw Ndosi and Mueller enter and from above the spit-mask he was forced to wear, his eyes blazed with hatred. Muscles strained against his bonds and the bed creaked and rattled as he snapped at the straps. "Oh look! It's the fucking Nazi and his pet. Fucking let me out of here you fucking bastards!"

Dr Van Den Berg acknowledged their arrival as he held the boom mic near Dave's face while Dr Horvath busied himself with the recording equipment.

"Let me out of here or I'll fucking kill you" he screamed. "Or I'll just kill you anyway, you useless fucking bastards!" The lunatic known as Dave continued to rant and rave and scream unintelligible abuse at her as she showed him pictures of atrocities committed in London, Sydney and New York back when there was a London a Sydney and a New York.

At first, the international community was at a loss to explain what came to be known as "The Madness" in the UK, the US, Australia, Canada and New Zealand. The enormous rise in murders, the streets literally flowing red with rivers of blood, the thoughtless brutality, the mass rapes. But these were just on the individual scale. When groups of murderers joined together there were riots and when the riots became larger and spilled out across national borders there were wars. Husbands killed wives, fathers killed sons, neighbours killed neighbours. That there was a reason for the Madness seemed obvious—its onset was so sudden it was clear that it was no natural phenomenon. The International Community tested the air, the water, searched in vain for some kind of viral or bacterial pathogen. Autopsies of those they found, whether they had been murdered or whether they had bashed their own brains out in fits of insane self-loathing, revealed nothing. It was then that a Chinese team had found Dave, trapped in the rubble of Tipton, unable to harm himself or others, shouting his hate and rage out to the ruins.

He had been subjected to a battery of tests—psychological, toxicological, genetic—none of them finding any cause for the cause of his insanity. And it was then that Dr Lem posited his hypothesis; the cause was the English language itself. Lem hypothesized that neither thought nor culture was possible without language and that the reason the Anglo-

Sphere had succumbed to mass insanity was that the English language itself, the means of thought for over a billion people, was in itself utterly schizophrenic, forever changing and taking elements from other languages, pillaging words and thoughts that were supposed to be used to express different personalities and cultures, and instead ramming them together, conflicting ideas and thoughts smashed together to express things that they were not intended to express. Surely, Lem claimed, madness could be the only result of such cognitive dissonance, linguistic schizophrenia on a global scale.

So, they had recorded literally hundreds of hours of Dave's ravings in the years since the Madness had ended, sending the transcripts of his rants to international teams who would pick out words that shared etymological roots with their own languages. They would then be passed on to another team who spoke a different language who would do the same and on and on until eventually they could work out what he was saying.

"You fucking bastards, I'll murder the lot of you!"

Mueller wrote down the word, 'Murder'. "Mord"? he said under his breath. Van den Berg blinked and muttered, "Moord ..."

The fact that the English language itself was the cause of The Madness has now been proven beyond question, although how it could cause such devastation in such a short period of time was still unknown and the sole reason for the continuing research into Dave.

"Just come a bit closer and I'll beat you to death!"

"Dood?" repeated Van den Berg, growing pale and unsteady on his feet. And so now Ndosi had to listen to the unintelligible ravings of the last lunatic on Earth, recording his rants in a dead language so that those who were left could work out how this linguistic insanity manifested almost instantaneously across the globe.

"Oh, if I was free, I'd show you bastards a million levels of pain."

"Pijn ..." said Van den Berg, putting down the boom mic and rubbing his eyes. "Pijn ..."

At least one thing is clear, thought Ndosi. Despite the horror of the affliction, at least as the Madness is linguistic in nature, it cannot be infectious.

Van den Berg muttered, "Pijn," his face contorted with hatred, as he reached for a nearby scalpel.

SCARECROW

ALYSON FAYE

Out in the field, tied up on its pole, Harry's scarecrow twitched. The button eyes were always open. It watched Harry's ma creep out to meet her beau. It watched Harry's dad following, shotgun prepped. It noticed Harry wake screaming from a nightmare. "Mum!" Fuelled by the memories of Harry's love in its creation, the scarecrow hauled itself up from the mud. "I'm coming Harry," it slurred. With stiff legs it stalked the furrows.

Harry sat huddled. He heard a shuffle, then a stumbling on the landing. "Dad's drunk again," he thought. "I'm here, Harry."

Lice crawled under the door.

JACK IN THE BOX

MATHIAS JANSSON

My name is Jim. I am six years old. My brother is a Jack in the box. His name is Jack and I have put him in a small box. When I cranks the handle, he pops up with a scary look. It was very funny in the beginning. But I do not like my new toy anymore. It has started to smell and his eyes have popped out. I also have a little sister. She is called Jane. I think I will cut up her into a jigsaw puzzle instead. Thousands of pieces and all will be blood red.

FRACTURE CLINIC

RICHARD J. MELDRUM

Smith watched with trepidation as the man before him left in a wheelchair, his leg in a cast. Smith was next in line. The room was well lit and clean. Biohazard and x-ray signs were dotted around. Nurses and doctors bustled around him, as he waited for his appointment. The technician arrived.

"Mr. Smith? Come this way."

The private room was cool.

"Mr. Smith, our records show an outstanding balance to the government of $500. Parking fines."

"Yes."

"Standard penalty is a wrist. Don't worry, treatment is free."

The technician reached back and lifted a small, but adequately heavy hammer.

DAVID AND GOLIATH

RICHARD J. MELDRUM

The laboratory was badly lit, the mains electricity had been off for a week. Paul was relying on a diesel generator to power minimal lights and essential equipment. The place was deserted, none of the staff had turned up that morning. Only he and John were still working, and that was because they'd been camping out in the lab, rather than going home. Paul guessed the rest of the team were either dead or dying.

Paul looked round at the piles of dirty glassware, discarded plastic and latex gloves. He didn't have the time or the inclination to clean up. Instead, he continued to run the assay, his mind elsewhere. What would the latest results show? There were some interesting new compounds, they might be effective. Would they be saved? The door opened. John entered, his white lab-coat stained with blood.

"I've got the results."

"I was hoping you had. Anything?"

John shook his head.

"The delta-blockers had zero effect. Same with the chloro-quinolones. Nothing is touching it. It's still completely resistant. Every time we hit it with a new molecule, it spits out another set of enzymes to destroy it."

Paul felt a wave of disgust and despair. He looked at the window, at the world outside.

"We don't have a chance."

"What do we do now?"

"See if any of the other labs have made progress. Check London, Geneva and Rome. They were all working on different formulations."

"Will do, but I doubt ..."

"I know," interrupted Paul, "but do me a favor and check anyway."

John nodded and headed out. Paul stood and walked to the window. The lab was on the fourth floor of the university building. He looked down at the street below. The cultists were still there, standing behind the barricades. They were protesting the research, as they did every day. They wanted the world to end, they wanted the world to burn.

"You got your wish," whispered Paul. His head felt hot against the cool glass.

Two years, that was all it had taken to turn the world to shit.

"From inconsequential beginnings, dynasties will fall."

It was a popular quote from the cultists. He stared at a Petri dish sitting on the bench.

"Just a wee microbe. Nothing special."

Paul thought back to how quickly disaster had overtaken the human race. The first case had been in Spain. An infection, acquired in hospital. It was considered routine until the clinicians realized the patient wasn't responding to any antibiotic. The bacterium causing the infection had developed complete resistance. The woman had died in agony.

That was just the beginning. The germ that killed the patient in Spain spread, first to rest of the hospital, then to the local city. Thousands were affected, hundreds were dead. The local authorities had requested help in containing the infection. From that point onward, Paul and his colleagues kept a close eye on the spread of the disease, hoping it would be checked. It wasn't to be.

Within a month Spain had declared a nationwide epidemic. By this time every global health organization was involved. Travel bans were imposed, but it was too late. Two months after the first Spanish fatality, cases popped up in the U.S. and China. Six months later a global pandemic was declared. The fatality rate was 98%. This organism didn't discriminate. If you got it, you died. It was as simple as that.

Paul remembered the day the email had arrived. It was a call to arms. Laboratories all over the world had rushed to find a way to destroy the organism. Pharmaceutical companies, universities and governments all frantically collaborated. Some were tasked with finding a new antibiotic. Others were challenged with developing a vaccine.

Hundreds of people, including Paul and his team, worked round the clock to achieve these twin goals, while the number of the infected grew exponentially. Hospitals were overwhelmed. People were told to stay at home, no matter how ill. Schools and colleges were closed. Subways, buses and other mass transit systems were suspended. Funeral homes refused to take the dead. Corpses were collected by the military, until there weren't enough healthy soldiers available. After that, the bodies piled up in the streets or quietly decayed in their homes. When Paul heard that news, he knew it was over. Humanity was finished when there was no one left to bury the dead.

It didn't take long for the tipping point to be reached. Hospitals shut down. Transport ceased. Stores closed. Paul's laboratory was one of the few that still functioned, thanks to the judicious purchase of the generator and supplies of diesel, but the chance of finding an effective antibiotic was now remote. Finding a vaccine was even more unlikely. Too many scientists and physicians were dead or ill. The critical mass for such large-scale research had been lost. But, a few laboratories kept working, kept hoping.

Paul continued to stare at the small yellow colonies on the Petri dish. So far, he'd been unaffected. His parents, his wife, his kids and most of his friends and colleagues were dead. He suppressed the grief he felt. John re-entered the lab.

"Nothing. They've all got the same results as us. They're shutting down."

"I expected as much. Well, that's it. There's no more drugs to test, we've exhausted all possibilities."

"Even if we found something that worked, how we would get it manufactured and distributed?"

"We wouldn't. It's too late. It was always too late."

"I don't feel well."

"We're all infected, John. You know that."

John started to cry.

"I'm going home. I know my parents are dead, but I want to be with them."

Paul embraced his friend, then walked to the window to watch him push his way through the cultists. He knew he would never see him again. He could feel the bacterium in his gut, spewing its toxin into his bloodstream. There was no treatment, nothing he could do. He regarded the Petri dish. He put his finger onto the surface of the agar and scooped up a layer of bacterial colonies. He sucked his finger clean and swallowed.

"Might as well give my killers some allies to help their cause."

He smiled. In the end, it hadn't been a comet, or nuclear apocalypse. Nature herself had finished humanity. The smallest creature on the surface of the Earth had doomed the most intelligent, the most advanced species. David had once again defeated Goliath.

THROUGH THE JUNGLE

STUART CONOVER

Jack's arm ached as he brought the Machete through another set of vines. Darkness would be coming soon, and he needed to make the cave by nightfall. The going had been slow since his guides had abandoned him.

He only needed to make it another mile but nature itself was trying to keep him away.

He smirked.

If he was right, what lay in the cave was by no means natural. At least not to this world.

His arm screamed as the Machete cleared the path before him.

Nothing would stop him from reaching his destination and what lay within.

SUNDAY ROAST

STEPHANIE ELLIS

"We need food, not words."

"Then let the words of the Lord feed your soul," said the priest.

"Gave up on our souls a long time ago," grinned Jackson. "It's our stomachs we need to take care of now."

"Listen to me. I can give you sustenance."

"On that we are agreed, Father."

The priest smiled, a hopeful expression filling his face. "Perhaps a prayer?"

"Of course, Father. I have one that is pretty apt."

The priest smiled as the men formed a circle around him. His flock.

"For what we are about to receive," said Jackson.

The smile vanished.

LITTLE LOUIS

ERIK BAKER

Louis was such a sweet boy. He always helped me with the groceries, wanting no reward for himself. When my husband would go away on business, Louis would always come around. I could tell he had a crush. It was sweet in a way, him only being at the ripe age of twelve. He would look at me with his big brown eyes with such infatuation. Although delightful, I had hoped Louis would have been faster. He screamed more than I had thought as well. Didn't put up much of a fight either. I'll bury Louis's body in the morning.

OUTLAST

KATE BITTERS

The alarm blares, plucking me out of dreamland. It's mid-winter, still dark, and my feet are twin blocks of ice, hanging off my bed in the chilly apartment. I pick up my device and silence the alarm. The screen flashes a wash of electric color; I blink and roll onto my side, tucking my feet under the blanket. The room comes to me in shapes and bruised colors. Then I remember.

It's the first conscious thought I have in the morning, routine as black coffee. I roll back to my device, click it awake, and watch the thin flex-screen rise from its base. My device knows I want to check the app before I issue the command.

The app. The one that's consumed my time, my focus for the past six months. It pops onto the screen.

OUTLAST

Blocky letters fill the green back-lit screen; the app loads. My heart thrums. Hands and feet prickle, turn liquid. My frosty skin now blazes under the heat of those seven white letters.

I wipe a sweaty hand across the blanket. I could never be a spy. My body betrays my nerves with an instant soak of sweat. It's a flaw that struck during puberty and, unlike my acne, decided to hang around into adulthood.

A chorus of trumpets blast a victory tune and I read the familiar message scrolling up the screen.

CONGRATULATIONS! YOU ARE STILL IN THE GAME.

A pause. The app gathers data from across the world. I scratch at my wrist, knowing my microchip is sending data to the global cloud, knowing its harvesting information about me in real time—my location, health, vital signs. I don't think about it much anymore. You get used to being watched after a dozen years of surveillance.

It takes a while for Outlast to compile the information it needs. The status bar crawls forward, sluglike. I like it that way. The anticipation ignites my curiosity, makes me wonder about today's number.

The app stops churning and the screen changes. Another scrolling message.

133 MILLION 926 THOUSAND 129 PEOPLE WERE BORN IN THE YEAR 2004. YOU HAVE OUTLASTED...

A counter box spins numbers.

… 30,581,020 OF THEM.

My heart seizes. *So many more than yesterday …*

The number always astounds me. Tens of millions of people born in the same year as me, gone. Kaput. Dead before their thirtieth birthday.

The counter box ticks up. Every few seconds, a fresh body piles onto the death toll.

This is the part I never get used to, watching death in real time. Human lives boiled down to a fleeting number on a screen. It coats my mouth with a grimy film.

And yet, I can't deny my vague pleasure when I see the number climbing. I'm winning the game.

I pull myself out of bed and into my apartment's chill. It wouldn't cost much to heat the cramped space, but *not much* is a lot when you have next to nothing. I rely on the heat from my downstairs neighbor to permeate through the floor and provide enough warmth to keep my studio hovering above freezing. My thick, hooded sweatshirt does the rest.

I make coffee. It's cheap, but iron-strong. I boil water for oatmeal and check the app again. The trumpets give me goose bumps.

CONGRATULATIONS! YOU ARE STILL IN THE GAME.

I wait to see how many people I've outlasted. The counter box slows to a stop.

42,007,831

I stare at the screen. Over ten million 2004 babies perished in the past ten minutes? Not possible. Usually it's a million in an entire *year*. About 2,500 each day. Two per minute. *Two* deaths, not millions.

I gaze, bug-eyed. The counter spins upward. Fast. Too fast.

I slam the app to one side of my screen and pull up the news. My fingertips, palms, armpits trickle sweat. I scan headlines, frantic. No super volcanoes, no earthquakes. No alien invasions. No bombs dropped on Tokyo or Bombay.

Mind spinning, I close Outlast and reload it. The app greets me with ever-cheery brass and a new death toll:

47,852,203.

No.

It's a glitch. Has to be.

My coffee has turned tepid and I have to catch the commuter train soon, but my feet won't move. I'm tethered to my device and the dizzying numbers surging through the counter box.

I have to call Hailey. She'll talk me down from my mania. Always does.

My voice is a bark when I command my device to dial. Hailey picks up instantly.

"Lee? Hey. Don't you have work?"

"Yeah, but listen, Hail. Something strange is happening, something with—" I pause, force out the word. "Outlast."

I see her cringe. We never talk about the app, even though I know she uses it too. Most users keep their obsession to themselves. The game has a dirty reputation. It's meant to be played alone, enjoyed in sinful bites.

"What about it?" Her voice slow, a creaking train.

"The toll for 2004 skyrocketed in the past ten minutes. We're talking a *million* people every minute. Is…is yours doing the same thing?"

"Lee," Hailey protests, "you're acting crazy. Why don't you just—"

"Come on, Hail. Please. Could you check yours too?"

"Fine."

Hailey mutters a few commands to her device. The screen splits in two, the left side showing Hailey's dimpled chin and chicory skin, the other side loading Outlast. I hold my breath, body slippery with sweat.

The trumpets, the greeting.

The death toll.

YOU HAVE OUTLASTED …

… 54,030,901 OF THEM.

The numbers surge.

"Holy shit, that's almost half our year."

"I told you, Hailey." I shove my hands inside my pockets and hug my torso. My shoulders rock away from my device, then back. Away, back. "Something crazy is happening."

"Did you check the other years? Is it just 2004?"

Without waiting for my response, Hailey navigates to the app's settings and changes her birth year to 2020. We wait for the numbers to load.

14,600,223.

Then, 14,600,224.

A slow tick. Normal.

A handful of dead pre-teens.

Hailey's eyes deaden. Her cheeks pale to ash. "I—" she stutters, shakes her head like a clogged salt shaker. "I don't know, Lee. Must be a glitch. Why don't you go to work and forget about it?"

"Are you kidding me? Even if it *is* a glitch, there's no way I can work today. I'm a total wreck. Can you come over? Please? I don't want to be alone right now."

Hailey sniffs. "Unlike some people, I care about paying my bills. Sorry. I'm going to head to work and try to forget about this whole thing."

A knock. Coming from Hailey's end.

"Someone's at the door. Gotta run."

"What? Hailey, no! Are you crazy? People from our birth year are dropping like dominoes and you're answering the door? Please—"

"You've come unhinged, Lee. Maybe lay off Outlast for the day, okay? Let's grab a beer at the Bassett tonight. My treat."

"Hailey, dammit! Listen to me. Don't open that door!"

"Bye, Lee."

The call disconnects and Hailey's image evaporates.

I slump into my kitchen chair and knock the coffee cup with my elbow. It hits the floor and I watch it through a fog, like it's happening in a room on the other side of the world. The liquid slides across the linoleum and my eyes flick back to the device.

Numbers roll and I wonder if one of them represents Hailey.

I pull my hoodie closer. My skin is clammy; it reminds me of a dead fish. I sit, rock, mutter to myself like the crackheads who live in the elbows of Dixon Bridge. I wait.

For what? Time to pass? Everyone in 2004 to die?

A voice floats into my head. *You wanted to win the game, right?*

"Yes," I say out loud to the air, to my bleeding coffee, to the device sitting in front of me. "Yes, I wanted to win. But not like this. Not until I reached one-hundred and four. Not until old age claimed my organs and shut me down. Peacefully. In bed. Surrounded by doting friends and family."

"Not like this. Ruler of the blood bath."

My brain's a circus, spinning and twisting, a riot of color. I'll leave town, I decide. I'll take the next bus out west and lose myself in the canyons and scrub brush. Details later. I have to pack.

I jump to my feet. My left sock has absorbed some of the coffee, but there's no time to change it. I have to move.

I start cramming belongings into my backpack. Some clothes, a couple granola bars, all the cash I had stowed inside an empty soup can in my cupboard. I zip the bag and glance at my device.

Over 70 million now.

Damn.

I coax the screen back in its shell and slide the device in my pocket. I reach for the doorknob at the same time a knock sounds on the other side.

KITTY CAT

ALYSON FAYE

Reversing out of the driveway, Jake glimpsed the quick streak of white behind his back wheels. THUNK. He'd hit Mrs What's-her-face's cat. Damn animal never learnt. Too late now. He shrugged.

Home late after a few drinks, Jake didn't notice several small white shapes flitting into his garage.

Drowning in his water bed, he didn't pay attention to the soft tugging on his duvet.

Six tiny white kittens sought his body warmth; snuggling, cuddling, smothering his face and mouth till his snoring ceased.

Tiny claws hooked into his skin, slashed his eyelids and licked his cooling skin clean of blood.

DATE NIGHT

RICHARD J. MELDRUM

It all had to be just right. She chose her best dress, the one she wore on the most important occasions. She'd had her hair and nails done. Her make-up was flawless. She was, by her own admission, beautiful. Perfection. She had to be, this was the most important date she'd ever had.

She arrived early, nothing could go wrong, she simply wouldn't let it. She'd been planning this night for months.

She glanced around, her date was nearly here. She counted down in her head, then, just at the perfect moment, she stepped out in front of the train.

THE EBBING TIDE CALLS

DANIEL PIETERSEN

Svensson lies in his bed, a berth the old shipmaster has rarely left in the past few years. He watches as the accusatory finger of the lighthouse sweeps across the harbour, in through the bottleglass window and onto the long, blank wall. Each pulse shines a zoetrope puppet-show onto the whitewashed brick.

An empty room. Darkness. The door, still closed, swings its shadow-self into the room. Darkness. A woman, his wife, crosses the threshold. Darkness. Halfway across the room, her features blurred as if underwater. Darkness. Sea-water drips from her hair, her out-stretched hands, as she stands above him.

Darkness.

BARFIGHT

FRED ROCK

Todd awoke on his back in a puddle of beer and broken glass with his ears ringing and his vision blurred. He lay still, watched the ceiling fan spin lazily without seeing it, and thought about nothing. A few seconds passed and he sat up. He closed his eyes tight and waited for the room to stop sliding around, the colors to stop smearing. Finally, his eyes came open, focused, and looked without expression at overturned tables and overturned chairs.

There was a dull ache on the side of his head. With tentative fingers, he found a ragged shard of glass protruding just above his ear. With a shaking hand, he gripped the shard and pulled. Warm blood streamed, sticky and purple, over his fingers and soaking his hair. The blood joined with the suds on the floor, and turned pink. Todd held the glass shard close to his face and gazed at it. Now squinting, he looked past the shard and discovered a big man standing over him, his hand gripping the neck of a broken bottle. It was then that Todd remembered.

"Wanna go again?" the big man sneered. He wore a denim vest with no shirt beneath. His nose was bloody and gruesome, smashed over to one side.

Todd looked at his own right hand, found its knuckles slick and red, and smiled. With a torn voice, he said: "I'm good."

The big man's eyes glittered. "You ain't that good." He tossed the bottle neck to the floor and left. The crowd parted to let him through, Todd noticing their presence for the first time. A red-haired woman with green eyes and freckles appeared with a white terrycloth towel and squatted beside him on her haunches. The vertical green and white stripes on her shirt told him she was a waitress. A name tag told him she was Becky. "Ambulance is on the way," Becky said, wiping his bloody ear and dabbing at his sopping hair. "I called the cops and gave them that guy's description."

Todd blinked. "Ambulance? I don't need an ambulance."

"Yes. Yes, you do. Hey now! Stay still and let's talk a little until they come."

Todd went to stand but his tennis shoe slipped in the beer and he sat down with an awkward splash.

"See?" Becky said. "You can't even stand up."

Todd's eyes were big and white. "What time is it?"

She blinked and put a crease between her eyebrows. "I don't know, nine-fifteen? Sit still a minute."

Todd got his feet under him. He wobbled and stood. "I'm fine. I've gotta go now," he said, batting the towel away.

Becky took his arm and pleaded with him. Two middle-aged men who appeared to be customers came over and folded meaty arms in front of their chests like bouncers. Todd watched the men but spoke to Becky. "Head injuries always look bad. I'm fine. I have to go. I can't be here when the ambulance comes."

The middle-aged men exchanged a glance. One of them said: "Sorry, buddy, we can't let you go. You might as well take a seat at the bar and relax."

"You're kidnapping me?" Todd demanded.

The second man shrugged. "For lack of a better word."

Todd's shoulders slumped and he exhaled, defeated. He shook his head slowly and bolted for the door.

Becky let out a small scream and the two men sprang. Todd stumbled halfway across the room before they caught him. The crowd came over now and encircled them and worked as one to walk Todd slowly back to the bar. Someone slid a chair behind his legs and he sat.

At the bar, Todd sobbed bitterly into his hands. His whole body shook. Finally, his wet face came up, his eyes crazed. He screamed: "You don't understand! The moon is full tonight! I will gut you all!"

A murmur passed through the crowd, as people expressed to one another a muted concern for Todd and his obvious head injury. Becky patted his arm soothingly and sirens drew close. One of the middle-aged men reached in with an icepack but Todd pulled away. He threw back his head, and howled.

TRISTAN

STUART CONOVER

Tristan knew his lineage but until he was eighteen it never seemed real. A normal life by day and a student of darkness at night. As a child, he believed his wards knew his place was to usher in the end of humanity.

At thirteen he realized that were bat shit crazy and ran away. Life on the streets was hard but he was smart. He adapted, his upbringing left him morally flexible. He thrived. Until he was eighteen. When the prophetic dreams began. His wards hadn't lied. He was destined for greatness. Tristan was meant to end the world.

REDUNDANT

STEPHANIE ELLIS

"Our time has come at last," said the first horseman, urging his mount through the fiery gate.

Across vast, frozen lands he rode with his three companions, only to find tanks already in place and dissension rife. Turning towards hotter climes, he discovered camps swarming with refugees and famine flourishing.

As the group looked around in dismay, a figure galloped towards them, handing a letter to each. *We regret to inform you that you are now surplus to requirements ...'*

Man did not need the Four Horsemen to bring about the End of Days; he could manage on his own.

NOT EVEN A MOUSE

RUSCHELLE DILLON

The tiny Christmas tree was beautiful; flocked with snow and gilded with gold and silver ornaments. Its perfectly fanned boughs sheltered presents gently arranged on a bed of snow.

Tina's eyes swelled with tears as she stared at it.

She knew she would never celebrate anything as long as she was with her husband.

He heard her sniffle and yelled for her to stop being a sentimental cow.

She wiped her eyes on her sleeve.

He was right. She was too sentimental.

So she bashed his head with the little Christmas tree snow globe.

This year, Christmas would be merry.

THE HANGING LIGHTS SWAY

ANDREA ALLISON

We explored the house with some reservations. The realtor insisted we would love its historical charm. Stained walls and dust-coated surfaces filled our hearts with dread. We were prepared to make our escape when I spotted them. Two amber globes hanging from a tarnished brass chain, swaying slightly above the hallway. Nothing special about them but yet I couldn't look away. Back and forth they pulled me in closer. My companion's voices drifted into the void. My body went numb until a car horn forced me to return. My gaze traveled down to the crimson liquid dripping from my hands.

DAD

G.A. MILLER

"Wha?" Bobby shook his head, still groggy.

A nightmare. Screams, and a heavy, wet, thumping sound, then silence.

He opened his eyes, letting them adjust to the darkness, and gasped when he saw the tall silhouette standing between his bed and Jimmy's bed.

As the figure turned, Bobby relaxed. It was just Dad, probably came in to check on the boys. Maybe he'd yelled in his sleep?

As Dad turned, he lifted Jimmy's baseball bat, which looked different somehow. It was darker, and looked wet in the dim light. Bobby saw a grim smile on his father's face.

"Now, you ..."

CHRISTMAS EDITION

A LETTER FOR SANTA

JESSICA SHANNON

On the floor in front of the fireplace was a woman in a nightgown that splayed around her body like a snow angel. A dark red tree skirt surrounded the Blue Spruce. Multi-colored Christmas lights flickered in time with a dancing snowman on the television screen. A plate of reindeer-shaped cookies with their antlers bitten off on the coffee table. A large glass of milk teetered dangerously on the edge.

He felt silly in the Santa suit. He had come straight from his final night on the job at the Oxford Pines Mall. No more kids on his lap with sniffling noses and gooey hands. No more prying questions from his boss about his home life. The background check had come up clean, what more did the nosy man want?

It had been a close call, but it helped that he used his brother's ID.

His brother was hundred miles away, celebrating traditions with his own storybook family. Handing out the Christmas Eve pajamas like they did every year. Telling his daughter that she better be a good girl so Santa would show up. Little Cora, with her strawberry blonde hair on the top of her head in a bow that her mother made. He missed her the most out of all of them. Which is why the little girl in the green dress had called out to him. She looked like his favorite niece.

In his front pocket, he had the little girl's letter.

Dear Satan,
Please come see Mommy for Christmas. It's her last one. I don't want her to be alone.
—Vivian

He had smirked at her attempt to spell Santa. Guess she had mixed up her letters, like most of the kids at the mall seemed to do. Heck, he mixed up his letters sometimes too. Never was able to win a spelling bee, or write a poem that made sense. "Some kind of learning disorder," he had heard his mother utter in the middle of the night to his father through the paper-thin walls of his childhood home. "Don't give that boy an excuse," his father answered. "He'll think he's some kind of special kid who deserves things. That's the last thing that kid needs. He ain't special."

On the bottom of the letter was a hand drawn map with the little girl's address. *15 Hawthorne Avenue.* He didn't do this kind of thing for kids, but there was something desolate in her brown eyes. She struggled to talk to him. He had asked her what she wanted for Christmas about a dozen times before she handed him the tattered red envelope.

She was a little girl who knew too much for her age. She knew that her Christmases would never be the same again. She knew that no one would make them special for her like her mother. Would anyone ever be Santa to Vivian again?

He could give her one special Christmas. One magical memory.

He took a deep breath like he always did when he started his shift at the mall.

Showtime. Remember to be Jolly.

With a small push, the door creaked open. It creaked so loud that it should have woken the world. At least it should have woken the woman on the floor. But she remained as still as the tower of stacked presents in holly patterned paper that sat next to the tree.

He stepped inside, adjusting his red and white-trimmed cap.

"Miss? I'm here to see Vivian. I met her at the mall. She gave me a letter."

The woman didn't respond.

Maybe she wasn't feeling well.

The television repeated the snowman scene from earlier except this time the screen flickered like when a VCR would adjust its tracking with black and white snow.

His tongue slapped the roof of his mouth, nearly sticking to it. He knew he should have picked up a drink at the food court before he left the mall. The glass of milk on the table looked cold and before thinking too hard, he grabbed it from the table and swallowed it down in one gulp. Vanilla and sugar, his favorite. Just like he had told the little girl.

"Miss?" he repeated a bit louder.

He reached down to shake her arm and as his hand touched her shoulder he realized that she was cold. Too cold to be living.

He stumbled backward, slipping on the floor, his feet nearly coming out from under him as he put his hand behind himself so he wouldn't fall flat on his back.

He felt something wet. It was the dark red tree skirt. Except it wasn't a tree skirt. It was blood.

His mouth opened into a gasp as he sunk into the syrupy human fluid on the floor. It smelled like the pennies that were in the empty fountain at the mall, next to Santa's workshop. The scent was so strong that he could feel his stomach wretch.

A giggle echoed in the room.

The little girl in the green smocked dress stood in the door to the kitchen. A smile crept over her face.

"Vivian, we need to get out of here," he said as his heart began to race. He looked down at his stained clothing. The white parts of his costume were matted with crimson. He couldn't go out into the dark in a bloody Santa suit on Christmas Eve. It wasn't even his own blood. No one would believe him. They'd learn about his criminal record. They'd pull up the fake ID. They wouldn't believe that he "found" the bag of presents at the mall. He wouldn't be able to explain it away.

"You drank the milk!" she said as she pointed at the empty glass.

"Come on, Vivian. Let's go," he hissed.

He looked into the little girl's glossy eyes. He had never seen that look in a child before. And he had seen scores of kids at the mall. Nice ones. Bratty ones. Scared ones. But none like this one.

This was pure evil.

He swallowed an acidic burp as he tasted the vanilla and sugar again.

"Satan! Satan!" the girl cooed.

Something inside of him told him to flee, but his body was stick. He was sinking. His limbs were heavy. He fought to keep his eyes open.

He shook his head slowly like the animatronic elves that stood next to his workshop at the mall. "I'm Santa! You spelled my name wrong on the card!"

"Satan," she repeated with a new smile. This time it was larger than before. Her eyes darkened.

He slumped to the floor, his face hitting the thick pool of blood with a squish. He stared into the dead woman's face. The missing sugar cookie reindeer antlers were in the spaces where her eyes should have been.

"Now Mommy isn't alone."

X-MAS TWIST

MICHAEL BALDWIN

Father Ralph parked in the spot reserved for ministers near the entrance to Conway Nursing Home. He hurried inside, minimizing his exposure to the chilling wind that had frozen much of North Texas this Christmas Eve.

He greeted Luella at the front desk, signed in, and made his way thru the lobby. A large, extravagantly lit Christmas tree took up much of the lobby area. On the wall near the tree was a garish cross, created by several strands of lights that flickered erratically. The cross appeared large enough to crucify a full-sized man, but there was no Christ figure on it. Glancing at it as he passed, Father Ralph thought the cross's mad flickering might be enough to cause an epileptic fit if one was so inclined. *Why is the cross here on Christmas?* he mused.

He didn't have time to appraise the decorations, however. He had been called to attend Mrs. Santos, whom Nancy Lomax, the head nurse, thought must be near death. Mrs. Santos was only in her 60s, but had evidently had a hard life and was now in advanced dementia. He found her in a wheelchair in the hallway, pushed by Nancy Lomax.

"If she's dying, why isn't she in bed?" asked Father Ralph.

"Well, Father, when I called you she had passed out and we thought she might not awaken. But she came to and seemed to be a little better. She's been babbling like crazy ever since. I thought it best you see her in case she maybe relapses into a fatal coma. She's acting very strange."

Father Ralph bent down to look the old lady in the eye. "Mary, are you stirring up trouble around here?" he asked lightly.

She grabbed his wrist with a gnarled claw and whined, "They never get it right. There weren't any shepherds or wise men. No presents either. It's not fair. But he's coming, he's coming!"

"What do you mean, Mary. I don't understand," said Father Ralph. Then he turned to nurse Lomax. "What's she mean about no shepherds or presents?"

"Oh, haven't you heard her story claiming to be the Virgin Mary? I thought she had told just about everyone by now. Well, let me see if I can make it coherent for you. As you know, her name is Mary—Mary Santos, which I think means Saint Mary. She claims that when she was a teenager, she became pregnant, but not thru the normal process. She was adamant that she hadn't been with any boys. Her family was mighty strict, so when they discovered her pregnancy, they kicked her out. But her older boyfriend, Joe, stuck by her and took her into his house. Well, you can see the parallels to the Christ story. She claims she is actually the latter-day Virgin Mary.

"She even says she gave birth in a barn. Seems Joe had a temp job at a guest ranch down near Palestine. So, the two of them were there when she had the baby, or rather babies. Seems she had twin boys. Named one of them Jesus, of course. Care to guess about the other? No? Well, Judas, no less."

"Holy macaroons!" said Father Ralph crossing himself.

"Yeah, she couldn't deviate that much from her illusion, so she left Judas with the owners of the guest ranch. She and Joe hot-footed it back here with baby Jesus. Joe gets a job building custom wooden coffins for the mortuary trade. Jesus does that too for a while as a teenager, but then disappears for several years.

Word was he went out to the coast and became a surfer dude. Some said he became a marijuana grower. Could have spent some time in prison. Anyway, next time Mary hears from him, he's become a rock singer and he and Judas are reunited in the same band. You see where this is going, of course. Well, they've been traveling around quite a lot, but she's claiming Jesus is supposed to show up here tonight, it being Christmas and all."

"That's quite a story," said Father Ralph. "So, she came out of her coma because she thinks Jesus is coming?"

"Could be, but we haven't heard anything that would give her reason to think so. No mail or phone calls from anyone."

Just then there was a commotion from the lobby. Nurse Lomax and Father Ralph wheeled Mary down the hall toward the noise. Several of the residents and staff were gathered in the lobby watching a group of musicians setting up their equipment to play. A banner for the group read: 'Jesus and the Apostles'. A thin young man with a scraggy beard detached himself from the others and came to embrace Mary Santos.

"Mother, I've come to see you and we're going to play some music for you and your friends."

Mary glared up at the man. "Don't try to fool your mother. You're Judas! Where's Jesus?"

The front door flung open and another thin young man entered who was obviously twin to the first. "I'm here! Don't start without me. Thanks for filling in for me Judas, but I'll take over now."

The two brothers embraced, but Judas said bitterly, "Maybe I'd better take the lead this time while you see to Mother. There she is, give her a kiss. She's been waiting for you, not me."

Jesus looked at his withered mother, then back at Judas. "The sign says 'Jesus and the Apostles'. I'll do the show as always."

"You always have to be in the spotlight, don't you?" sneered Judas. He gave Jesus a little push to get around him. Jesus must have lost his balance or stumbled on a speaker cable. He did a slow-motion fall against the flashing cross on the wall. Glass broke. Electricity crackled. The lights went out. Jesus gasped.

When the lights came back on, Jesus' body was stretched grotesquely against the now dark cross. There was a haze of smoke and the smell of burnt flesh. The cross had evidently shorted out and electrocuted him.

Mary screamed, "Jesus!"

Judas groaned, "Oh, my God!"

Father Ralph exclaimed, "Holy macaroons! This is Christmas not Easter!"

DEAD WATCH

R. M. SMITH

It's a chilly one tonight. The cold goes right through the bones if you let it; but I shan't let it. I'm warm here in this small room with its small bed and small desk. The light of the candle sitting beside me on the desk is fighting with the light of the fireplace behind me; a to and fro battle my shadow cannot win. I'm sitting with my fingers firmly gripping my quill. I plan to write my love Cynthia who has gone off to visit her family in New Brighton for the Christmas holiday.

Marty, the undertaker of the mortuary and my dear friend, asked me to take the dead watch for him tonight saying that he had previous plans with a visiting cousin. With Cynthia gone, I had nothing else to do. I suppose I could have run down to the tavern with some of the others or even asked to run along with Marty and his kin; but the cold kept me in.

During the dead watch I oversee the dead who have been brought here after Marty prepared them for viewing or burial, or a cremation which will take place the following day; or after a holiday. I have watched the dead before, a few times, not much. Most of my time is spent with my dear Cynthia.

The watch is quite simple, really. I merely stay in a back room of the mortuary ensuring that the building is secure and no one breaks in during the night. It is quiet. No one disturbs me.

The only duty I must perform during the watch is to turn off lights situated above each occupied coffin. The lights are perched above the head of the deceased in case a loved one or a policeman may drop by, perhaps an investigator. Loved ones may stay with the deceased for some time before I must usher them off for the night whilst outside, trolley cars continue their rounds about the snowy city.

As soon as night has fallen, I lock the front hinged door of the mortuary, chain and bolt it, and then make my rounds turning off all of the lights in the building including those hanging over the deceased.

Back in my small room, I settle down with a few sheets of paper, my quill, and the fire warming my back. The only light now is in the room with me, shoving my shadow here and there. The dark open viewing area of the mortuary is through an open doorway to my room.

I begin to write Cynthia, my love. My words of love for her easily flow through my quill. Sometime later, a rap at the front door startles me. Hurriedly I throw on my cloak and quickly walk to the bolted door. I pass the coffins in the dark noticing that I left one of the lights on by one of the coffins near the far wall. How silly of me. I thought that I had turned it off. With a slight laugh, I arrive at the front door, unlock it, and am surprised to see a night patrolman.

In a cold shivering whisper of a voice he asks, "Can I sit in by your fire for a bit, lad?" His moustache is covered in small bits of frozen ice. His hat and shoulders are covered in fresh snow flakes.

"Sorry old boy," I say. "But I am not allowed to let anyone in now that visiting hours have passed. You might try the tavern. They may let you sit for a bit."

He smiles. "Well done. Marty wanted me to check in on you. I see he's hired himself a good man. Goodnight then."

Graciously, I nod, closing the door on him and relocking it. Of course Marty picked a good man for the job! I wasn't going to let a good friend of mine down. He had helped me on many different occasions. Sitting here in the dark was not such a hard thing to do to repay a kindness, now was it? And not only that, Marty was going to have Cynthia and me over for dinner as payment. His rabbit stew was such a treat.

With a shiver, I folded my arms and rubbed my sides as the front door sealed the cold away. "God its bloody cold out there," I said making my way back to my room past the coffins. Entering the door to my room I stopped in my tracks. "Ah, the light." I walked back to the one which was still lit, pulled the chain, and off it went.

The light of the fire beckoned to me. Just that short time of talking to the night patrolmen had brought such a chill to my bones. I could feel the cold air around my ankles.

Hurrying now, I entered my room and stood in front of the fire. I pulled my hands out of my pockets and spread my fingers toward the heat of the flames. The cold left my body and warmth filled me.

Out of the corner of my eye I saw that a light was coming from the room full of coffins. With my head cocked, I walked back out into the coffin room and saw that indeed one of the lights was on over one of the coffins. It was the same light that I had turned off only moments before…right after the night patrolman's visit.

I stood with my fingers on my lips, my thumb under my chin. "I thought I just turned that light out," I said quietly.

So cold. The room was so damned cold. It felt like the chill of death in here.

I walked back over to the coffin. I pulled the chain down and the light went out. I stood for a moment—or at least as long as I could until the cold pushed me back to my stateroom and the warm fire waiting there.

"I know it's out now," I said with my hand on the back of my chair preparing to sit down. Instead I went back to the door of my room. The room full of coffins was dark.

With a sigh I took off my cloak, laid it on the bed and returned to my desk. I thought that I should at least finish the letter before retiring. I picked up the quill; feeling the warmth of the fire on my back; and continued the letter.

A bit later, I felt a wisp of cold around my ankles.

"Did someone come in?" I asked. They couldn't have. The front door was locked with a bolt and chain. Still, it felt like wind was blowing around my feet.

I pushed back from the chair. Putting my cloak on once again, I stopped in my steps when I stepped into the room of coffins.

The light was on again over the same coffin.

The pull chain was swinging slightly.

"Is someone playing tricks?" I asked to the cold room. "Come out now. There's no time for this."

No one said anything, just the icy wind blowing outside through shutters, between the barren trees, over the rafters.

"Now, I know I have been turning this off," I said in an angry whisper.

I walked over to the coffin.

In it, an old dead man lay, his hands folded over his chest. His hair was white. His face clean shaven. I could see tiny ice crystals covering his skin. I thought about closing the lid of the coffin, but Marty distinctly told me to leave the coffins open. He didn't say why, however. I just assumed that it was for the undertaker to do before the bodies were transported away from here.

I stood looking down at the old man.

Was he really not dead? Was this one of Marty's friends playing a trick – his cousin? Or a different night patrolman? No. It couldn't be. No man could lay in a coffin so long, especially not in this cold. The man was only wearing a suit. He wore no cloak!

I could see my breath pluming out in front of me.

The old man was not breathing.

"I will make sure this light stays out," I said pulling down on the chain. The light went off. "There. It's out."

Back at the door to my room, I turned around to look back.

It was dark.

I stood in front of the fire, again warming my hands. I kept turning my head to see if the light was on again in the other room. It wasn't. It stayed off.

"Ok. It's off," I said, sitting and tapping my quill on the desk. The letter to my love sat unfinished. I wouldn't be able to finish it now. My mind was racing too fast. I couldn't understand how the damned light kept coming on!

"I won't get this letter done tonight," I said to myself. "I can finish in the morning."

I leaned over the desk and blew out the candle. Now the only light was from the fireplace. Shadows danced on the wall.

I slipped off my shoes and got into bed leaving the rest of my clothing on. It would be too cold to sleep in the buff, and I also wasn't certain if a night patrolman might stop by.

Pulling the covers up to my chin, I closed my eyes then shot them open again seeing a reflection of white light on the ceiling above me. The fire wasn't emitting a white light. It must have been from out in the coffin room.

"No," I whispered. "It cannot be."

I threw the covers back, slipped on my shoes and walked over to the doorway. I stood, my hands on either side of me resting at shoulder height on the door jambs. I stared into the darkness, my eyes stuck on the single light.

"It can only come on if someone pulls the chain," I said, my breath short. "Who is pulling the chain? Who is out there?"

Only the wind outside answered me.

"Who is out there?" I said louder. "Who is out there?"

It was deathly quiet.

Quickly turning around I marched over to my desk and plopped down in the chair. "No one is pulling the chain. How can the light be coming on?"

I shot a look over my shoulder, fear gripping me, causing goose pimples to run up and down my body.

"Unless … unless the old man is reaching up and turning on the light himself."

I stood up quickly.

"I must find out. I will stand and watch him."

Quietly, I walked back into the dark room over to the lit coffin. I stood over it, my arms folded, my breath freezing in front of me.

I reached out and pulled the chain down.

The light went out.

I waited.

There was no sound, only the wind. I didn't hear a grunt or a sad, or perhaps angry moan from the old man in the coffin. He didn't sit up in the coffin and grab my neck, strangle me, yell in my face with his rotting voice "Leave my light on!"

It remained dark.

"I've been hallucinating," I whispered. "This has been my imagination. I am standing here in this dark room expecting a dead man to turn on a light." I laughed with a cold shiver. "I am a fool."

I went back to my room. Entering, my body was lit from behind as the light came on once again.

"No."

The dead man lay with his hands folded over his chest.

With fear shaking me, I went back into my room, kicked off my shoes, and jumped under the covers.

I was not cold.

I was not shivering from the cold.

I was afraid. Fear was holding me tight.

"How can this be happening?"

Loud rapping on the door woke me the next morning. Groggily shaking my head, I hopped out of bed, threw on my cloak, put on my shoes and went to the door.

My eyes never left the coffin as I passed it.

The light was still on.

Marty stood outside the door. He was looking around, his breath pluming out in front of him. He held a large Christmas wreath.

He met me with a smile as I opened the door. "Good morning, James."

I nodded to him. "Good morning."

He asked, "How was your night?"

"Fine. Fine." I didn't want to tell him about the man turning the light on in the coffin.

Shaking snow from his shoulders he came into the room. He looked around. "Oh, that damn light," he said with a sniff.

"What about it?" I asked.

"The damn thing has a short. Every time a trolley goes by outside, it comes on," he said. "Didn't you notice?"

"No," I said in the calmest voice I could muster. "I didn't even see it."

Marty laughed and nodded toward the open doorway.

I turned.

"Merry Christmas, James," a sweet voice said. Cynthia stood in the snow shivering, her arms wrapped around her. She had a large red Christmas bow tied around her waist. She came in and kissed my cheek.

Marty slapped me on the back with a grand smile. "Merry Christmas, old boy! When would the two of you like to come over for dinner?"

THE DAY BEFORE

CHARLES REIS

It was the day before Christmas, so it was a busy time at the department store. For Catherine, who started college last autumn, taking on a second job as a gift wrapper for the store during the season helped with the bills. The job also helped her save up enough money to get her parents a cruise to the Caribbean for Christmas, and she was excited to have them receive it.

Her workstation consisted of a table that was covered by a red cloth and the items she needed to wrap were scattered on top of it. There was also a small tip jar, and she had received a lot in tips due to her upbeat and hospitable attitude. Though she had been working nonstop for a few hours now, she enjoyed the job.

"Happy Holidays, Mr. Leroux," she told a gentleman she just finished helping.

Her next customer was a woman in her mid-fifties who wanted several baby clothes wrapped, "They're for my first grandchild!" the woman cheerfully proclaimed.

Catherine smiled, "OH, congratulations!" She loved children herself, which was why she was going to school to become a teacher. This was when a loud bang coming from the other side of the store was heard that startled her and the customers.

"What was that?" the woman wondered.

"Someone must have dropped something very big," Catherine brushed off the incident, "Anyway, what's your grandchild's name?"

"Jennifer," the woman replied with a big smile.

Catherine smiled back, "Jennifer … that's a pretty name." More loud banging noises were heard in rapid sequences, accompanied by people screaming. This was when a crowd of screaming people ran towards her direction. When another bang noise was heard, a man in the fleeing crowd fell dead to the floor from a bullet to the head. Blood splattered over the tile floor as the body hit the ground. The people in her line started screaming and running in terror.

Catherine froze as fear filled her veins and mind. A gunman, armed with a semiautomatic weapon, was walking in her direction. She believed such events happened elsewhere, but now it was happening before her eyes. The shooter looked odd because he dressed like Jesus. He had long black hair and a beard. There was a crown of thorns on his head and dried blood along the scalp. He wore sandals and a white robe that had blood stains on the right side near the chest. There were additional dried blood stains on his feet and palms. She was paralyzed from shock, but when he pointed the weapon to his left and yelled out, "Keep Christ in Christmas," Catherine ducked. As he fired upon a crowd of people, she hid under the table. While she knew this wasn't the smartest decision, it was her only option. However, since the table cloth hid her well and he wasn't looking in her direction when she went under it, she felt it was a good hiding spot.

The only light under this table came from the small gap between the table cloth and the floor. This allowed her to see the shadows from the people that were running away as sounds of gunfire and screaming plagued her ears. Her heart started to beat so loud that it almost drowned out the noise of the chaos. Then, the man shouted "Sinners!" After hearing that, she could judge that he was less than ten feet away, and he was getting closer.

She tried to control her breathing, which was heavy due to fear. Another shot was fired, followed by a woman screaming. Seconds later, a shadow appeared and stopped right in front of her. A chill went down her spine because she knew it was the shooter. She could see threw the gap his feet, and noticed that each foot had a self-inflicted wound. Catherine assumed that he was such a fanatic that he self-inflicted stigmata on himself as part of some blind religious devotion. He stood in front of her table, and she could hear that he was reloading his weapon. Luckily for her, it appeared he was unaware of her presence. She wanted to scream, so she placed her hand over her mouth to control herself.

"But those mine enemies, which would not that I should reign over them, bring hither, and slay them before me," he said to himself. His sinister voice brought pure terror throughout Catherine's body as she struggled to keep herself quiet. All she could do was pray that he wouldn't find her. This was a nightmare she couldn't wake up from.

He finished reloading and started shooting again. A group people were heard screaming several yards away, and he ran towards them. For her, there was a slight sigh of relief knowing he was no longer near, but she still wasn't safe. She decided that if she had the chance to escape, she would do it. So, she listened.

Now, it was eerily quiet in the store, as if death took over it. Seconds felt like hours within this silence of horror. After what felt like an eternity had passed, Catherine heard screaming and gunfire coming from the far end of the store. This was her chance as she believed the gunman was far enough away that she could escape unnoticed. Catherine's plan was to run with all her energy to the nearest exit and not look back. Wasting no time, she gathered what bravery and adrenaline she had and crawled out from under the table.

Salvation was just a few yards away, but once she crawled out into the open, there was nothing but damnation. Still on all fours, she looked up and saw a gunman pointing his weapon at her. Though this man was dressed like Jesus, his hair was blond, not black, indicating that there was more than one fanatical killer.

"God told me what you said to Mr. Leroux. It's Merry Christmas, not Happy Holidays!" he yelled. His words brought her questions on whether this was fate, divine judgment, or just a coincidence. While this confused her on how he knew what she said early, it didn't matter in the end. She trembled as she faced her own mortality.

The man aimed the gun directly at her forehead and said, "That whosoever would not seek the LORD God of Israel should be put to death." She didn't want to die as tears fell from her eyes. What followed was the last sound she would ever hear: *BANG!*

FIVE LETTERS TO SANTA

DAVID RAE

The great thing about homicide is what it does to retail values. We would never have been able to afford the house if it hadn't been for the murders; two murders and a suicide to be precise. That put a big dent in the asking price, and Amy haggled it down still further. After all, it's not everyone that is willing to move into a crime scene. Even then we had to stretch to the limit to afford it. Luckily the banks were still happy to loan out high.

People get so spooked about these things; I mean, why? Do they imagine they're going to find ghosts haunting the place? The past, in my opinion, is firmly in the past. Ghosts are all just in your imagination, and the one thing I don't have is much imagination. Amy doesn't either. She's like me only more so; practical.

The house was in a bit of a state when we moved in. It looked like it had been rented out as a multiple occupancy unit. There were locks on the bedroom doors, and there were separate fridges with locks on them too. We were going to remodel anyway. We had budgeted for that when we bought the place and got some further discount. But we were going to have to do most of the work ourselves. That's ok. As I said, I'm practical. We stayed in the basement flat to begin with and got to work. Of course, there was more work than we expected, there always is. First thing to do was to clear out all the trashy, old furniture and fittings. I ripped out the kitchen and threw all the old appliances in a skip. I know you think that I could have got a house clearer in to take the furniture and white goods, but seriously they were not worth anything. We did get some local house clearers round to look at it, but they all wanted money to haul it away. My guess is that whoever inherited the house sold the original furniture and, like I said, set the place up as bedsits.

The house was going to need a new kitchen; the bathrooms needed to be redone, a complete redecoration, rewired, new heating. That was before we could even think about the landscaping. Still, we knew we could make money from it; not least because eventually, people forget about the past. We just had to hold onto it long enough.

We made pretty good progress. We refitted the kitchen, and we got an electrician in to do the first fit on the rewiring, and we got heating done. We'd had to replace some of the doors due to the locks that had been stuck on them, but we managed to keep most of the original features. We even took some of the fireplaces out and had sold them to bring in some extra cash for the work.

I stripped out the fireplace in the back bedroom. It had been boarded up and a heater had been stuck in front of it. I was going to take out the chimney breast and get a bit more room anyway. But it was a nice fire surround and I was pretty sure I could make good money from selling it on to the salvage merchants.

When I pulled out the fire, there were five yellowing envelopes lying in at the back. Amy, who was helping, leaned over and picked them up. The envelopes were all different sizes, but all of them were addressed to Santa Claus. I guess a kid had written then and stuck them in there.

"Cute," I said. "Let's read them."

"I don't know," said Amy. "Let's just bin them with the rest of the rubble."

"Nah, go on read them," I insisted.

"Well, alright," said Amy. And she tore open the first letter. It was written on Mickey Mouse notepaper and scribbled in crayon. The kid must have been about five when he wrote it.

"Dear Santa," Amy read. "Please make Daddy come home from the hospital. I miss him so much and Mummy is sad because he is not here. She cries a lot and looks worried even though she tries not to."

"That's a bit of downer," said Amy.

"Poor kid," I said. "I wonder what was wrong with his Dad. I hope things turned out all right. I guess they must have if he wrote more. Let's read the next one."

"Alright," agreed Amy. "I'm not sure which one it is. I guess this one going by the handwriting. That one was on top of the pile so it must be the last so I guess this is next."

"Dear Santa, thank you for letting Daddy come home. It's great to see him, even although I need to keep quiet because he's not well. Mummy says that he'll get better and this is for the best. She says that the doctors will fix him and that why he needs his special medicine. I'd like special medicine too. Sometimes I get sad, just like Daddy, although I don't shout and break things when I feel sad. Mummy hugs me when she feels sad. I wish Daddy would hug Mummy or me. But Mummy says he can't because he's so ill. Do you get sad, and does Rudolf give you a hug when you feel bad?"

"This isn't any better," said Amy.

"I don't know; it's kind of cute. You should give me a hug when I'm sad," I said.

"I do," said Amy. That made us laugh.

"Next one," Amy said, opening the middle letter from the pile.

"Dear Santa, I'm sorry I've not been a very good boy this year. I've tried to be good but I keep making Daddy mad. He keeps shouting at me. When I make him mad, he hits Mummy and makes her cry. Mummy should go to the doctors but she won't. She says Daddy is very ill and that if we tell the doctors, then they will take him away again. She says he is ill because the doctors won't give him enough of his special medicine. When Daddy gets his special medicine, he can be lots of fun. He tells all sorts of funny jokes and things. I know this letter is from me, but can I ask you to give Daddy more special medicine for Christmas."

"Wow," said Amy, and put the letter down. "Let's not read anymore."

"We can't stop now," I said. "I want to hear what happens next."

"Then you read them," she said and handed me the two last letters.

"Ok," I agreed. "But this is not like you."

I opened the fourth letter. It was written in copperplate handwriting with a fountain pen like a schoolboy. Who knows what age the kid was now; I and guess twelve.

"Dear Santa," I read. "Thank you for the presents last year. I liked the cowboy suit and the train set very much, although I'm a bit big for them now. Dad took them and sold them. He said that they were too babyish for a boy my age. Dad is well, and so is Mum. They send their best regards. I am doing well at school and working hard. Dad is fine now that he has enough medicine. I help Mum to look after him and clean him up after he's been sick or fallen asleep on the floor. He has a friend that comes and stays sometimes. She is very nice, although I think Mum does not like her. Sometimes I hear Mum and Dad arguing about her. Mum says that she is a whore. But when I asked the teacher at school what that meant, I got into trouble. Mum cries a lot now, and I have to help her look after the house. I love my Mum and Dad very much. Please help us to be happy this Christmas and keep Dad's friend away."

When I finished the letter, Amy took it and screwed it up.

"That's enough," she said. But we both knew that we had to read the last letter. I looked at her and took a deep breath. She was shaking her head. But we had to. We owed it to the kid at the very least.

"Alright then," she said at last, and tore open the envelope with shaking fingers. There was only one line of writing.

"Dear Santa, For Christmas I would like a new bicycle, a new phone and a .22 hand gun. Thanks."

Like I said; ghosts only exist in your head, and now there was the ghost of an abused, twelve-year-old kid with a gun that shot his parents and then turned the gun on himself living in my head.

We lost a fortune on that house when we sold it. And of course, Christmas was never the same.

CLACK!

DJ TYRER

"Brilliant costume!" shouted Steve.

A 'soldier' in a red jacket and a tall hat was marching up the street towards them.

"Yeah, brill!" muttered Harry. Their mismatched Santa outfits seemed quite pathetic.

"Hallowe'en all over again ..." groaned Bill.

Then, another figure in uniform rounded the corner. And, another. And, another. Dozens, marching in unison.

"Something's not right," said Harry.

A man with flashing antlers on his head stumbled out of an alleyway. The nearest soldier swung around and its jaw dropped.

CLACK! Its jaw snapped back up and took the man's head off.

"Nutcrackers ..."

They were everywhere.

CLACK! CLACK! CLACK!

THE GRUNGLE

KEVIN FOLLIARD

The Grungle is a critter
That hides in Christmas trees
Its seven eyes are black as coal
Its spiny legs deceive

The Grungle looks like evergreen
It blends with colored lights
It tip-taps on glass ornaments
And lingers through the night

When children come to open gifts
The Grungle plays a trick
Its poison stinger fires out
To make the child sick

The child wakes up in his bed
Away from Christmas cheer
And the Grungle crawls upstairs
To grant the gift of fear

Underneath the child's skin
The Grungle lays its spawn
Teeny-tiny grunglings
That wriggle out by dawn

WRONG NIGHT

ADAM MILLARD

The sound of bells wakens me, and my heart instantly fills with joy. I listen as, downstairs, heavy boots move around the house. Do mother and father hear it, too, or is the magic of this moment just mine?

There is a clatter and a grunt—a stifled curse-word I never expected to hear from Santa—and I sit upright in bed, turn to face the door.

This is when I notice the advent calendar hanging there, two doors yet to open, for it is only the twenty-third.

Panic sets in as the boots stomp up the stairs toward me.

Printed in Great Britain
by Amazon